PALADIN

ELEMENTAL PALADINS: BOOK TWO

MONTANA ASH

This is an IndieMosh book
brought to you by MoshPit Publishing
an imprint of Mosher's Business Support Pty Ltd
PO BOX 147
Hazelbrook NSW 2779
www.indiemosh.com.au

Cataloguing-in-Publication entry is available from the National
Library of Australia: http://catalogue.nla.gov.au/

Title: Paladin
Author: Ash, Montana (1984)
ISBNS: 978-1-925447-54-5 (paperback)
        978-1-925447-55-2 (ebook – epub)
        978-1-925447-56-9 (ebook – mobi)

Cover design by Montana Ash, author, and Ally Mosher,
IndieMosh.
Stock photography from Adobe Stock

PALADIN

ELEMENTAL PALADINS: BOOK TWO

Dear Tracy!.

Happy Reading!.

Montana
Ash xx.

Dedication

To Montana's Minions!

You are everything women should be; mighty, pervy, funny, weird, fierce, dirty, loyal, special, strong, beautiful, smart, unique, witty ... and very, very appreciated!

Thank you, thank you, thank you!

Rock on, Minions!

The Order of Neptune thanks Marcia;
Cinder thanks Kirsty;
Mordecai thanks Fran.

PROLOGUE

It had been a fierce battle, but a good one, Sir Darius thought, as he made his way through the killing field to his liege. Over four months they had warred in order to secure this piece of land. Three other Orders had also taken up arms in the Crusades, Earth, Life, and Fire, and were spread throughout the city. He hoped there had been no casualties among his fellow soldiers. Distracted, he noted a sword among the bodies on the stained earth. The Earth Warden would have a tiresome time attending to the battered grounds here. The glinting metal was tarnished with red, evidence that its owner had fulfilled its purpose. The distinctive pommel caught his attention almost as surely as its owner had weeks before. The death paladin was second in command to Verity – Warden of Life – and Darius was ashamed to admit he had been admiring her from afar from the very first moment he had laid his eyes upon her. She was breathtaking in her beauty, with eyes the colour of polished grey river stones, her hair black as night and her curls unrelenting in their chaos. Twice he had found himself distracted with thoughts of tugging on those tresses. But those were wasted thoughts, he knew, as he bent to retrieve the weapon.

Unbeknownst to him, the sword's owner was also reaching to retrieve the it. The skin of their hands brushed against each other, causing an almost literal spark to flare between them. Heat shot up his arm and very unexpectedly, directly to his groin. He somehow had the presence of mind to stifle his groan even as he heard the feminine gasp from the other paladin.

"What was that?" She asked, her grey eyes beseeching and lovely.

No, Darius thought, *this cannot be.*

"What 'twas what?" He replied. Any other acknowledgement would be seen as encouragement.

"Do not act as though you are ignorant, Sir Darius. You understand me completely." The Lady Diana responded sternly. "I am referring to that … tingle … that heat!"

Oh, yes. Darius understood very well, to what she was referring – *attraction*. Instant, spontaneous, dangerous, *attraction*. Darius swallowed hard in order to formulate the lie he knew must be uttered. Any form of relationship between the two of them simply could not be permitted. His responsibility was first and foremost to his liege. Not only was he honour-bound to his sovereign as a sworn paladin, but he was also blood-bound due to their family ties. Any relationship, any *feelings* would prove an unacceptable distraction to his duties. Especially in times such as these, when his liege had sworn to aid the humans and help them fight their Holy wars. As paladins, they had little choice in regards to personal life as it stood. But given the current climate fraught with violence and change, their choices were now non-existent. So he voiced the only response he was able;

"I do not know what you are implying. I did not feel a thing. And if you are as good and as loyal as you appear in battle, then you will never admit to feeling differently either."

The Lady's grey eyes appeared to darken as if a storm cloud had suddenly passed o'er head. She raised her chin and somehow managed to give the appearance of looking down at him, despite the discrepancies in their statures. "And this is your final word on the matter?"

Darius nodded curtly, "It is."

"Then I will consider this matter concluded. But know this, Sir Darius Magne," she continued, the hot wind picking at her glorious curls, "I will ne'er approach you again. When you come to regret your decision – and you will – you must approach me ... and pray you find me in a forgiving mood."

Diana retrieved her bloodied sword from the hard earth and strode way without a backward glance. He couldn't help but admire the pride in her stiff shoulders and the purpose in the sway of her feminine hips. It was already too late for regrets he knew – his regrets had begun the second he saw her magnificent hair waving wildly on the battlefront as she swung her sword with lethal grace. For the first time in his life, he had regretted being a knight.

"You believe you are doing a great service to your liege by denying your truest emotions."

He jumped in alarm from the deep voice at his back. Verity, Warden of Life and Lady Diana's liege was standing behind him. Clearly, the Warden had been there long enough to surmise the gist of their conversation. Or perhaps not, given a Life Warden could see into his very heart and pluck out the truth. Hoping to bluff his way through, yet not cause offense, he bowed low, "My Lord?"

Verity merely shook his head, gazing fondly at his sworn paladin in the distance, he continued, "This is a lie, son. The greatest disservice one can commit is being false to oneself."

He leaned forward, placing a kindly hand over his coat of arms. "Even the strongest of us cannot best Fate, son."

The most senior sovereign in their society took his leave as quietly as he had appeared, leaving Darius with naught but confusion, doubts and regrets.

ONE

More than eight hundred years had passed since the capture of Lisbon where Darius had first laid eyes on the paladin of death. Eight hundred years when his fate had been sealed in her eyes; never to know her touch, her affection, or her love. She had told him she would never offer herself to him again, that if he wanted her he would have to go to her, and she had held to that vow, despite living in the same house for the last twenty-odd years. Who knew the woman would have the capacity to be so stubborn? And why was he up at five in the morning dwelling on the actions he took some eight centuries ago? Likely, it was due to all the recent upheaval in the household.

Max, a pint-sized, redheaded, whirlwind of trouble had descended upon them in a flurry of questions and impossibilities. Not a month ago, Darius himself had discovered her sitting alone in a local pub, legs swinging back and forth on a too-tall barstool, communicating with the wind as easy as you please. To say he had been surprised would be an understatement. Wardens, those who possess a kinship to specific elements from nature, were fated caretakers of that element; Earth, Air, Fire, Water, Life, Death, or Beast. They had the ability to create, restore, see, feel and shape their element. Without wardens, balance could not be maintained and the world would spiral into chaos. The only problem was; people were born wardens and the birthright was a heavy burden to bear. Constantly using their own energy and resources in order to ensure their element – or domain – remained happy and healthy, resulted in them always losing what was essentially their life force. On top of that, they were like beacons to the evil beings of their society – the chades.

Darius hated the chades with every fibre of his being. They were foul creatures, monsters who had turned their backs on their honour and instead chosen a life of pain and depravity. They stalked, stole and killed until warden numbers had withered to a small percentage of their once thriving population. But luckily, Mother Nature had accounted for all the obstacles a warden faced, he supposed. And that was him – well, him and his fellow knights. As a paladin it was his born duty to provide service and protection to wardens in general and to his liege in particular. He always prided himself on his exemplary service and his family had been one of the most respected and sought after paladin lines for centuries. He had served under the one liege for a millennium until those unspeakable chades had taken everything away from him and his family. Thousands of years of service and honour, eradicated in an instant. As a result, he hadn't been in an Order or served a liege for almost forty years. Instead he volunteered at the training centre with a few other misplaced paladins.

But all that was about to change, thanks to Max. Following what he assumed was a lost Warden out of the bar, he had been completely appalled and shocked when she had fought expertly and decapitated their enemy. Passive. Wardens were supposed to be passive. Well, in recent years anyway, Darius silently amended. After all, his liege had fought in the Crusades. After weeks of educating the young Warden of Life about her powers, about shielding, about their roles in society and their laws, he had begun to see that Max was never really going to fit into the traditional Warden mold. She was easy-going, honest and had no social airs whatsoever. She didn't understand their caste system and didn't *want* to understand it – she thought it was outdated and 'dickish' – her words. And despite all their best efforts to convince her they were not suitable candidates to be her personal paladins, she had claimed them anyway. In turn, he had offered her his service just the evening prior. It was a huge step for him and although he didn't regret it per se, they definitely needed to discuss a few more things before any bonding and branding occurred. The biggest issue in the light of day?

Max was a Custodian.

A Custodian.

Not a Warden like they had originally – and rightfully – assumed. But an honest to goodness daughter of Mother Nature herself. Which meant that Max was a real live Goddess. The woman walked around with no shoes, a slater bug on her shoulder and a spoon of Nutella permanently attached to her face, and she was a Goddess?! Darius barked out a laugh and was glad he was alone on the beach – he was famous for his controlled demeanour at all times. He was also the resident researcher and historian of the group, which implied he would be the one responsible for trying to unravel the mystery that was Max. Darius was pretty sure it was going to be an impossibility and he didn't think his poor, ordered, mildly OCD brain was going to be able to reconcile the chaos that was a darn Goddess in his house!

He sighed as the wind caressed his face, cooling his flushed skin. He was a paladin affiliated with air and although he couldn't create it or control it like a warden could, it still recognised him as a friend and ally, and he was able to take comfort from the element. Although it seemed nigh impossible, Darius knew in his heart that Max was indeed a Custodian. A child born directly from the Great Mother herself ... and not seen or heard of in thousands of years. How Max came to be roving around the streets with no memory he had no clue, but he sure was going to try to find out. He was also going to dig deep into the archives for any mention of a Custodian in a corporeal form. As far as he was aware, they weren't supposed to be in human form. Darius scrubbed his fingers over his close-cropped scalp; yep, Max sure was upsetting his carefully ordered world.

Seeing movement out of the corner of his eye, Darius automatically reached for his sickle. Even though it was barely dawn and he was on private property, he kept his blade with him always. He relaxed as he recognised Cali's slender form silhouetted against the now-rising sun. She was obviously going for her morning swim. Although there was not much light and it was still chilly this time of year, he knew she could swim like a fish and therefore wasn't concerned about her being alone in the water. The water would never harm her anyway, given the paladin was affiliated with the water domain. With his thoughts somewhat more in order, he decided to head into the house, where the others were probably already stirring to begin their morning routines.

*****

He found he had another hour to himself before the masses began to descend. In that time, he had made a pot of tea, eaten breakfast and listened to the morning news as was his usual ritual. There was nothing noteworthy in the local news to suggest any warden-related issues, so he felt better about informing Ryker he'd be spending the day hitting the books. Clearing the table, Darius felt himself go still as Ryker entered the room. It wasn't because his Captain was a commanding presence – although he was. He figured Max assumed they all followed him because Ry was an *Alpha*, as she called him, and although the title was incorrect, the description was spot on. Ryker was a *potentate*; one of those rare few paladins born with the legacy to lead.

Although, he himself was the oldest and most experienced knight in the camp with the purest bloodline, he was not a born potentate. He could fight chades with the best of them, work the politics better than most, and provide a warden with vitality, but none of that mattered if he couldn't maintain a link within an Order. Only a potentate could act as a bridge between a Warden and their Order, allowing communication and a flow of the bond. A potentate also exuded strength, purpose and loyalty from their very pores and commanded respect just by breathing. Ryker was definitely that man, despite his 'outcast' role in recent years. Darius couldn't think of a single other paladin who could have survived the madness of The Great Massacre other than the man standing before him.

But all that was kind of a moot point now, Darius mused, given that Ryker was now officially bonded to Max. Ryker had little choice but to accept the title of Captain regardless of his potentate status. Besides, he was so in love with the fiery Goddess, there was no way he would allow any other to be in charge of her safety. Clearly it was now very official, he thought, and the reason for his continued stillness. Ryker now sported a brand new coat of arms – he and Max must have bonded as paladin and liege overnight. He was wondering how that would work, given she wasn't actually a Warden. But a binding was obviously possible, evidenced by the full sleeve of dark ink covering Ryker's left forearm and disappearing under the sleeve of his white tee shirt on his bicep. *Damn! That was one big Heraldry!*

"Well, that's different." Axel stated, breezing into the room in workout shorts, shoes and nothing else. Darius managed to hold back a cringe at seeing the fire paladin unclothed in the kitchen and so casual. He was from a time when things were more ... formal. Although he thought he had adapted admirably to the changing customs of the modern world, some old-world decorum still clung; like not eating communal meals half naked! But he was the only one who thought so apparently, given the regularity of the act, so he had learned to accept the more casual ways of his fellow knights. He could not, however, accept Axel guzzling directly from the milk carton!

"Axel!" He shouted.

The blond with the surfer-boy good looks simply gave him a thumbs up and continued drinking. Shaking his head, he gave up. Axel was never going to change. He was reckless, sarcastic and defiant of all authority figures. Darius also felt he had some growing up to do, but at the end of the day, he would follow him into battle anywhere. He was a fierce soldier with a backbone of steel and trustworthy to a fault. His somewhat wicked and dirty sense of humour had even started to grow on him. Not that he would ever give Axel the satisfaction of knowing he found him to be refreshing and funny.

Milk-chugging now done with, Axel focused on Ryker once more. "That's some piece of artwork you have there."

"Indeed it is." Darius agreed, frowning. "Not exactly inconspicuous."

He watched as Max's brow furrowed and her bottom lip extended in a pout, "You don't like it?" She asked.

Although that pouting lip made her look even more adorable – Darius could admit he was well under her spell – he could also see the genuine worry in her eyes. A Warden's coat of arms or Heraldry was a huge point of pride to their Orders and their lineage. It denoted their domain and the strength of their abilities. They were always unique, like a fingerprint, and were reflective of the Warden and their ancestry as well. They never knew what the brand would look like until they bonded and formed an Order. It was an honour to see one's coat of arms branded on those loyal to you – those sworn to protect you and serve you throughout your life. And Darius figured it would be rather humbling as well. But to Max, he knew it must mean even more. With no memory, unstable powers, and chades haunting her every step, she hadn't been able to set down any roots. Any friendships she made only put them in danger and having been raised in foster care as well as time on the streets, there wasn't anyone she could call family.

To finally learn who and what she was and to be amongst her own kind, must be an unbelievable relief. Max soaked up affection like a sponge, having gone so long without any. The fact that all of his fellow paladins had fallen head over heels for her was like a balm to her lonely heart. So to see her brand on the man she loved? Well, Darius knew just how important that had to be to her. Treading carefully, he offered;

"It's not that I don't like it, Max ..." And it truly wasn't. The sleeve was a thing of beauty. Axel had been correct in calling it artwork. It looked to be a series of black and grey lines interwoven in some sort of intricate pattern. The only hint of colour he could see anywhere was the druidic symbol for life. Given Ryker was a paladin of life, he figured that must be significant. Walking over to take a closer look, he could see the small rune was centre stage on Ry's inner forearm, right where a typical coat of arms would be. A mixture of vines, branches, thorns, flames, and feathers swirled around and branched over his entire arm from wrist to shoulder. The complex shading seemed to flow like water. He could also make out six more druid symbols interspersed in the flames and vines – they were perfectly matched with Max's own domain symbols tattooed on her back. He really wasn't surprised. Ryker had discovered the seven druid elemental runes hidden in Max's tattoo the night before and had figured out they were her Heraldry. She had instinctively melded them into her art without realising their significance.

What did surprise him though, was seeing the shimmering pale purple, almost white quality of the life symbol. And as Ryker moved his arm, it seemed almost three-dimensional. It wasn't large, no bigger than a twenty-cent piece, but the fact that it shimmered in the light and seemed to stand out from his skin, made it the first thing you saw. Reaching out his hand, he raised an eyebrow for permission. Ryker nodded and extended his arm out further. Darius tentatively ran his hand over the intricate vines and thorns.

"Holy –" He barely managed to cut off his expletive as he jumped back, putting distance between him and the now *moving* coat of arms. The dark lines of twisted branches appeared to writhe in the wake of his touch. After a couple of seconds, they were once again still, bar for a couple of leaves settling as if they had been ruffled by the wind ... or by someone shaking a branch. Ryker's symbol for life had also glowed and it definitely looked three-dimensional – it wasn't just a trick of the eyes.

Darius knew he must look like an idiot – standing there, jaw hanging open, eyes wide, staring at Ryker's inked skin like it was going to attack. But jeez, moving Heraldry was just not normal! It was almost as if ... it was alive.

"Cool, huh?" Max chirped happily, seemingly ignorant of his internal freak-out. "It's almost as if it's alive!" She finished, repeating his own thoughts back to him – which served to freak him out further. A Warden shouldn't be able to hear their paladin's thoughts until they bonded.

"Darius?"

"What?!" He didn't mean to snap at the tiny female, but, well ... Ryker's coat of arms had been *moving!* At his abrupt retort, Ryker's brows slammed down and he stepped in front of Max, his large frame completely blocking her from view.

"Watch your tone, Darius." The rumbled words were practically growled out and there was no mistaking the implied 'or else' threat in them.

Darius winced. Yeah, Ryker would wipe the floor with him if he said or did anything to upset his new lover and liege. Still, you'd think he'd cut him some slack, given all the insensitive and harsh comments he'd been spewing the past few weeks. But Darius hadn't gotten to be over a thousand years old by being stupid, so he wisely kept his mouth shut. Instead, he peered around Ryker's body mass at Max. The adorable pout was gone and this time real concern shone in her turquoise eyes.

"I'm sorry, honey. I didn't mean to snap." He held out his hand, which she immediately grabbed, and he kissed the back of it as was his habit in the past. "It just surprised me is all. Not only is your Heraldry encompassing Ryker's whole arm, but, well, it *moved!* That's not ..." Seeing Ryker's fearsome glare, he quickly amended the word 'normal' to, "... typical."

Quick to forgive, Max rolled her eyes. "Yeah, no shit. I figured that out when Ryker screamed like a girl in the shower this morning when it did its thing."

"I did *not* scream like a girl!" Ryker scowled and crossed his arms over his chest.

Max merely snorted and made her way to the refrigerator, "Did so too."

Axel, who had actually been quiet for more than five minutes for once, snagged her arm and dragged her onto his lap. "I believe you, sweetheart. The man is easily startled, like a mumma grizzly bear." He teased, ruffling her port-red hair. Ryker growled even as Max giggled and Darius couldn't help but smile at the sound. Yeah, Axel really was an asset to the team and he had appointed himself Max's overprotective big brother – if you ignored the constant flirting, that is.

"I think your Heraldry is great! Completely badass! Puts all those other puny, non-moving ones to shame." Axel continued.

"Axel ..." Darius began warningly. Talking about other Heraldry and Wardens in such an insulting manner, could earn one serious reprisals. Nothing like the public floggings and whippings of the past, but still ...

The fire paladin merely levelled serious blue eyes at him and Darius knew without a shadow of a doubt that Axel considered Max his liege. He would die to protect her and offer her loyalty and friendship to the end of his days. Darius felt the same way, he truly did. But he couldn't help his concerns or his few reservations from forming front and centre in his mind. He liked things ordered and in control. Max was very ... unordered. The mere fact that she was a Custodian was enough to rock him to his core. In time, he knew he would reconcile all this new and chaotic information, but he needed to be able to process, assess and act accordingly. So first up would be trying to pry some more information out of the tight-lipped Goddess, then it would be research time with the books.

Before he could start asking anything, however, the rest of the household breezed into the room. They were at least fully clothed, although Lark and Beyden also wore workout gear. Cali's long blonde hair was still damp and her loose summer dress was sticking to her – she rarely dried off completely after a swim before donning her clothes. And then there was Diana. The woman of his musings from ages past. She was fully dressed in designer jeans and a muted green singlet top. Her curly hair was as perfectly styled as curls could get, and she had a light dusting of makeup on. She was, as always, perfect.

Darius forced himself not to linger on her visage longer than any of the others. He had become rather adept at it over the years. "Good morning." He offered to all. A series of 'good mornings' followed as everyone made their way to the coffee machine, fridge or pantry. Paladins were big eaters. He noticed Beyden and Lark subtly eyeing Max as if she were a ghost. Clearly he wasn't the only one to find the whole Custodian situation a little unnerving.

"How is our little Custodian this morning? Still a Goddess?" Cali asked, cheekily. Apparently, it didn't bother her in the slightest. How she could be so flippant about the whole thing, Darius couldn't fathom.

Max shrugged, "I guess so. Ryker explained a little about it last night; how the Druids were the original guardians of the world, born from Mother Nature herself to protect, guide and create the elements. But it became too much for the few Druids and so some humans were given similar abilities – the Wardens." She buttered her toast casually as if she were telling a fairy-tale instead of recounting the most sacred facts of their history. "He also said the Druids – or Custodians – aren't supposed to be so fleshy."

"Fleshy?" Beyden asked, confused.

Max waved her toast around before pinching the skin on her arm, "Yeah, you know, *fleshy*, like skin and bones. They were like spirits or something. Given that I am indeed very fleshy, I'm not sure how I can be one of these Custodians. But, it does feel … more right. It always sounded a bit off whenever you called me a Life Warden. This doesn't – it's *comfortable*." She ate her last bite of toast before continuing, "And apparently my Heraldry is different to other wardens, so I guess that's more proof."

"Your Heraldry?" Cali asked, latching onto the end part of the conversation with interest. "Who'd you bond with?"

"Who do you think?" Axel rolled his eyes, "My room is the closest to Ryker's but I swear I'm moving bedrooms! I don't think I can function if I keep hearing all those squeals and grunts bleeding through the walls every night." He shuddered.

Ryker merely slapped him upside the back of his head as he passed, flashing his new brand in the process.

"Oh, wow! That is so cool!" Cali exclaimed, eyes widening. Turning to Max, she stated, "I want one!"

"Okay!" Max squealed and bounded over to her friend, placing one hand on Cali's left arm and one over her heart, before anyone could move.

"No! Wait!" Darius cried out, trying to stop Max before it was too late. But the air had already started to charge with electricity as wind whipped around, lifting hair and rustling clothes gently. A pleasant warmth engulfed the kitchen and he saw Max's eyes go opaque before they began to swirl with a rainbow of colours. Cali gasped as a series of branches, thorns, vines, feathers and flames began to swirl their way up her arm from wrist to shoulder. Darius watched in wonder as all seven of Max's domain symbols began to appear against the black and grey tapestry. The whole scene was over in a matter of seconds and as Max removed her hands, he could see the shimmering, luminescent, somehow three-dimensional water symbol, centred and blue on Cali's forearm.

Darius pinched the bridge of his nose, his only outward sign of distress. What should have been a sacred ritual witnessed by the most supreme members in their society, had taken place in the kitchen with bare feet, sweaty bodies and saltwater hair. Yep, Max sure was a strain to his perfectly ordered world.

TWO

Diana watched in awe as Max casually bonded Cali to her as easily as if she were blowing out a candle. Typically, when a paladin wished to pledge their allegiance to a warden, they first submitted their application to the Local Warden Council. After ensuring the paladin's bloodline, reputation and completion of training, the local council would then recommend the paladin to the International Domain Council. The IDC had the final say of who would be bound into what Order – although they did attempt to ensure a natural bond was present – the overall goal was creating a powerful Order. Once approved, a ceremony took place in front of the IDC, the local council in their area, and all other local paladins and wardens. Bonding ceremonies only happened twice a year and were a very big deal. Not only did the swearing of allegiance need to be witnessed, but the warden's coat of arms, or Heraldry, needed to be observed and documented in the Chronicles. Max had just made a big boo boo as far as their councils and traditions were concerned.

Casting a glance around the room, she assessed the various responses from her fellow knights. Ryker was resigned, Cali thrilled, Lark and Beyden appeared a little frightened and a lot awe struck, Axel was smiling indulgently, and Darius? Diana shook her head. The poor man was valiantly struggling to hide his reaction. She could only imagine what the whirlwind that was Max was doing to the staid, ordered psyche that was Sir Darius.

Diana really wasn't surprised to see the look of strain on his handsome face. It wasn't really that obvious and others who didn't know him so well probably wouldn't have even noticed, but the lines around his clear hazel eyes were pinched and his nostrils were slightly flared. Diana had been studying his perfect countenance for hundreds of years and recognised the tell-tale signs of agitation easily. He had always been one of the handsomest men she had ever encountered. Too bad he was also one of the most stuck-up. Not stuck-up as in snobby or posh, but he was a rule-follower to the nth degree. He believed in duty and responsibility above all else, almost to the point of obsession. Most certainly to the point of sacrificing his own needs and desires in order to ensure every rule or law was adhered to precisely. As a result, Diana had gone centuries without ever knowing the intimate touch of the air paladin. Sure, she could have tried harder over the years, maybe taken advantage in his rare times drinking or in his time of grief. But she had meant it when she told him he would have to ask her.

Prideful? Yes.

Stubborn? Most definitely.

But just as Darius had a personal code he followed, so did she; she didn't beg for anything.

But he sure was looking good this morning, she acknowledged. Dressed in their uniform of black cargo pants and a black tee shirt, newspaper spread in front of him and a cup of tea at his elbow, the man looked dangerous and sophisticated at the same time. How someone could pull that look off, Diana didn't know, but he always somehow managed to do it. He was just so ... *fine*. The instant attraction she had felt for him when she had first laid eyes on him eight hundred years ago in the Battle of Lisbon, still perplexed her. She had known who he was of course – every paladin and warden knew of the famous Magne brothers. His lineage was distinguished and could be traced back to one of the original wardens from the time of the Druids. His family line had been producing powerful wardens and paladins alike for centuries. Too bad it resulted in Darius being a pathological rule-follower.

Even now, Diana couldn't understand why Darius's rejection of her that day had hurt so much. It wasn't like she had known him then other than the magnificent way he had swung a sword. She flexed her hand in remembrance of the heat that had flared to life between them when their skin had touched. She hadn't felt anything like it before nor since. And Darius had denied it. *The big coward!* She thought, silently. He couldn't bend the rules for just one minute to consider the potential that had been standing in front of him. And here they were, thrown together again after eight centuries, and he was still ignoring the possibilities. All because of an esteemed family legacy in a society that had turned their backs on him because of one incident that had been no fault of his own. Their society needed a swift kick, Diana knew, and watching Max ooh and ahh over her new coat of arms, gave Diana hope that said kick was imminent.

"Max, I think we need to have a little talk." Darius's deep voice was just as attractive as his face and had Diana shaking herself out of her stupor. Dwelling on the past never resulted in changing it, so why bother?

Making her way to the table, she gave both Max and Cali an affectionate kiss on the cheek, "Congratulations, ladies. The Heraldry suits you both." She then reached up and dragged Ryker's face down to her level, before planting a kiss directly on his lips. "Good job, Boss-man. You snagged yourself a winner."

Ryker grumbled good-naturedly and a slight flush dusted across his smooth cheeks. Diana still found it strange to look at her Captain and not see that horrendous scar covering half his face. Although he didn't look like a mass murderer anymore, he was still an imposing figure and Diana figured his bad boy rep would still be solidly intact.

"Ryker, please." Darius's voice was now a touch sterner and had the Captain's eyebrows rising. "We really need to address the elephant in the room."

Max's eyes narrowed, "I know you're not calling me an elephant, Darius."

Diana contained her snicker when Darius's eyes widened in horror as Max questioned his wording. That man was just too easy. No doubt he was concerned about potentially offending a higher member of society. When was he going to accept that Max was different and she was always going to be different? Ryker was very clearly on board, despite having the deepest reservations at the beginning. Most likely because he was sleeping with her, Diana acknowledged, but still …

"I didn't mean to imply –"

Max cut him off with a wave of her hand, "Relax, Darius. Geez, lighten up dude. You're totally ruining my moment of triumph here."

"I'm sorry Max, but I'm going to be spending the day researching Custodians – if that is fine with you, Ry?" He asked.

Ryker nodded. "I was going to suggest the same thing. Thanks, man."

Darius smiled, revealing his even white teeth. *The man even had fine teeth*, Diana thought. "I was hoping you could answer a few questions for me." He asked Max, politely.

Max crinkled her nose, "Like what?"

"Well, like your first memory. You said you woke up in Sydney as a teenager and couldn't remember anything ..." He trailed off.

Max shifted a little uncomfortably now. Diana knew she didn't enjoy sharing her past. She got the feeling there were many aspects to the complicated woman they had yet to discover and many things in her past that she wanted to keep private. Diana could relate, she honestly could. Everyone here had things in their past and most were yet to disclose those pasts to Max as well. But she also agreed with Darius. If Max was indeed a Custodian – she *totally* was – then they definitely needed to figure a few things out.

"That's right. Nothing." Max confirmed. "I couldn't even read. I told you that."

"I know. But I'm just hoping for some clues as to where you're from."

"Why?" Max asked.

"Why?" Darius repeated.

"Yes. Why? Is it that important? I'm here now. I found you guys, I'm not running for my life from phantoms, I'm not sick anymore." She looked at Ryker lovingly but a little pleadingly, "And I have Ryker now too. Does it really matter where I came from?"

"Not to me." Axel replied.

"Or me." Beyden followed. Diana wasn't surprised by their immediate support. Axel had appointed himself protector and biggest fan and Beyden was a real sweetheart – too mellow to want to rock the boat.

"It doesn't matter to us. Not in the way you're worried about it." Cali assured her. "But it's sure going to matter to everybody else, including the IDC."

Bless her, but Cali was just so practical. She understood where Darius's polite questioning was heading. She was absolutely correct. The IDC had a hard enough time believing

Ryker when he had reported Max was a Life Warden. But Diana knew they had been giddy as school girls to learn that another female had been found with powers over the domain of life. It was the rarest and also one of the most powerful of the seven elements. When they finally divulged Max was actually a living, breathing Custodian ...? They would probably pee their pants. But they would have questions – lots of questions! And puppy dog turquoise eyes were not going to work on those hard-arses. It was better for all of them to be prepared.

"Well, I can't tell them what I don't know. I literally woke up in a park wearing a plain grey tracksuit. It had no tags and no logos. It was natural fibres though – one hundred percent pure cotton. I was maybe fifteen, sixteen ..." She disclosed.

"How do you know you were that age?" Darius asked, his fingers twitching. Diana knew he wished he had a pen and paper to be writing things down but didn't dare interrupt in case Max closed up again.

Max shrugged and leaned more heavily against Ryker who immediately dropped a kiss to the top of her head. "I looked about that age – the authorities thought so anyway. Plus, I had boobs."

"Boobs?" Axel perked up.

Max grinned at him, "Yep. Boobs! I obviously went through puberty years earlier, oh, and I was always this height. I never got any taller. That was around twenty-five years ago so I'm like, fortyish now. Is that helpful?"

Darius grimaced. "Not especially ... But thank you!" He hastily added when Ryker glared at him.

"You don't look more than thirty, maybe even late twenties." Lark pointed out. "Wardens age slower than normal humans and even paladins because they are constantly recharging their vitality. It's what gives them their longevity. Paladins age much the same as normal people and slow down when they form a bond with their liege. It's possible you are far older than what you think. Wardens in their twenties often look like they are in their teens; they mature much slower."

Diana smiled when Darius stilled, his face revealing nothing much but she knew he was piqued that he hadn't thought of that angle. Diana wasn't surprised; Lark was very intelligent. She was extremely curious as to what his IQ might be. She was suspicious that he may actually qualify as a legitimate genius. But his happy nature and his reading habits didn't lend one to the assumption that he was an Einstein.

"That's good thinking. Maybe you should join me in my research?" Darius acknowledged and offered.

Lark ducked his head as he flushed. He was far too modest and given the number his father had done on his self-esteem, she wasn't surprised he underestimated himself. "I'm sure you've got it handled. Besides, I'm on Lodge duty with Axel and Cali. I'd be happy to pitch in later though if you think it would help?"

"I think it would help a lot." Darius's smile was warm and genuine. She locked her knees to keep from swooning a little.

Presently, Ryker surged up, effectively dwarfing his new liege and lover. Max was only five foot three in shoes and Ryker was six foot four bare foot. But somehow ... they fit. He clapped his hands once, "So we all know what we're doing today; Lark, Cali, Axel – get to the Lodge. It's sickle training today. Darius, I want you to put your historian hat on and report back to me anything you discover – no matter how small. Bey and Diana, we three will be on guard duty. Max is ours now, we protect her with our lives."

"That was so hot." Max breathed, looking to Diana and Cali for confirmation. Diana nodded her head and shook out her hand as if burned. Boss-man was *definitely* hot!

Cali waggled her eyebrows suggestively as the men started to move, clearly choosing to ignore the pervy women in the room. "Oh, one more thing ..." Cali's voice rang out and halted everyone in their tracks.

"Wha-at!" Max whined out. Her patience was well and truly gone.

Cali ignored her. "While Darius is off doing his thing figuring out how you're a lowly Goddess, and we're at the Lodge kicking trainee butts, maybe Beyden and Ryker can work on your shielding some more and controlling the bond."

"What do you mean, more shielding? I'm good at that now. I haven't even drawn any phantoms to me in weeks!" Max exclaimed.

"Chades, Max. They're called chades. And yes, your shielding is much better. Go team!" Cali gave a double thumbs up. "But the link in our new little Order could use some work."

Max was frowning now. "What do you mean? What does she mean?" She asked Ryker.

"The bond is almost like a path or a bridge, linking all the members within an Order to their liege. Its purpose is to ensure we can be connected to you at all times so we can best anticipate your needs, safety and happiness. It's a two-way street though. You can feel us and we can feel you." Ryker explained.

"You can feel what I'm feeling? Can you hear my thoughts too?" Max asked, clearly dismayed over the notion that her privacy was being invaded.

"It's not like that. Yes, when the Order is fully knitted together and you learn how to control it better, you will be able to speak to us in our minds, but it's not like an open door, don't worry." Darius appeased.

"But it is kind of flowing like a waterfall right now." Cali pointed out bluntly. The woman really wasn't great at subtle. No wonder her and Max had clicked the moment they met. "Beyden and Lark are the experts with shielding but Ryker is the expert at controlling the bond. So you get to spend the day with your new man. Yay!" Cali cheered, before continuing, "He's a potentate, which means he can maintain the bond between you and your Order. Although, with you being a Custodian, I'm not sure if this is going to work the same ..."

"Let me get this straight; first, I'm leaking and now I'm gushing like a waterfall?" Max's hands went to her hips, her jaw tightening.

"It's just a matter of control. It's not a big deal. We'll work on it." Ryker drew her in close to his side.

"I can control myself. I'm awesome at control!" Max assured the room at large.

Even Diana had to laugh at that one. The woman was spontaneous to say the least and prone to random and unprovoked fits of violence and lecturing. Control and Max were not words that were synonymous.

Max stomped her foot. "I am! See!"

Diana watched as Cali and Ryker abruptly reeled, Ryker caught himself against the edge of the table and Beyden managed to prop up Cali before she took a header into the marble benchtop.

"Whoa there, girlfriend." Cali shook her head, "You can't just cut off the link like that. Cold turkey is not fun for anyone."

Max looked genuinely startled as she bit her lip. "I'm sorry. Too abrupt?"

"Maybe just a little." Ryker said, grimacing as he rubbed his chest with a large palm. He immediately opened his arms to Max though as she leaned in, smoothing her palms over his pecs.

"I'm sorry. You're right. I need to learn. Will you teach me?" She beseeched.

Diana remembered Max asking Ryker that exact same thing almost six weeks ago when they had all mistakenly told her she was a Warden. And now those same words were obviously like some kind of trigger to the man. His eyes darkened from their usual warm milk chocolate colour to a much darker bitter cocoa and he growled, the sound rumbling deeply in his muscled chest. Diana shared a look with Cali – the masculine sound of want was damn potent! Deciding to give the love birds a break, she clapped her hands like a school marm;

"Okay, since we all know our jobs now, perhaps we should get to them, hmm?"

Ryker was already moving in the direction of the stairs, pulling a very willing Max along behind him. Max glanced back long enough to mouth a silent thank you before disappearing in a breathless giggle.

THREE

One week later and Darius was no closer to finding any answers and solving the mystery that was Max. He had been researching Custodians morning and night for six days and had read every last available piece of information. Beyden had even managed to get his hands on an electronic copy of the Warden Chronicles. The Chronicles documented hundreds of years of history and covered information about wardens, paladins, domains, vitality, chades and endless laws and rules as well as battles fought and won. Unfortunately, an incalculable amount of history had been lost during The Great Massacre fifty years ago. The Chronicles had not been stored electronically back then and the main library housing the priceless documents had been razed to the ground. He had been able to learn a little more information about Custodians in general, as well as vitality exchanges and the origins of wardens, but nothing that really provided them with more answers as to why Max was a Custodian and why she was, well, *fleshy*, as she had so eloquently put it last week.

Lark had proven himself invaluable and Darius felt quite ashamed that he had been living with the younger man for almost ten years and he had not known that the earth paladin was a borderline genius. They had been able to piece together a vague history of the Custodians, using the odd mention of them here and there over the years. They had even managed to put together a timeline of sorts on Max's history before she had stumbled across them. Still nothing before she woke up in that park though and it irked him to no end! How was he supposed to form a clear, concise and logically reasoned out theory if he didn't have all the facts?

He and Lark had shared what they had discovered. Max had thanked them and Ryker had congratulated them on a job well done. But the job wasn't done – well or otherwise! Darius raged internally. He needed answers so he could make order out of the chaos. But he was apparently the only one who thought so. The others seemed more than willing to accept the situation for what it was and seemed to care nothing for the potential ramifications Max was going to have in their society. Their nonchalance irked him also, and so that morning, he figured a good old fashioned spar might just help relieve some tension. Max deemed it a brilliant idea, informing them she wanted to train as well. Although a couple of the others had pitched themselves against Max's considerable skills, Darius had been unable to bring himself to do it. It had been difficult enough sparring with her five weeks ago when he had thought her a mere Warden. After all, she was female, half his size and also his superior – not an opponent he was comfortable fighting. But now it was even worse. They had confirmed that she was the single most important person on the planet and she wanted him to wrestle with her in the dirt? Not going to happen.

Ryker had been more than willing to put him through his paces though. And paced he had! He had used brute force as well as practiced technique to throw Darius to the mat again and again. Darius prided himself on his own strength and was able to break through Ryker's defenses a handful of times, only to have his victory short-lived. Ryker was taking no prisoners and had even nicked Darius a couple of times with his sickle. They rarely went so far as to draw blood during training. It was like Ry was determined to guarantee that anyone responsible for ensuring Max's safety was at the top of their game. Darius couldn't really blame him. And although his body was sure to feel it tomorrow, his mind did feel lighter.

Now he was watching Cali and Diana critically as they attempted to take down Max. Max was between them and fighting hard against their constant attacks. Both Cali and Diana were striking simultaneously, not even taking turns to give the outnumbered, shorter woman a fair chance. The very flexible Cali delivered a high round-house kick that sliced over Max's head at the last second. Max immediately flipped herself back up from her now prone position on the ground where she had landed after allowing her limbs to go loose. She gave a slash with her tanto sword at Cali's midsection and Darius knew she was holding back. If she had have straightened her elbow out completely, he had no doubt Cali would be gutted on the floor. Diana charged silently from behind but Max anticipated the attack, catching her sickle along the length of her blade. The clang of metal caused all the other occupants in the room to still and watch the show.

Darius thought Ryker would put a stop to it before anyone got seriously hurt, but he merely crossed large arms over his chest and eyed the scene with ... lust. Darius rolled his eyes. Of course Ryker was eyeing his woman like she was a prime steak on the menu. He glanced at Axel, Beyden and Lark and sure enough, they also wore expressions of manly appreciation. Fortunately, Darius was far too superior to be ruled by such base emotions. Nope, there was no way that Diana's perfectly shaped rear-end and perfectly flared hips caught his attention. Her plump breasts, now encased in form-fitting lycra, in no way made him want to tie her to his bed while he lavished attention on them all night long. And there was absolutely no way that the vision of her, grappling with him in such a forceful manner, had him harder than he could remember being in all his long days. Nope – no way!

The sound of singing steel refocused his attention just as Max flipped Diana over her shoulder, maintaining her hold on the female paladin's weapon. Diana landed heavily on her back and wasn't quick enough to spring back up before Max landed on her, holding her own blade to her throat. Cali was behind her instantly, sickle raised, but frozen in place. At first, Darius couldn't understand why, then he saw that Max had her sword pressed snugly high up on Cali's left thigh. It would take very little pressure to sever her femoral artery. Silence reigned for a full ten seconds before Cali grinned and offered Max a hand.

"Good job! I didn't even see you until I felt the blade against my skin." Max grinned and they both reached down to help pull Diana to her feet. *Thank the Great Mother!* Darius prayed silently. Despite his amazing and mature restraint *not* to get turned on by the display of women fighting, the sight of seeing two gorgeous women straddling each other had been beginning to get to him. *He* wanted to straddle the Lady Diana.

Impossible, Darius! Focus!

"Well fought, My Lady." Diana bowed in a courtly manner of old as Max flushed with pride.

"Thanks!"

"But fess up. You were good before – like really good – but now you're brilliant. What's going on?" Diana asked, leaning over to rest her hands on her knees as she gulped in harsh breaths. Her latte skin was dotted with a fine layer of perspiration in further testament to her exertion and several springs had escaped the confines of her bun.

He wanted to pull on them.

"Just call me Master, young Padawan." Max replied, grinning and barely out of breath. Darius narrowed his eyes. Max did seem to be sparring with ease today, blocking and dodging the fists and sickles coming at her with an effortless grace. Perhaps it had something to do with the constant vitality she was now receiving. Lark and Diana had also bonded with Max over the past week – despite his continued warnings to the contrary that they should all wait. As a result, Max was recharging her essential energy on a daily basis. The results were astounding. Obviously, she was much healthier and Darius couldn't be happier about that. She barely resembled the pale, exhausted woman with dark circles and cracked lips of six weeks ago. He was pleased to see that she had more colour in her cheeks and a healthier glow overall. Darius couldn't believe the state Max had been in when she had first arrived. She was so low on vitality – the energy Wardens needed to function – that she had been having seizures. It was absolutely deplorable. Typically, for a warden to be showing such extreme outward signs of ill health, they were almost at death's door. And Max had been suffering from seizures since she was a child. Of course, she had no idea she was supposed to be recharging her energy. She had somehow been able to survive by borrowing minute amounts of vitality from the world around her. Darius couldn't even begin to imagine how much pain Max must have been in all these years. And although, not a Warden like they had originally presumed, she clearly still required a vitality exchange from a paladin in order to be healthy.

Her constant recharging and newfound health also meant that the landscape surrounding the camp was undergoing constant maintenance and upgrades. It had always been beautiful; kilometres of private beach, generous picturesque gardens and natural bushland, encircling the stunning house of logs. But now it was like a paradise; the lawns were a lush green and all the plants were blooming in abundance. The fish in the pond had somehow multiplied, as had the resident animal life. There were honest to goodness koalas in the trees and kangaroos grazed every evening out the front. Despite what the rest of the world seemed to think, koalas and kangaroos did not roam free range around everyone's neighbourhoods. On top of that, Darius knew Cali was now sharing her morning swims with dolphins and even a whale or two. The world around them was thriving.

"Are you cheating?" Cali demanded, clearly still focused on how Max was suddenly a ninja.

"Cheating? *Moi?* I would never!" Max's oceanic eyes were wide with innocence.

Yep, Darius thought, smiling. She was *so* cheating. There was nothing innocent about Max.

"You are! You're cheating!" Cali exclaimed, pointing an accusing finger.

Max burst out laughing as she walked over to Ryker, accepting his kiss as if it were the most natural thing in the world – and to them it probably was. They were perfect together, they really were, and he couldn't be happier for the smitten couple. But Darius feared the repercussions of their relationship. Emotional relationships were not allowed. It caused too many issues, not the least of one being a distraction and torn loyalties. But there would be no going back for them and Darius knew Max would never hide their commitment to each other, so he and the rest of his fellow knights were just going to have to support them the best they could ... And threaten anyone who dared stand in their way.

"She's not really cheating." Ryker defended. "She is simply using every resource at her disposal. I would hope all of you do the same when you're fighting."

Obviously, Ryker was privy to Max's secrets. Darius knew Max kept her bond with Ryker more open than with the others. Since the week before in the kitchen when Cali had told her of how open the bond was, Max had been working diligently to control the flow better. She could easily turn it on and off at will – something only possible from the oldest and strongest among them. But sometimes keeping the balance of in and out was still a bit tricky for her. Being a very private person, used to her own space, she tended to prefer to close the bond when experiencing high emotion rather than just turning it down. But just yesterday in his private study, Lark had revealed that he was having horrendous nightmares almost every night. He didn't disclose their content but he said he would wake up petrified and shaking and sick. He thought he was sharing Max's nightmares with her.

When she had first come, her screams had been a nearly nightly occurrence. Since sharing Ryker's bed every night, the blood curdling sounds had stopped and Darius had assumed the nightmares no longer plagued her. But if Lark was correct, then she was still suffering through night terrors. Lark was worried about upsetting Max and didn't want to approach her, adding on; *"Besides, she is my liege and I her paladin. If she must suffer nightly, then it is my duty and privilege to suffer with her."* Darius couldn't have been prouder of the young earth paladin. Lark had never been bound in an Order before, having been deemed unfit firstly by his pathetic excuse of a father, then by the local council – also coloured by his father's remarks. But he had taken to his duties like a true knight.

Beyden began laughing, drawing Darius back to the present. "I agree. We should all play to our strengths." He said smugly.

Cali's ice-blue eyes narrowed in mock danger at their resident gentle giant. Darius knew it was in jest because none of them could ever get mad at him. "What do you know, Beast-boy?"

For some inexplicable reason, the comment made Max and Beyden laugh even more. And that's when Darius noticed their guests. They were inside the gym – a separate building from the house – and the gym opened right up with a set of concertina doors, effectively creating a huge indoor-outdoor area. Given the fineness of the day, the doors had been opened wide and now that he was focused on something other than three sweaty, semi-naked females wrestling in front of him, he could see they had some extra spectators.

There was a parliament of owls perched in the doorway and even in the rafters. Although it was very unusual to see the normally nocturnal birds out in the light of day, Darius now had his answer as to Max's impressive skill. She literally had a little birdy sitting on her shoulder. The others noticed his line of sight and several gasps followed. Beyden picked his way over the practice mats and over to a particularly large brindled owl. It hooted softly, nudging his hand.

"Owls have binocular vision. It means they can judge height, width and depth all at the same time and even estimate distances the same way humans do. When you add in they are able to rotate their head two hundred and seventy degrees, their field of view is amazing." He explained.

"Are you trying to tell me the *owls* told you what to do?" Cali asked, sounding incredulous. Darius couldn't blame her. It was his understanding that Beast Wardens could communicate with animals, but he didn't think it was as clear as actual words. And those who could 'speak' to the animals held the most power over their domain. Max couldn't possibly be as powerful as the oldest and strongest wardens of their society, in every single domain, could she?

"Of course not!" Max said, everyone relaxing at her words. "They were simply watching your body's projections. You know, how your left shoulder twitches before you strike and your head dips slightly down when you're about to execute a kick? Their eyesight picks up everything!" She blew kisses at her new feathery friends. "Then they relayed that information to me."

"You were communicating with the owls the entire time you were engaged in battle with Cali and Diana?" Lark asked slowly as if in need of further clarification.

Max nodded her head, "Uh huh!" Oblivious to the shock and awe her flippant answer caused, she headed out of the gym, "Come on. I'm starving!"

Darius shook his head even as Axel asked, "Is she really that strong already?"

Ryker nodded. "Yes. She is."

FOUR

"So, I need to borrow a car please." Max stated, after everyone had cleaned up and were enjoying a mid-morning snack. It was Saturday and nobody was due in at the Lodge for anything. Diana knew Ryker had been working his butt off in order to find suitable replacements for them at the training centre. Now that they were bound to Max, they could no longer be working with the new recruits. Their sole responsibility was now to their liege and they would follow her and protect her and offer her vitality wherever she may be. The problem was, they couldn't yet reveal that some of them were indeed bound to Max, let alone that she was a Custodian. Ryker had strictly forbidden anyone to discuss Max outside these walls. They were all on board with the secrecy until Max could be introduced to the International Domain Council.

The seven heads of each domain travelled the globe almost constantly, each having a different home base somewhere. They usually travelled in pairs or small groups, settling disputes, doling out punishments, approving Orders and whatnot. They only appeared *en masse* every few months or so and had been due to arrive in their sleepy little part of the world at the beginning of the week. Garrett – the Life Warden and most influential member on the council – had called to let Ryker know they were held up dealing with other issues and their scheduled meeting would be delayed until further notice. They had asked Ryker how they were dealing with their new 'warden' friend and if they had any luck finding suitable paladins for her to bond with. Ryker had managed to fudge his way through the conversation by assuring them that Max was happy, safe and healthy and she had decided to stay on under their care temporarily. Ryker had revealed to her that he felt Garrett was a little too knowing – almost as if he was postponing the meeting until all of them could bond with Max or something. Diana had no idea why the Life Warden would want to encourage Max to bond with them let alone facilitate the process, but she had always liked him. He and his wife had been a part of the IDC for hundreds of years.

For her part, Diana was glad they were given the timely reprieve. She, along with Lark, had also bonded with Max a few days ago and they were all slowly muddling their way through the new link within their small Order. Cali had been correct; Max needed some guidance when it came to the link. It was either all or nothing. All was ridiculously intense, the power behind Max's thoughts and emotions were like nothing Diana had ever experienced in all her years. And her old liege, Verity, had been one of the most powerful Life Wardens ever to be born. Ryker, in true potentate style, was able to regulate the flow to a degree and she was sure he was directing it a lot in order to maintain Max's privacy. The initial peek Diana had gotten into Max's mind and her heart had left her shaken. Max was all goodness and light but also pain and sickness, and her vitality flowed from her in waves almost constantly. That was despite all the extra shielding techniques and all the holes Ryker and the other bonded members were plugging up. Diana could only imagine what that energy flow had been like before Max had met them, when she was ignorant of her origins. No wonder the poor thing had chades chasing her down like prey for so long. There would have been nowhere for her to hide where those power-hungry fiends wouldn't have been attracted to her.

And then there was the flip side; Max closing off the link altogether. They all struggled with it given it was just so unnatural. A very old and very powerful warden would be able to seal off the bond within an Order at their choosing very rarely. But the majority were not able to. Besides, most would never consider it because the whole point of the Order was to maintain a constant link to their liege. Max had other ideas however, and insisted on maintaining her privacy as well as theirs. It was actually very thoughtful and once Max learnt how to dial down before shutting off, Diana was sure she would even appreciate it. She had been without an Order for fifty years now and had grown accustomed to being alone in her own head. She was also worried about what she may inadvertently reveal to Max and the others about her attraction and feelings to a certain air paladin.

Said knight had been steadily showing signs of agitation all week. She knew he was frustrated that he couldn't find all the answers he wanted. His mind was very structured and rigid and she was concerned his self-perception of ineffectiveness would make him feel out of control. And a Darius not in control of his environment? Well, she had never really seen it but she was worried they were all about to. He had taken to muttering to himself, frowning constantly, and his temper was getting shorter and shorter. They were all sure signs that an individual was about to blow. And given she didn't believe he had blown a gasket in a thousand years ...? Well, it was going to be a doozy.

She was also very worried that Darius was yet to pledge his allegiance to Max again. She knew he wouldn't be able to feel secure in Max's Order until he attained resolution regarding her origins and potential. She also knew that was not going to happen. The answers as to why Max was a Custodian and just what it meant for their society and indeed, the world, was not going to be found on the pages of a book. If she were being honest with herself, she would admit that the thought of Darius not being in their Order terrified her. She knew. She just *knew* that the seven of them were supposed to be bound together. For what purpose, she had no idea, but Verity had always told her to trust her instincts. Axel and Beyden had not yet reaffirmed their pledge either, but it wasn't from lack of desire to do so. Ryker had thought it best to add to the Order slowly so as to not overwhelm Max or the fragile and novel bond. Axel couldn't wait to get his moving tattoo. That was another issue Darius had – Heraldries should *not* move.

Despite all of the above concerns, Diana was eternally pleased and proud to be bonded to such a wonderful liege. The natural bond had been there from the start and the feeling of rightness of *portent* even, just proved to Diana that this was where she was supposed to be. Her new liege, however, clearly wanted to be somewhere else at this moment for she was still busily asking Ryker for the loan of a car.

"Why do you want to borrow a car?" Ryker asked and Diana was glad to see he wasn't just going to say yes because they were sleeping together.

"I need to go into the city. I need to shop." Max said bluntly.

"You *need* to shop?"

"Yes! I have been here weeks and weeks now, living out of my beat-up pack and mooching off Diana and Cali for clothes. I need clothes. I need toiletries. I need supplies for my work. I *need* to shop." She said determinedly, and Diana couldn't blame her. The woman had shown remarkable strength of character to get this far living out of that damn bag of hers.

"Can't you just order it online?" Her idiotic *male* lover asked.

Predictably, Max felt it was a very male question as well. "No, Ryker. I cannot just order it online. I'm a human being. I have ovaries. I have needs."

"What do your ovaries have to do with anything?" Darius asked, causing her more alarm. There was no way Sir Darius would ever normally talk about the female reproductive system, let alone call one of its organs by name. She was tempted to feel his forehead for signs of fever.

Max narrowed her eyes at him, "My ovaries often dictate my whims, like the spontaneous and immediate need to shop. Just like your testicles often dictate your whims, like the need to masturbate furiously in the shower every morning."

Hey, what do ya know, Diana thought, eyes really could bug that far out of heads and not fall out of their orbital sockets. Evidently choosing to ignore the testicle laden occupants of the room, Max spoke again, this time directing her words to Diana and Cali;

"I also have a bunch of stuff in storage that I would like to get shipped here. I just need to get in contact with my friend where my stuff is stored and –"

"You have friends?" Ryker interrupted, surprise evident in his voice. Diana shook her head. Silly, silly man. That level of shock was totally insulting. Max clearly felt the same way for she aimed darkening eyes in his direction.

"Yes, Ryker. I have friends. I am actually likeable to some people. And I am capable of forming relationships."

Ryker winced, "I'm sorry, Max. That came out wrong. I didn't mean it like that. It's just, you don't talk about friends much and you always said you moved around a lot ..." He trailed off.

"No, I don't talk about my friends much. Yes, I did move around a lot." She repeated in acknowledgment. But that's where she stopped, not giving an inch to her poor chastised man. She was such a hard-arse, Diana thought with pride. And that prissy, cold tone of hers sure made one squirm.

Ryker walked over and took Max's hands in his. He towered over her and his large hands completely enveloped Max's petite ones. Raising her hands to his lips to kiss and nuzzle softly – a gentleness she never thought she would witness from the ruthless paladin – he apologised again, adding;

"Why don't you give your friend a call and get everything shipped here. And then we'll all go shopping and you can buy anything you want."

"Anything?" Max asked, still appearing stern.

"Of course! Anything!" Ryker was quick to assure her.

Max seemed to contemplate the peace offering for a moment, running her tongue over her white teeth as all the males in the room held their breath. *Damn, that girl is good!* Diana silently acknowledged.

After a strained thirty seconds, Max finally nodded, "Okay. I'll call Jazz now and then we can get ready to go."

"Sure thing."

"Of course."

"We'll be ready whenever you are."

The men commented as they all rushed off, obviously to weapon up in record time. As soon as they were out of ear shot, Cali released her pent up laughter, "Woman, you are just mean!"

Max giggled, all pretence of anger miraculously vanished. "What? That man deserved it. *'You have friends?'* Insensitive much?" Max asked rhetorically. "He's been so good these past couple of weeks, I thought he was cured of his dickish comments."

"Honey, he's a man. There's no cure for that." Diana pointed out.

Max nodded, "True. Very true. But at least we get to spend the day shopping!" She clapped enthusiastically. "I am dying for a wardrobe upgrade. Especially after seeing yours, Diana. I am in total wardrobe envy!"

She did have an exceptional wardrobe, she acknowledged. One she was very proud of. She was a little snobby when it came to clothes. She liked natural fabrics and believed it was worth spending a little more in exchange for quality and the best fit. When she had first moved in, she had twenty-five large boxes and suitcases; twenty-three of them had consisted of clothes and shoes. Ryker had been horrified. But to his credit, he had offered her the adjoining two rooms at the far end of the house, with their own bathroom. One room she slept in. The other? Well, she had converted it into a walk-in wardrobe ... a very *large* walk-in wardrobe. She thought Max was going to have one of her seizures when she had first shown it to her. She had stiffened, eyes wide, before squealing like a stuck pig and rummaging through everything like a kid in a candy store. Diana didn't mind. Although Max had been very handsy, she had left everything exactly in its place and hadn't disrupted a thing. She had also sniffed all of her leather shoes like a junkie needing a fix. It just made Diana like her more.

"Well, you know ..." Diana started, "Ryker did say you could get anything you wanted. That is extremely vague and open for interpretation."

"It is indeed. One could interpret it to mean, for example, that *anything* could mean *everything*." Max grinned and winked.

Laughing, Diana gave her a one-armed hug. "I do like how you think, my liege."

FIVE

Six hours later and Darius was considering slitting his wrists with his own sickle. Max, Cali and Diana had descended on the city's stores like an apocalyptic locust plague! They had gone from shop to shop, decimating the racks and locking themselves away in the fitting rooms for hours now. "When will this nightmare end?" He muttered, head in hands. He was out the front of a particularly large shoe store with Ryker, Axel and Beyden.

Axel bumped his shoulder, "It's not that bad."

Darius felt his eyes widen in disbelief, "You cannot be enjoying this."

Axel shrugged, popping a sauce-smothered fry into his mouth, "I enjoy all things female."

Of course he did, Darius grumbled silently. Lark was in the shoe store with the women – not for protection, no – the knight was almost as bad as they were! If Darius didn't know how lethal Lark was with a blade and such a badass solider, he would have been ashamed of his friend. He had followed them from shop to shop, smiling and laughing, getting just as excited over the sales as they were. The man loved to shop – who knew? Apparently, having Max around was allowing everyone to show their true colours without fear of shame or embarrassment. After all, Ryker was now meek as a lamb – around Max anyway. He had to give his Captain credit today though. The vein pulsing above his eyebrow indicated that he was experiencing the same type of hell as Darius.

Looking to his left, he eyed Beyden – who was also eating … again. The man must have consumed his weight in junk food throughout the day. How he could eat so much, Darius had no clue. He didn't share the ambivalent look of Axel or the tortured look of Ryker, no, he looked … indulgent. Which, in his opinion, was far worse. The man was absolutely smitten with their Custodian. "What about you, Bey? You about done for the day?" He asked, just to be sure.

"I don't mind." He responded amicably, as predicted. Darius could do no more than sigh.

Bey pinned him with those feline-like eyes of his, "What? They're happy." He stated simply. "What more can you ask for?"

Despite his impatient mood, he couldn't help smiling at the paladin of beasts. He was so even tempered, all of the time. Just so mellow. He wasn't sure if he had ever seen him yell or throw a tantrum. Although, to be fair, most of them probably hadn't seen Darius genuinely upset either. He didn't think of himself as even-tempered, but he did pride himself on his control. When he was a young paladin, the laws and rules governing their society and also the mainstream human one, were very strict. He had grown up knowing his place, never questioning his status or that of the wardens. He was a soldier and would always be a soldier, even when he wasn't bound to a liege. Old habits were hard to break … and so were first impressions. That was also something that was bothering him, he admitted. His first impression of Diana had been a blood splattered knight, fighting fiercely beside her liege. Cali had likewise been armed and dangerous at the Lodge. But this here, today?

They were undeniably women, not just paladins. It made him twitchy. He didn't need to be thinking about Diana as a woman, his nerves were already fraying.

"I guess I didn't realise how girly they all were. They're usually trying to prove how un-girly they are." Darius spoke without really thinking. "But then, most women love to shop I suppose."

Beyden did smirk at that, "Not all women. And I'd be careful how loudly you say things like that if I were you." He balled up his empty hot chip bucket and shot it into the garbage bin over five metres away with ease. He continued, "My sister wouldn't be caught dead shopping."

Ryker made a strangled sound – whether it was from the ridiculous imagery of Bey's sister shopping or something else, he couldn't be sure.

"Nothing could kill your sister, man. She's too mean to die." Axel softened his teasing words with a shoulder nudge and a twinkle in his blue eyes so his fellow knight understood he was joking.

"I sincerely hope that's true." Beyden's deep voice resonated with affection. Although he didn't see his sister often, they were still close.

Darius had only met Beyden's sister a handful of times but he had been impressed by her every time. It was a little hard not to be impressed really, the female earth paladin was a Ranger. The Rangers were the boogeymen of their society. They were paladins just like those serving in Orders so far as they also produced vitality and were able to share it with a warden. That was where the similarities ended though. A Ranger never bonded to a liege or formed an Order. They were loners by nature and design, their duty was to punish the guilty amongst them, whether they be Warden or knight. They hunted and killed chades with a merciless economy and were responsible for maintaining their prisons. They helped identify wardens abusing their powers or wardens with unstable powers, thus halting the threat of their conversion into a chade. Darius had no idea what actually transpired in the Ranger encampments and he wasn't sure he ever wanted to. He'd had the occasion a few times throughout his long life to deliver wardens and paladins into the care of the Rangers and each time he had shuddered in distaste at their establishments.

How Beyden and Ivy were related, Darius had no clue. They were polar opposites in everything from looks to personality. And it wasn't because they were only half siblings. Half siblings were extremely common in their society because wardens and paladins generally procreated with the aim of producing wardens or paladins of a particular kind. It meant they picked and chose who they wanted to produce a child with based on what they wanted the outcome to be. As a consequence, romantic relationships were few and far between and full siblings were a rarity. Darius and his brother had been one of those rare few. Not willing to focus on old, painful times, Darius decided to address new times instead;

"How is Max finding her feet within the Order?" He asked Ry.

Ryker smiled, his white teeth flashing. Although that horrendous scar no longer covered his face, his cheeks were by no means smooth, Darius noted. It looked like the guy hadn't shaved in days and a dark growth of stubble dotted his face from chin to hairline. He had never been particularly fastidious over his appearance but he had never shown any interest in growing a beard before. Darius wondered if maybe he was feeling a little self-conscious now that he didn't have the scar to hide behind and was compensating with the scruff. No doubt Diana would know the correct terminology and the exact psychology underlying the new behaviour. She was as equally skilled in analysing human behaviour and thought processes as she was with a sickle. He sincerely hoped she kept her head shrinking to herself where he was concerned. He didn't want the perceptive, intelligent, gorgeous, stunning, talented female clueing on to his deep-seated and long-standing infatuation with her.

"She's doing great! After the initial issues with the strength of the flow, she's really gotten the hang of it ... kind of. She still doesn't really understand it but at least she doesn't balk at us sharing vitality with her anymore." Ryker responded to Darius's previous question.

"What's with that anyway? She was positively horrified with the thought of recharging from us and downright judgy to be honest." Axel pointed out.

Darius noted the way Ryker's shoulders stiffened almost imperceptibly before he forced them to relax in a show of feigned casualness. "It was just so new to her, that's all. Using someone else's energy in order to sustain herself? It was just such a foreign concept, it made her uncomfortable. She's more relaxed about it now that she understands it's her – and our – birthright."

Axel and Beyden nodded in understanding and Darius flashed Ryker a quiet look; *what's the deal?* He projected with his eyes. He knew the younger paladin would get the message. All of them were familiar enough with each other now that silent communication was easy – even without the bond in place. Ryker gave a small shake of his head in the negative as if to say; *not now.* He nodded back once in acknowledgement. Evidently there was more to the story than he wanted to discuss in front of everyone. Given they shared practically everything – barring secret unrequited feelings of lust of course – he knew Max must have specifically asked him not to discuss it. Although he was curious, he also respected Max's wish for privacy.

"Although she is taking on vitality every day now, I'm still not convinced she's at full strength. I wonder if she should be recharging more regularly and also from more of us."

Beyden frowned. "She looks so much better, Ry. And I know everyone has noticed the surge in nature at the camp, so it's obvious her energy is disseminating out into the environment."

Axel snorted, sitting himself down heavily on the bench next to Darius and propping his feet up on the garden plantar box next to them. "Yeah, no shit. It's like a freaking menagerie there!"

"I know. It's not even intentional." Ryker said. "But there's still a ... *sickness* stemming from her, especially when she sleeps."

Now it was Darius's turn to frown, remembering Lark's concerns and revelations regarding Max's sleep patterns. He didn't want to raise it in front of a group and it wasn't really his information to share. Perhaps he would speak to Lark again and encourage him to discuss it with Ryker.

"Well, I'm more than willing to get the decoder ring. Just tell me when." Axel stated, merrily.

"Me too. I mean, I would be honoured to serve Max formally as one of her personal paladins." Beyden's rejoinder was somewhat shy but heartfelt nonetheless.

Darius hesitated before asking, "Is that wise?"

Bey's amber eyes looked a little devastated as they turned his way. "You don't think I should be in the Order? I know my local council didn't approve my request to join a –"

"No, Bey! That is not what I intended, I swear to you on my lineage. You are one of the most trustworthy and skilled paladins I have ever had the privilege of meeting. You would be an asset in any Order." He assured him. Damn the man's local council back in Spain. They had really done a number on his self-confidence.

"So you just don't want her to be healthy then?" Axel asked, half sarcastic and half serious. Jeez, Darius thought. They were all so touchy when it came to the tiny redhead. It just served to prove to him that he was taking the correct course of action in being more reserved and practical, and not rushing into things.

"Don't take me the wrong way. I want her to be healthy just as much as you do." He assured them all firmly, "I just mean, we still haven't figured out how she's even a Custodian, let alone if Custodians are even supposed to take on vitality that way. What if you're not doing it right or something?" He wasn't trying to be a downer – he was just being realistic. They could be doing more harm in the long term even though she seemed to be thriving right this second.

"She's sick without it and sharing vitality makes her well." Ryker responded simply. "That's good enough for me."

Darius held up his hands in surrender at the three sets of frowns aimed in his direction. "But you also saw what she was able to do, just with Diana's vitality that one time. I mean, seriously Ry, she healed your fifty-year-old scar! That wound was made by a chade's claw – we all know how toxic those things are. I've been researching all week as you know. Even the most powerful Life Warden alive would have had trouble healing that scar, and Max did it fuelled with one paladin's vitality and two minutes on the beach! A paladin she wasn't even bonded with, I might add. Have you considered what might happen if she were to finish bonding with all of us and recharge daily?"

Ryker eyed him cautiously, "I have actually. But it seems like you have too."

"Damn, Ry. Her powers could prove limitless!" Darius was afraid he'd gone too far. Expressing his concerns to his Captain was one thing; expressing his concerns to Max's lover was another matter altogether. But, once again proving he was a born potentate, he merely nodded, eyes straying to the shoe store which housed Max, in contemplation.

"I understand your concerns, Darius. And I'm grateful you feel comfortable enough to share them with me. But I think you're missing a key factor here." Ryker's brown gaze was serious as it stared into his. "She's a Custodian. She's a daughter of Mother Nature herself. She's *supposed* to be powerful. It's her purpose, Darius, her duty."

Darius understood all about duty and purpose. His last millennia of life proved that. "But where did she come from?" He burst out, quite spontaneously.

"I know it must be driving you crazy, not being able to find answers. You hate puzzles, you like solutions. You like control. I get it, man." Ryker actually stepped over and patted him roughly on the shoulder. Darius figured he must have looked pretty darn pitiful. "I don't know how she came to be here or why. Fuck! You know I'm not whimsical or any of that shit. But … what were the chances that there would be seven of us, all from a different domain, with no bonded liege, all in the one place?" Ryker blew out an agitated breath, "Makes you wonder, man."

Darius couldn't quite suppress the shiver of portent that whispered through his system at Ryker's words. Still, he wasn't a fanciful man, so he forced himself to ask, "Wonder what?"

Ryker barked out a laugh that held more exasperation than amusement. "I don't know, man. I don't know what I'm saying. All I know is, I trust my gut. And my gut is all about that woman."

Darius felt a strange fluttering in his own gut. Ryker's words essentially alluded to a higher purpose or fate or some such thing. His faith in the Great Mother was solid. He believed the original being was real and didn't doubt the influence she had on nature and the world in times past. But it had been many millennia since a direct sign or action could be attributed to the holy female herself. Once again, his research had hinted that at least one Custodian – one of the original creatures and direct descendants of Mother Nature – must have some presence in the world somewhere at some time. But never was there any whiff of a mention that a

Custodian would be in human form. They were spirits. They didn't require vitality from a paladin because they were essentially nothing but energy – nothing but vitality. And yet, the mere thought of calling Max anything but a Custodian made his stomach cramp in instinctual wrongness.

Max was a Custodian. Full stop.

Feeling it was more than time to lighten the mood, Darius slapped Ryker on his back, forcing him forward a step. He always loved doing that. "Are sure it's just your gut that's all about that woman?" He teased.

Ry threw him a cocky grin as his eyes roved over Max's curvy frame appreciatively. The four shopping musketeers were blessedly exiting the store. "Well, maybe not *just* my gut."

SIX

"Stop the car!" Max's sudden shout startled Diana out of her post shopping binge stupor. After arriving in the city, they had shopped non-stop all day; from clothes to lingerie to cosmetics, they had devoured every shop they came across. And Max had been happy as a pig in mud, which had surprised Diana. Max wasn't exactly a girly girl nor was she vain or particularly feminine, so she had just assumed that shopping wouldn't really be Max's thing. Wrong! She was like a little retail whirlwind, trying things on, sniffing scents, and of course spending money – a *lot* of money. Once again, Diana had been surprised by the amount of money Max had at her disposal. Given the look of her battered pack and limited faded clothes, she had figured that Max didn't really have a lot of money. That was not the case, apparently. She just hadn't been able to access her accounts in months and had been at the end of her cash. She also had been too worried to access anything online for fear of being tracked. But now she had no obstacles in the way, she had arranged for her things to be shipped from storage and also made a big dent in her royalties. Diana was so proud. Cali had also joined in the fun, as well as Lark – much to the disgust of the other men – and the four of them had been wallowing in the spending endorphins as they split into two cars and made their way back home.

At Max's shouted command however, they all sprang into action. Ryker slammed on the brakes, causing Beyden to do the same in the car behind them, Diana reached for her sickle and Axel reached over Max in a protective gesture as he began scouting the area with intense blue eyes.

"What is it? What's wrong?" Ryker demanded, eyeing Max from head to toe, dual sickles already in hand.

"Sheesh! Calm down guys. Nothing's wrong. I just saw the park ..." She pointed to her left and sure enough there was a small reservation with picnic tables and a park area. "... and the swings. I love swings! Can we go swing?" She asked, wide-eyed.

Ryker's eyes widened in disbelief. "You almost gave me a heart attack over some swings?" He shouted.

"Don't exaggerate. Please can we go swing? Do you know how long it's been since I was able to just play?" Max cajoled. Nobody could resist the blue-green depths of her eyes and Diana could practically feel the resigned sighs throughout the car. They were going to play on the swings and Max clearly knew it too for she already had her hand on the door handle.

Ryker sighed, more in aggravation than defeat, "Fine. But you stay near one of us at all times." Max squealed happily and started to get out of the car, "*And*, you wait for us to clear the area first." He added, sternly.

Max rolled her eyes but stayed where she was as Ryker gave his orders and Lark, Cali and Beyden burst from the other car. It took less than ten minutes for their Captain to be satisfied the area was safe, and less than ten seconds for Max to shoot from the car and jump on a swing.

"Someone push me ... please!" She demanded. Diana smiled as big, bad Ryker pushed Max on the wooden swing, her small feet kicking out into the darkening sky.

"Not the usual demands we're accustomed to obeying from our lieges, is it?" Axel asked, standing guard beside her.

"Not at all." She agreed.

"Do you think she'll change? You know, when everyone finds out about her and she begins to see that she is literally royalty?" Diana didn't turn to face him but she did cast her eyes to the side so she could make out the handsome paladin's profile. He was watching Max with clear affection but his normally dancing blue eyes were clouded with concern. He would probably take it the hardest if Max were to suddenly change her behaviour, given the history with his previous liege. Once a carefree young warden, innocent of the ways of their society, she had been a charming woman who had fancied herself in love with one of her knights. Diana knew that Axel had returned the feelings tenfold and had been utterly devastated five years later when she had thrown him over for better prospects with a more renowned bloodline. Ever since, Axel didn't bother to hide his disdain of the ruling class and to him, betrayal was the greatest sin one could commit. While Darius also had a pet peeve for betrayal, his was based more on abandonment than duplicity like Axel.

Feeling for him, after all he was not only a part of her Order but had also become a very close friend over the years, she looked back at Max ... and grinned. She nudged his arm, "Why don't you take a really good look at her and answer your own question?"

He frowned but did her bidding. After a few seconds he smiled too and chuckled, "You're right. Nothing's going to change that girl."

Max was pumping her legs back and forth in an effort to get as high as she could. Her port-red hair was flying behind her in a tangled mess and her breathless laugh could be heard echoing throughout the entire picnic area. But what she knew Axel noticed the most was the way nature seemed to respond to her. The grass surrounding the swing set was greener and more lush than minutes before, the air was neither too cool nor too warm, birds graced branches of nearby trees, the horizon was awash in a spectacular array of colours and new plants were popping up like daisies.

Looking around, Diana saw that the others had noticed the amazing display too. They were watching the metamorphosis with awed eyes and shaking heads. It was a powerful display of a guardian of nature at work ... and Max wasn't even trying. In fact, Diana would bet that she didn't even know what was happening. When they had first met her, she had been leaking out energy like this from her very pores, so maybe she was used to such things. And although she was definitely filtering out power at the moment, this was somehow different. Diana didn't sense a drain in her vitality like she was losing it. It was more of a sharing she supposed. Even among their most powerful wardens, Diana had never seen such beauty created with such ease.

"They're not going to believe us – the IDC, I mean." Axel said.

Diana grunted and looked him in the eye, "I'm more worried that they will."

Axel frowned but before he could question her, a sudden chill in the air had them spinning to eye the trees surrounding the park. The park backed onto a large nature reserve and was rather remote, a little off the main highway between the city and their camp, about forty minutes from home. Max abruptly stopped swinging, jumping off when she was high in the air. She landed gracefully and said one word;

"Phantoms."

"Chades." Darius corrected automatically before processing what the one word meant. When he did however,

Diana saw his whole demeanour change. He went from a courteous gentleman of old, to a battle-hardened warrior. The only time Diana ever saw Darius show even a modicum of loss of control was during battle with the chades. Oh, he was never unprofessional and always aware of his surroundings and fellow paladins, but he always seemed to ... *unleash* when he fought the ghastly spectres. Back in the Crusades, he hadn't been that way, but now he had a personal vendetta to reconcile – one that was impossible to do – and Diana was worried the hatred was eating him alive. If only she could talk to him, like really talk to him. Unfortunately, such an act was impossible, given the attraction between them and the fact that they both desperately fought to ignore it. They were friends of a sort and comrades in arms, but confidants they were not. Which was a real shame, for she wanted nothing more than to help soothe his fears and ease his pain. And if that led to the soothing and easing of other things, then more the better, Diana thought. But alas, that was not likely given her vow to herself and his strict adherence to the rules. And now was surely not the time to be contemplating such things given the beautiful sunset was fading to a bleak grey and the wind was now biting in its intensity.

Inky black fingers stretched outward from the tree line and Diana shivered in the moment where shadows became pale imitations of men. The transformation from shadow to solid always perplexed Diana. Because of her affiliation with the element of death, she could easily sense death or those near the brink. The chades weren't dead but they didn't feel alive either. In fact, they didn't really feel like anything – other than creepy of course. It was almost as if they were a void or an abyss. They just felt like ... nothing. They were neither spirit nor man which meant she had no idea where they resided when they weren't attacking and no idea how they managed to transform from nothing to something. She knew such answers had alluded their leaders for centuries also.

As four skinny, pale chades with stringy black hair began to inch their way toward them in an almost graceful glide, Ryker ordered grimly; "Max! Stay with Cali and Beyden. The rest of you – standard offensive positions."

"I can fight!" Max stated, her tanto sword already in her hand.

Ryker spared her a glance, "Do as I say, Max. Please. There is a reason why paladins and their lieges are not supposed to form an intimate relationship. It's a distraction. Please don't distract me."

Diana saw that Max was torn. The woman had been taking care of herself for years and had fought the chades – and won – on many occasions. It also wasn't in her nature to be idle when a threat was imminent. But she clearly didn't want to upset her partner and Diana was relieved when she bobbed her head, allowing Cali and Beyden to box her in protectively.

When Diana glanced back, she saw that the advancing chades had covered a lot of ground and were almost in striking range. But they didn't attack, instead they were eyeing Max with their cold, dead eyes like she was the main course at a banquet. Darius was the first to break ranks, launching his sickle at the closest one. His aim was true and the steel lodged with a dull thunk in the pitiful creature's chest. It stumbled back a step but didn't go down. It didn't bleed or scream or yell or do anything that showed it could feel pain. Somehow though, its eyes took on a sheen of hurt and disappointment and its mouth gaped open unnaturally wide as it suddenly charged forward, sickle still in place. Diana took a precious second to watch as Darius's lips quirked in satisfaction and his eyes shined, fevered for the fight to come.

The charging chade seemed to awaken some emotion in the others for they all advanced swiftly, one of them pinning accusing eyes on Diana.

They don't feel, Diana assured herself; they don't feel, they don't bleed, they don't stop, and they chose to lose their humanity, she repeated to herself, swinging the sickle in her left arm while blocking a blow with her right. No matter how many times she fought them, she could never quite lose the small spark of pity she felt. A triumphant whoop accompanied by a whoosh of flame demonstrated that Darius had no such reservations. He had dispatched his chade, who had clearly once been a Fire Warden. Hearing a rush of air, Diana ducked just in time to avoid a swipe with those poison-tipped nails of theirs. Going low, she made two deep cuts in quick succession along the creature's upper thighs. It wobbled but didn't go down and Diana saw Lark move quickly, his blade slashing in a downward arc, effectively removing the head. She couldn't help cringing as the chade appeared to disintegrate before her very eyes, dissolving into millions of droplets of water, spattering the earth with wetness. This pathetic being had once been a Water Warden, she thought.

Moving quickly, she saw Ryker and Axel had another well in hand and it would be dispatched within moments. That only left one. It had stayed back somewhat, eyeing the spectacle impassively but as she watched, Diana saw it lift its head and sniff the air. She shuddered; it was just creepy, especially because she knew it was sniffing out Max like she was game.

"No bloody way." She muttered, bringing up her sickle once more in order to launch it as the thing started to move.

"No!" Max yelled, "Not that one!" The command in her voice was so strident, Diana felt her sickle falter and point uselessly to the ground. The chade kept moving forward, eyes locked on Max, but Diana's hand felt frozen and she couldn't raise her sickle to stop the chades progression. She could hear yelling and knew the others were warning her, trying to get her to move. Pounding feet accompanied the arrival of Darius. His shirt was partially singed and a lot holey now and she knew he must have been damn close to the chade when it had erupted into flames. The burnt shirt was sticking to his heavy chest, outlining every hard muscle on his torso. Despite the dire circumstances, she couldn't help the way her heart jumped and her adrenal glands chimed in with an extra little push of adrenaline. The man was so damn *fine*.

Raising his sickle aggressively, she watched as the remaining light glinted off the metal. The chade didn't seem to notice, its black eyes focused purely on Max behind her, like it was determined to reach her. No way was that happening, no matter what the hell Max was thinking, freezing her like she was. As Darius swung, Max shouted again;

"I said, no!" This time, the force of her voice was echoed by the force in her power and Diana watched in shock as Darius found himself flung backwards, landing heavily on the hard ground.

"Max! What the fuck?!" Ryker's voice was a mixture of bewilderment and anger as he also began to run in their direction.

Completely ignoring everyone, Max moved quickly to Diana's side. So quickly, in fact, it didn't look like she had even moved her feet. She looked directly at the chade and said one word;

"Go."

Diana felt a burst of hysterical laughter bubble up. Max was treating the chade like it was a mischievous puppy ... and she was going to get herself killed. "Go, now." Max repeated quietly, in direct contrast with the mayhem around her.

And then Diana witnessed something she never could have imagined. The chade stopped and tilted its head as if it were listening. It's dull, onyx eyes never changed but it did close its misshapen, elongated mouth. It then seemed to crumple in on itself, before whisking away within the trees, apparently being absorbed by the dense shadows. And just like that, the meagre sun was resurrected again and the wind stopped its mad whipping. Max let out a sigh and suddenly Diana could raise her hand again. She was very tempted to use it to tan Max's hide.

What the hell was that all about?

SEVEN

Back at the camp, Darius didn't bother wasting time on pleasantries; "You had better tell us what you were doing back there, Max. You're bleeding heart has no place on the battlefield!" He knew his voice portrayed exactly how angry he was. She had knocked him on his butt! With no more than a thought, Max had laid him out flat, his arse still hurt and he wouldn't be surprised if his tail bone was bruised clear to the marrow. Not only had she flung him aside, which had the added benefit of bruising his ego, but she had placed herself and the rest of the Order in mortal jeopardy. Unacceptable.

"Be careful how you speak to me, Darius." Her voice was chilling – the ice queen was making an appearance. "*You* had better tell *me* more about the chades. What exactly are they? They're not just a balancing presence in the world like you told me six weeks ago." It wasn't an accusation or a question, but a statement; she knew there was more to it. Well, Darius didn't rightly care at the moment. She had chosen one of those foul creatures over him. Okay, perhaps that was a slight over-exaggeration, but right now he felt as though Max had hurt him in order to save a chade – his personal nemesis.

"Now is not the time for a tutorial. What you did was unacceptable! It was reckless and stupid and naïve and everything else you can think of." He spouted. "Fuck! What the hell, Max?!" He knew all eyes were on him, and given that he never cursed, he was sure they were all enjoying the show. Well, let them enjoy it. Darius was beyond caring.

"Watch it, Darius." Ryker rumbled,

"You can't possibly be okay with this?! Ryker, she just let a chade go! She put herself and everyone else in jeopardy over a *chade*!"

Ryker scowled fiercely and if his scar would have still been present, Darius knew it would have been pulling taut. "I am most definitely *not* okay with the situation. But watch your mouth." His brown-eyed stare pinned him in place before he turned that look on Max. "What the fuck was that, Max?"

Max didn't even have the decency to look contrite, nor did she make any attempt to answer the Captain of her Order. "They are Wardens, aren't they?" She asked instead.

"Yes."

"No."

Diana answered in the affirmative at the same moment as his vehement denial. He glared in her direction. "No." He repeated, more firmly.

"I can see a lie, Darius – taste it too. And you taste very bitter right now, doesn't he Ryker?" Max turned to Ryker. Not only should Ryker be able to feel what Max was feeling through the bond, he was also quite empathic himself, given he was a paladin of life. He looked torn, wanting to discipline Max but also obey her at the same time. But in the end, Max was his liege and lover; Darius didn't stand a chance.

"Yes. They were once wardens. But Max, you –" He managed to grind out before Max interrupted.

"Why didn't you tell me this sooner? Why would you deliberately keep this from me?" She interrupted, her words lashing hotly in the air.

Ryker was pacing, tugging futilely on the long strands of his messy hair. "I wasn't deliberately keeping this from you. I didn't want to overwhelm you when you first arrived. Your powers were so unstable and I was worried how you would react if you knew what happened to wardens who can't control their powers." He explained.

"And I suppose there has been no opportunity since then to fix this oversight?" She questioned, archly.

"Max ..." Ryker looked pained but also frustrated with Max's attitude.

The lady of the house waved her hand impatiently in the air. "Forget about that for now." She turned to Beyden of all people, "They were once like normal wardens but something went wrong with their powers?" She asked.

Beyden looked startled that she would single him out regarding such an important question, but he rallied and answered her promptly, "Yes. The allure of power can be too much for some and they begin to take too much vitality from their paladins. The more they take, the more they need to sustain all that extra power. In the end, no amount of energy sustains them anymore and they become chades."

"They then seek out and hunt down wardens, draining them of their vitality and leaving them nothing more than wizened shells." Darius pointed out, furiously, not wanting the conversation to get side-tracked.

"But they don't seek out paladins? The original and natural source of energy for wardens. Why wardens and not paladins?" Max questioned Beyden again, seemingly more interested in asking irrelevant questions rather than accepting any responsibility for her earlier actions.

"They are evil, Max; disloyal, traitorous and vile. They choose power over their birthright, over their blooded duty and responsibilities. They no longer care about the Earth, about nature or their domains. They choose to exploit what the Great Mother gifted to them. Who the fuck knows why they do what they do!" He shouted into the obnoxiously quiet room. Darius felt like the skin on his head was shrinking – his brain felt far too tight, like it was going to explode. Why was no-one else taking this situation seriously?

*****

Wow. Diana thought. Two *fucks* in as many minutes when she hadn't heard him use that word once in twenty years. If that wasn't telling enough, Darius's voice was low and filled with hate. There was no hiding his personal animosity towards the most shameful aspect of their society.

"Although, what Darius said is all true," Beyden began, casting a concerned look at his fellow knights, "there is more to it than that. They seek out and hunt for what is lacking in them; vitality. Wardens are charged with that special energy, even though they can't produce it. They are the biggest energy source around, hence, the chades are drawn to them." Beyden explained patiently. Max had intuitively chosen the only other paladin in the room other than Darius who was the most knowledgeable in the area, given that his sister was a Ranger.

"They suck the life out of their fellow wardens, Max. They poison paladins with their noxious claws, incapacitating them so they can't defend their liege. Then suck their wardens dry. They are abominations." Darius's jaw was clenched so tightly Diana was afraid he would grind his teeth to sawdust.

Max roved her eyes between Ryker and herself and Diana felt a query through the bond for the first time. Sure, there was almost a constant flow of sensations since Max had branded her with her Heraldry, but it was very inconsistent and non-specific. This was a clear question and although she couldn't make out actual words, Diana understood what she was asking. *Why was Darius so bitter?* Diana and Ryker had every reason to despise the chades – they had lost their liege's in the Great Massacre to the chades and Ryker had lost his entire Order, but they weren't as hate-filled as Darius. Six weeks ago Ryker probably would have been spouting the same disgust and abuse, but they all knew Max had healed more than just their Captain's face. Maybe she could help Darius too. Diana hoped so. It was hard to see her strong, noble warrior so consumed with anger – even if he did have his reasons.

"So they stop being able to recharge their vitality ... they must be starving!" Max muttered, almost to herself, rubbing her arms.

"What nonsense!" Darius spat, and Diana felt the ripple of unease work its way through the bonded paladins. Cali straightened in her chair, Lark actually lifted his lip in a silent snarl and Ryker seemed to grow larger, placing both hands on Max's shoulders, his glare formidable. Even she found herself fighting the need to bitch-slap him. Max was her bonded liege and Darius was being aggressive. "What were you thinking? You let that animal go! And now it's out there doing who knows what – likely killing wardens and paladins! It's what they do!"

Max was oddly calm, apparently not responding to Darius's anger and accusations. She was frowning in a contemplative way, obviously mulling over the revelations and Darius's reactions. When she spoke, it was in a calm, reasonable tone;

"They're not animals, Darius. They are Wardens."

The quiet words landed in the room with the impact of an atomic bomb – like all the air was sucked out. Diana felt the bottom of her stomach drop out, like when you went down the big dip on a rollercoaster. She felt the sensation sweep through their Order, even to Axel, Beyden and Darius, who were not yet bound. Surely Max wasn't implying that they were good? That they were anything but the scourge of society? She was grossly misguided and her interpretation of what they had just explained to her was way off course! But then, what was with the dippy feeling in their stomachs? Like a veritable truth had hit too close to home.

"They are *not* wardens, Max." This time it was Ryker who responded, and although his tone was even, it was also very firm, brooking no argument.

Max raised an eyebrow, "Of course they are. You just said so. Not a normal warden, sure. But a warden nonetheless."

"Abominations. They are abominations." Darius was pale, all colour having washed from his face. Max's words had resonated with reason and truth, and Diana knew she believed each word she spoke. Max dialled back on the bond subtly, as if she were distancing herself from them. But Diana still noticed and so did the others if their uncomfortable shifting were any indication.

"I don't believe they are abominations or monsters or vile creatures." Max still had a speculative gleam in her turquoise eyes. "I think they are sick."

Silence. Nothing but silence for a heartbeat ... two heartbeats ...

"Sick? You think they are sick?" Darius was incredulous. "You're damn right they're sick! Sick fucks who have chosen to abandon their honour!"

"That's just it. I don't believe it's a choice. Who chooses to get a horrible disease?" She asked practically.

"You have no idea what you're talking about. You were calling them 'phantoms' not two months ago!" Darius's voice had now risen a few octaves and his face was an alarming shade of red.

"And? What's your point? I have been dodging them my whole life. And yes, fighting them and killing them. I have been in contact with them nearly on a weekly basis for over twenty years. I am *very* familiar with them. I could know more about them than you." She pointed out.

"I'm sure you did your due diligence trying to find answers, Max." Beyden's voice was gentle and reasonable. "And although it is an intriguing theory, it is extremely unlikely. The chades have been around since the time of the original wardens. Not in these great numbers, but wardens have been succumbing to their powers for millennia. Our governing body have searched and searched for answers and cures and solutions. There are none. If it was a sickness, don't you think they would have figured it out by now?" Beyden asked.

Max shrugged, "You would think so, yes."

Darius scoffed rudely, "So what? Now you're implying there is some kind of conspiracy at work? Max, you really are too much sometimes. Your *investigations* wouldn't hold a candle to the IDC's."

"Do you think I was blasé about investigating them? I watched them, talked to them, and tried to figure out what they were. But answers were hard to come by." Max said.

Diana watched as Darius swallowed convulsively like he was forcing bile back down his throat. "They don't talk." He gritted out, "They have no voice. They have no voice because they have no humanity. They are soulless, voiceless traitors."

Max's eyes swirled with colour for a mere second before her expression turned decidedly haughty and she appeared to taunt him, "Is that so? Me think you doth protest too much. Has a chade spoken to you, Darius?"

Darius's chair was flung with such force, it shattered into dozens of pieces as he jumped up abruptly in a fit of rage. Anger radiated from him in palpable waves and he was eyeing Max with clear dislike – something Diana never thought she would ever witness. Darius loved Max. As one of the three paladins to discover her sitting alone in that filthy bar, Diana knew Max held a special place in his heart. But she was clearly witnessing Darius snapping his collar. For her part, Max was sitting calmly, eyes narrowed as if she were taunting him. What game was she playing? Max didn't know Darius's history but she could obviously see this was a sore subject for him. Why was she pushing him? And Darius looked to be at his limits. Besides the fact that it was Max, he would never talk to a Warden with such disrespect and anger. Duty was his whole world – the last eight hundred years she had been alone was evidence of that.

"You're going to want to leave now." Lark's voice was a rough growl and he was eyeing Darius as if he were a threat. This situation had the potential to get real ugly, real fast. There was no threatening a bound liege and Max was officially bound to five of them – including Diana. It was taking a toll on her to sit there passively instead of sucker punching the hell out of him.

"Fuck, yeah. I want to leave. I don't need to hear this shit. And I can't believe you're all indulging her!" He spat the words out as he stormed from the room, slamming the door behind him.

"Was it something I said?" Max's question sounded innocent but she was anything but.

"Max ..." Diana began, warningly.

"Yes?" Max's question was almost a dare. Her turquoise eyes were direct and held a clear challenge; are you questioning me? They seemed to say. Diana was torn. Her allegiance was now to her liege and it wasn't her place to question.

Max's eyes softened as if she could hear Diana's internal debate, "Go after him." She urged.

Still, she hesitated, casting her eyes around the room. They all looked uncomfortable and tense. Max hadn't ever really acted commanding before. She was always a little antagonistic – especially to Ryker – but she was never mean, like some wardens. Diana figured it was a mixture of her normal nature and also her ignorance of her place in their society that made her so sweet. This was the first time she had acted like a Warden and Diana didn't like it.

"You should go after him before I do." Beyden said. "I'm half tempted to knock some respect back into him."

Diana sighed and ran her fingers through her hair – it didn't work. Her curls prevented it and she was left untangling a springy lock from a ring where it was caught. Beyden was the most non-violent one in their group. If he was simmering on the edge of violence, then the others were about to boil over. Diana wanted to check on Darius, but she feared there was no putting the lion back in the cage. It had been locked away for years and Max may have just successfully unleashed the beast. The thrill she felt in her nether regions was entirely inappropriate, as was the beading of her nipples.

Shit was about to get real.

EIGHT

Darius prowled angrily around the west side of the building that housed the gym. It was on the opposite side of the kitchen, away from prying eyes and the ocean. His view was only of thick bushland and he considered walking off into the dense trees and shrubs just to escape all the people back in the house. They had all lost their minds! When Max first arrived, Darius had found her refreshing, and believed she was just what they all needed. Her innate goodness and light seemed to spread through their ranks, drawing them closer together where they could all acknowledge they were a family in ways they hadn't been able to before. He loved the little midget and she was a true miracle to their race and their world. A Custodian? A daughter of Nature? She was an absolute marvel just by existing. But she was also ignorant to the point of stupidity. Weeks! They had all spent weeks, educating her about their society and their history and their laws. And still, after all this time, she insisted on remaining ignorant! And what was worse, she insisted on remaining antagonistic. Darius thought she had gotten all that out of her system with Ryker and the local council, but clearly she hadn't. No, she was now trying to goad him!

Aren't I just a lucky boy? He thought to himself snidely. He now had a greater appreciation of how Ryker felt all those weeks ago.

Darius continued to pace as he kicked at stones and muttered to himself. The more he paced, the more amped up he became. His thoughts were now a swirling mess of the conversation in the kitchen and no matter how hard he tried, he couldn't make her suppositions stop. *She has no idea what she's talking about!* He assured himself. Ryker had been correct all those weeks ago – she was nothing but an ignorant, clueless, reckless nobody! How dare she waltz into his life and make grand statements about things that had been facts for centuries before she had even been born?! She had no right to question the very foundations of their society or their proud history. And to question their leaders? The people who worked tirelessly and selflessly to ensure the world continued to spin on its axis for all the other ignorant, destructive human beings out there? Well, that was blasphemy, pure and simple.

"How dare she accuse the most honourable members of our society of conspiracy?! Doesn't she get it? She can't just walk in here and disrupt thousands of years of history on a whim!"

"Wow. Talking to yourself. She really got to you, huh?"

Darius literally snarled as he spun around, seeing Diana move purposely toward him. Just what he needed; the object of his one-sided lust. "What do you want?"

She shrugged casually but Darius could see her grey eyes were sharp, taking in his every movement. "To see if you're okay."

He laughed. Hard. "Okay? Am I okay that Max is trying to disrupt the basis of our world? Am I okay that you all seem to believe this nonsense about the chades being sick? No I am most certainly *not* okay. So run along and report back that Sir Darius is having a tantrum. I'm sure they're all waiting to hear about it."

Diana finally came to a stop in front of him. Although she was tall for a woman, he still topped her by four inches and she was forced to angle her head up to make eye contact. "We don't all just blindly believe her. But it's an interesting theory. You won't even consider the possibility?"

"Consider what possibility? That chades are just misunderstood? That they have some kind of disease? Bullshit! The chades are abominations and they get everything they deserve." He snarled in anger.

Diana leaned back against the wall of the gym, apparently at ease. "How long have we known each other? Like, eight hundred years?" She answered herself. "I have never seen you act this way. I know the chades are personal to you and I get it – I truly do. But this seems more ..." she paused, as if hesitating before speaking again, "... obsessive." She finished. "It also seems extremely defensive. Is Max right? Have they ever spoken to you?"

Fuck! Darius gripped his hair hard and yelled in frustration. He was *not* going to delve into memories long supressed – they were false anyway; artefacts of a traumatised imagination. "What is it with you? Is it all about the girl power or some feminine bullshit? Is that why you are suddenly ready to abandon everything you know to take the word of one faithless woman?"

Diana arched one perfectly plucked eyebrow. She was still wearing the slim black jeans and tightly fitted, emerald green shirt she had been when they were shopping. Despite the long day and the skirmish with the chades, she still looked absolutely stunning and neat as a pin. Well, except for her hair. Her hair was always in disarray around that gorgeous oval face. Seeing her so perfect and prim and so put together when he felt so out of control, aggressive and almost feral, made him want to throw her against the wall and dirty her the fuck up!

He looked down and saw that his hands were shaking. He never acted this way and never thought this way. He was a knight of old, from the most honourable of lines in Warden and paladin history. He had even officially been given the title of 'Sir'. He did *not* consider throwing women against walls or banging them stupid. Just as he was about to give himself a long, hard silent lecture and put the beast back inside the box, Diana made the mistake of speaking again;

"I think I'm looking at your abandonment issues with your brother. That's what I think."

He moved without even really thinking, pinning Diana roughly to the uneven wall behind her. He gripped her wild hair in both fists, forcing her head up. "Don't talk about him." He warned. Diana's grey eyes sparked with defiance but she made no move to escape his grip, even though he knew she could do it in an instant.

"What's the matter, Darius? I hit a little too close to home?" She taunted.

He gritted his teeth in an effort to beat down his sudden need to unleash forty years of pent up shame and disappointment, and yes, abandonment from his brother. One thousand years, Darius had served his liege – had served his brother – with faith, loyalty, and honour. He had been unwavering in his duty, forsaking his own happiness in order to serve. And that potential happiness was pressed against him right now. He also had eight centuries of pent up lust to unleash. Diana was in a very precarious position. His brother had abandoned and betrayed him and it still hurt so damn bad, even after all this time. Max was poking at an open wound and Diana had come out here to throw some more salt? Well, maybe it was time to for him to be selfish for once. For him to think about what he wanted. Clearly, that's what everyone else did.

And right now? Feeling Diana's generous body aligned with his, her riotous curls under his palms? Darius wanted with a hunger he hadn't known was possible. So he lowered his head and ... plundered. He forced Diana's mouth open with his own and pillaged the recesses of her mouth with his tongue. Her unique flavour exploded over his taste buds and he groaned harshly into Diana's very willing mouth. She gave as good as she got, both of them fighting for dominance, which served to fuel his fire even more. She wasn't going to be a meek participant and follow his lead like the women of his time. She was going to battle just as a warrior should.

Damn! He abruptly pulled away. She was a warrior – a *fellow* warrior! He really shouldn't be doing this. As long as she didn't open that fine mouth of hers again, maybe he could tamp down his raging arousal and save them both from the erotic assault that was about to happen and that he was sure he would never recover from. Instead, the next words out of her mouth this time? A taunt.

"Stopping so soon?" She asked, her lips swollen. "Why am I not surprised! You can't ever just feel, can you? Can't ever just think for yourself? The great Sir Darius, duty before all else."

"Oh. Did you think I was stopping?" He asked lowly, devouring her body with hard eyes. "I was just giving you a breather ... last chance." He had no idea his voice could go that low.

He watched as she took a deep breath before holding out a shaking hand. He moved, having no patience for buttons and saw them fly in multiple directions as her emerald green silk blouse gaped open. He sucked in a harsh breath upon seeing the lacy, violet bra she was wearing. The colour was bold and contrasted loudly with her lightly tanned skin. He could see the hard nubs of her nipples pressing insistently against the lace and he reached out gripping both breasts fully in his palms. He plumped her cleavage up before leaning in and placing a series of biting kisses along the exposed flesh. They weren't soft love bites either, but almost a form of erotic punishment for pushing him until his iron-willed control snapped.

Diana moaned and pushed herself closer to him and Darius realised she liked it. He ran his tongue over the small pink marks to soothe the sting, before pushing her shirt off her shoulders and unsnapping her bra. His knees weakened at the site of all her coffee-coloured flesh. Her breasts were high and round, her nipples dark and large. He didn't look at her face; he knew he would be lost the second he looked into those storm-cloud eyes, and although his control was already shot to hell, he still wanted a moment to play. He probably wouldn't get another chance. Banishing those thoughts, he caught a hardened peak between his teeth and flicked his tongue teasing and igniting her further.

Diana moaned erotically and grabbed his ears with rough hands, she then steered him toward her other breast where he took the hint and paid equal homage to the exposed flesh there. Running his hands down the curves of her waist, he pushed the heel of his palm against the feminine heat radiating between her legs. Now it was his turn to moan; she was scorching hot and he swore he could feel a tell-tale dampness under his hand. Greedy, feminine hands brought him out of his lust-induced haze and Diana had his burnt shirt up and off before he could blink. He watched from hooded eyes as she licked her lips and smoothed her palms over his chest and abs. She scraped her nails back up to his nipples, leaving train tracks of red marks behind. At five foot ten, her line of sight was almost directly level with his chest, so she had only to close the five-inch gap between them and open her mouth to lather attention to his nipples in return. He had never been into women fondling his nipples before. He was rather aggressive in the bedroom and used to being the one in charge. As her tongue lapped away, he decided she may have just made him a nipple-convert.

Her hands were by no means idle as they worked at the button on his cargo pants. Forcing his pants down just enough for his aching erection to spring free, Diana latched on the moment it was revealed. Her hands, calloused from hours of fighting, gripped him confidently as she gave an almost experimental tug. He shuddered, relishing the sensations flooding through his system. The wind picked up, causing her hair to dance around her face and cooling his super-heated skin as it brushed by. If he were prone to whimsy, he would have thought his domain was giving its approval for the act taking place.

But Darius wasn't whimsical and he knew how badly he was breaking the rules. A trickle of unease flooded him again but refused to take hold. Probably because Diana abruptly dropped to her knees and swallowed him down nearly to the root. He shouted hoarsely, his hands automatically gripping the thickness of her hair. Unable to stop himself he began to move his hips as her lips and tongue tormented the length of his dick. Diana unleashed her nails again, this time over the cheeks of his arse, and flattened her tongue, allowing him to slip further into her throat. Manoeuvring her head into a position that suited him more, he began to thrust against her in earnest, essentially fucking her lips. It was something he had always desired to do with lovers in the past, but something he had never allowed himself. Although he was a dominant lover, he was also a respectful one, always ensuring his partner's pleasure before his own. But he was so cocooned in his lust-bubble, years of anger and hurt and disappointment roiling inside him, that for once, he was taking what was offered.

For her part, Diana seemed to thrive on the rough treatment, moaning and closing her eyes in obvious pleasure. Her cheeks hollowed as she sucked and Darius couldn't believe how sexy she looked with his flesh disappearing between her lush lips and her breasts bobbing. On his next inward thrust, she swallowed; his eyes rolled to the back of his head, his body demanded release. Clenching his teeth, he forced her head off his impossibly hard erection – no way was he going to waste the opportunity to feel the paladin of death wrapped around him. Her eyes held questions as she stayed on her knees before him. Unable to articulate, he demanded one word roughly;

"Up." She began to move but not fast enough to satisfy his current state of mind. He gripped her upper arms and dragged her to her feet, delivering a scorching kiss to her bee-stung lips. He smoothed his hands over her hips and gripping her jeans, pushed them from her body. He nearly swallowed his tongue. She was wearing matching purple lace underwear and the smallest G-string he had ever laid eyes on. Did she walk around every day wearing this kind of thing?

Spinning her around, he nudged her face-first into the wall. Gripping the fragile lace, he tugged, ripping them clear off her body. Diana arched her back, her gorgeous arse and spine on clear display. He gripped the delicious mounds hard and squeezed, eliciting a gasp and shudder; *"Darius."* Was that a whimper? Smirking in satisfaction, he took a moment to test her readiness with two fingers. She was already so wet and her wanton movements were proof of her own desires. Releasing her left butt cheek, he felt a surge of male satisfaction when a red mark the size of his hand remained on her skin.

He thrust into her without delay, forging his way through her scorching depths. She gripped him tight and he took a moment to rest his forehead against the back of her neck savouring the feeling and burying the intense emotions it wrought. Snagging her hips, he began to move forcefully and was rewarded by a series of moans as he increased his speed. The wind picked up now, whipping around them as sweat made their bodies slick. His pants were still around his ankles, having never been removed completely, and they were outside where anyone could see. But everything about it was absolutely perfect. As was Diana's inner muscles flexing and clamping along his length. Knowing it wouldn't take much to nudge her over the edge, he gripped her breasts, briefly giving her nipples a sharp tug. He then spread his fingers, using his pointer and ring finger to spread her mound wide. It left his middle digit free to press down onto her clit, all three fingers gliding easily with each harsh thrust.

"Holy ... My God ... Fuck ... I ...." Diana babbled incoherently and began to buck her hips desperately. Two deep thrusts and strokes with his middle finger later and she orgasmed, archly strongly and crying out loudly. With no interest in denying his own release any longer, he pumped into her rippling sheath and groaned through the most pleasure he had ever experienced in his thousand years. Panting, he squashed the female paladin into the wall, willing the feeling back into his feet.

He didn't think it would be like that. Not even in his wildest fantasies did he dream she would take everything he had to give and still demand more. She wasn't supposed to be as into it as she had been. Rather than being intimidated by his dominant behaviour, she had flourished with it. She wasn't supposed to be so perfect for him.

"I didn't think it would be like that." His muttered words had Diana glancing over her shoulder, face half-hidden by her black locks.

"Huh?" She asked, a sanguine smile on her face. He did the only thing a man could do when confronted with everything he ever wanted.

He ran.

NINE

She'd finally done it. After eight hundred years of holding out and waiting for Darius to come begging to her, she'd finally unleashed ... and screwed Darius to within an inch of his life. Or had he screwed her? Either way, it hardly mattered. It was done now and she wasn't at all surprised by the explosive nature of their lovemaking. She was surprised though, by Darius's reaction. *He didn't think it would be like that?* Be like what? And what the hell did that even mean? Did that mean he didn't like it? She couldn't fathom that was the case – the man had made some very interesting orgasm noises.

Sighing she leaned against the window looking out into Lark's perfect garden, when she found herself almost bowled over by an exuberant miniature Goddess. Steadying herself and Max, she looked up and wasn't surprised to find Cali entering the room too. Looks like it was girl-talk time.

"Well, well, well. You dirty, dirty hussy!" Max teased. "Outdoor sex with the prissy, ordered, Sir Darius!"

Diana rolled her eyes trying not to smile. The woman was going to have way too much fun with this, she knew. When in actual fact, Max should be coming to discipline her for actions unbecoming of a sworn paladin. Paladins could sleep with other paladins, no problem. But not within the same order. Anything that detracted from their primary duties of serving and protecting their Warden was absolutely outlawed. So Max was perfectly within her rights to have Darius and herself reported to the council and punished by the Rangers. But Diana knew Max was not going to do that, and it wasn't because she didn't know their laws either. Darius had sat her down and explained every law in minute detail to the newly discovered Custodian. Max just didn't care.

"Sooo ... hit me with it." Max demanded.

Feigning innocence, Diana asked, "Hit you with what?"

"Diana!" Max whined, "Did I make you beg for deets? No! Hit me with Darius's dick of course!"

Stuttering out a shocked laugh, Diana saw Cali's ice-blue eyes widen before she too began laughing uproariously. Max, apparently just hearing what she said, slashed her hand impatiently through the air, "You know what I mean. Not literally. Although ..." She trailed off, humming to herself.

Diana whacked her playfully, "Greedy much? You already have a dick to play with. It's attached to a smokin' hot giant with nipple rings."

"I know, I know. But lookin' and listenin' is free, so ...?"

Diana roved her eyes back and forth between Max and Cali. Clearly their express purpose in seeking her out was to interrogate her about her sex life. She took a moment to think about how much she wanted to reveal. She was actually a private person by nature, loving her solitude just as much as her social time. She also came from a time when women did not speak of such things. Hell, they weren't even expected to like sex much. It had been a duty, an obligation between a husband and wife in order to produce heirs. And heaven forbid you indulged outside of wedlock. Women were branded as whores and their prospects of marriage and a family were ruined. Diana could only be forever grateful that she was a paladin and therefore blessed with long life so she could witness the evolution of women's rights.

Eyeing the other two women, who were practically salivating waiting for her to talk, Diana smiled, knowing her old sensibilities would not extend into girl-talk time. Besides, Max had held nothing back – as in *nothing!* She leaned forward and whispered, purely for theatrics;

"Darius's dick is glorious ... so wide, I'm sure I have rub marks and I bet he has friction burn."

Cali fanned herself and shook her head, "I knew it! I knew that man was packing. I'd heard rumours ..." She trailed off.

Diana had too. Now she knew they didn't do the man justice.

"And does he know how to use it?" Max asked, turquoise eyes all shiny with feminine hope.

"Oh, yes! The man was like a demon possessed. He literally threw me against the wall and ripped my pants off! He also did this thing with his hand ..." Diana went on to describe the air paladin's nifty clit-trick in detail, leaving them all breathless and a little in awe.

"Sir Darius; the Panty Destroyer." Max intoned sombrely when she was done, as if she were bestowing a title.

They all burst into unrestrained laughter again and Diana was so very grateful for these two women. Although, she was concerned about what this would mean for her and Darius's relationship and the dynamic of their Order, she couldn't bring herself to regret the act. She had wanted Darius for over eight centuries when she had first seen him wielding his sword in the Crusades.

All three women quickly cut off their evil cackling as Ryker, Beyden, Lark and Axel entered the room. All four men stopped in their tracks and eyed them with equal parts suspicion and wariness. Diana knew her girls all wore identical expressions of feigned innocence.

"What are you three up to?" Ryker asked, squinting through narrowed eyes.

"Nothing." Diana answered calmly.

Axel snorted. "Yeah, right! If I didn't know you three females were on my side, I'd be pissing my pants right now. Those doe eyes of yours are just plain creepy."

Diana shook her head at his exaggeration, but apparently Bey was on the same page, staying well away from them on the other side of the room.

Max, relishing any opportunity to make her man squirm, answered him, "We were just comparing you and Darius in the sack."

Ryker stilled, horror likely setting in. "You were not!" It was a statement but Diana heard the underlying plea. Poor man.

Max's grin widened, "We *so* were. Di, tell him about that thing Darius does with his left hand when he –"

"Woman!" Ryker roared, interrupting.

"What? Aww, babe. No need to feel insecure. Sounds like Darius has you beat in the girth department but you're still in the lead for length." She turned to Diana and Cali, "Seriously, guys. It's like my freaking tanto sword!"

"That's enough, devil-woman!" Diana quickly moved out of the way as Ryker picked Max up threw her over his shoulder like a sack of potatoes, before striding quickly from the room.

"One guess where they're going." Cali said dryly, sending them once again into hysterics.

"Diana." Beyden's soft baritone had her turning to see the beast paladin shuffling his feet in apparent discomfort.

"Yes, Bey?"

"I know it's none of my business but Darius is my friend. Is he okay? I was angry at him before but when I calmed down, I realised how much the discussion must have hurt him. That's why he was so upset."

Diana smiled gently. "Yes, he was upset. You all know he would never ever speak to Max that way if he was in his right mind."

"So he's better now?" Beyden asked again.

Diana barely contained her grimace. No doubt the man was feeling very relaxed physically. She had taken a power nap after her shower, herself. But emotionally? Yeah, she didn't think the whole screwing her brains out thing was going to be conducive to Darius's mental health. This was going to create disorder in his very ordered brain and he wasn't going to cope. Particularly when he seemed to be going through some kind of crisis of self. "He'll work it all out." She answered Bey.

"So, the Lady Diana and Sir Darius finally got it on, huh?" Asked the ever-forthright Axel as he plonked himself onto the exceedingly comfortable lounge.

"Axel!" Beyden scolded.

"What? That's what the evil females were discussing when we walked in." He fluttered his lashes in her direction and there was no way she could take offense at the charmer. "Don't tell me – my chances with you are now ruined, just like they are with Max."

"I wouldn't count yourself out yet." She answered, fluttering back. The easy comradery between them felt good.

"So are you two, like, a couple now?" Lark asked adorably.

"No. Not in the slightest." She answered quickly, ruthlessly shushing the tiny whimpering voice in her head.

"Why not? You two make as much sense as Ryker and Max. You're the perfect match." Lark was a true romantic at heart. Probably because of all those trashy romance novels he insisted on reading.

"It's not allowed for one." She stated. She really didn't want to discuss this given she hadn't had the opportunity to discuss it with the man in question yet.

Cali snorted, "Yeah, because your new Lord and Master, Max, isn't going to give you the freedom to do anything you want. She's going to report you to the council and the Rangers are going to come storm the place and that will be the end of you both. Max is a real heartless bitch and Ryker is going to agree with her."

Diana turned to her slowly, "Sarcastic much?" Cali could be a real hard-arse when she wanted to be. She had her own demons to slay when it came to Orders and lieges and even sex. She had been born in Sweden almost one hundred and fifty years ago and had been a member of the Order of Neptune – a traditionally male Order and a very misogynistic one. She had the bad luck to catch the attention of the Water Warden and the even worse luck that there was a natural connection between them. He had put in a bid to have Cali join his Order on the basis of that innate link – tenuous though it had been on Cali's part. Cali loathed the man. Diana could understand the depth of loyalty Cali felt toward Ryker – a male who had allowed her to be a true knight rather than a piece of eye candy who produced vitality. And now there was Max, her new liege, who was easy-going, a rule-breaker and a friend. Cali believed they should all just embrace the casualness of Max. Diana was half on her side. Yes, she craved the freedom and the changes Max represented, but she still understood the necessity of a hierarchy.

"I'm sorry." Cali was quick to apologise after hearing herself. "But you truly have the chance to be everything you ever wanted with Max here; a paladin, a friend, a consultant, a lover. Why aren't you embracing it?"

Diana had the feeling this was more about what Cali was hoping to embrace with Max here. She desperately wanted permission to just be herself – she wanted her cake and she wanted to eat it too. Well, Diana didn't think she could personally afford all those calories. "It's not just my choice remember? Or even Max's. It's also up to a certain ancient air paladin." And Darius was going to freak out, undergo extreme self-flagellation, and then cock the situation up further by being a man and acting like a moron. That was Diana's prediction anyway.

And what do you know? She was absolutely right.

TEN

He had fucked Diana. Like, really fucked her. Not even a little bit fucked her. But a lot fucked her. And he kept saying the word *fuck*. He never said the 'F' word. Never! He didn't believe in foul language. But there was just nothing else that even came close to describing what he had done ... other than that four-lettered expletive. He was pacing the length of his attic bedroom trying to find a sane solution to the madness that had been his day. First, there had been the shopping; second, the chades; third, Max's ridiculous theories; and fourth ... well, fourth there had been the fucking. He had been hiding in his room since the sun had gone down and it was now just after midnight. Even stargazing hadn't been able to soothe his frayed nerves, he thought, smoothing a gentle hand over the wide shiny surface of his telescope.

His Celestron telescope was his pride and joy. When he had left his home, he had left with nothing more than the clothes on his back. At the time, he had just wanted to escape and hadn't given any thought to taking any treasured belongings with him. And treasures he had – his astronomy collection was definitely a treasure ... as was his full set of

Star Trek VHS. Yes, he knew VHS was outdated but there was just something about forgetting to hit pause on the ads and catching a few seconds of annoying, cheesy advertisements that a DVD just couldn't replace. He had them all, plus more, on BluRay now with all the extras. He loved extras. It hadn't taken long for the others to figure out his two – very minor, in his opinion – vices. The stars and Spock. The first time he had watched the rigid, pointy-eared Vulcan he knew he had found a kindred spirit. Now that man truly appreciated the meaning of the word *rules*! He was economical, loyal, polite and unemotional. He was the perfect soldier!

He found it rather amusing that his two favourite things were linked with space – the vast unknown – given his aversion to the mysterious. But he couldn't shake the sentimentality associated with the stars and his childhood. After a vague reference to astronomy one day, Darius had walked into his room to find a top of the line telescope with perfect aperture, brightness and clarity. Ryker. Ryker had purchased it for him. And how had he now repaid the man for his continued nobility and kindness? By engaging in public sex with a fellow paladin! And on top of that, he had disrespected Max – the man's new reason for breathing. Hence, his current level of agitation. What if they decided to kick him out of the camp? What if they decided to notify the IDC? Max was well within her rights to do so. He didn't really believe she would, for that would mean severe consequences for Diana too. And although he knew Max was legitimately angry with him, he also knew that she adored Diana and had formed an instant bond with her. Surely she wouldn't do anything to purposely hurt her?

"Darius?" The sound of Max's voice had him thinking he might just be cracking for real before he saw the door push open an inch and the fall of dark red hair slither through the gap. A turquoise eye soon followed and he immediately strode forward to open the door fully. "May I come in?"

"Of course, My Lady. You needn't ask." He was quick to respond formally.

She frowned. "Why are you speaking so fancy? And of course I need to ask before I enter your room." She looked around curiously, taking in the black and grey scenery. He liked dark, neutral colours. Besides, they caused less reflection of a night time. She cleared her throat, "I wanted to apologise to you. I'm sorry Darius. You don't need to ever talk about the chades again if you don't want to. Please don't hate me!" She finished, her voice wavering, and Darius thought he might just cap off his day by having a heart attack. She wasn't going to cry was she?

One look at Max's stricken face and he felt immediately guilty for his continued anger and resentment at the young Custodian. "Come here little sister." He opened his arms wide and Max all but threw herself into them. He immediately wrapped his strong arms around her like a cocoon and rubbed his hands up and down her back in a soothing motion – the act a comfort to him as well. He felt like he could breathe for the first time in hours. "I'm not mad at you sweetheart. I'm so sorry, I didn't mean to yell at you. You hit a nerve is all."

Max sniffed, decidedly improper, as she peered up at him from under thick lashes. "I know I did. I meant to. Well, sort of meant to. I didn't mean to hurt you. I just ..."

"You wanted to force my hand." He said, realisation dawning.

She nodded her head. "Darius. I adore you. Everything about you, including your sense of duty and discipline. But honey, all that pent up pressure? It's just not natural. You don't need to hide yourself from me or from anyone in this house for that matter."

He turned, unable to stand the sincerity in her gaze. "I am from a different time, Max. Structure. Control. Equanimity. These are the values of my time."

"Silly man. You're from this time. Right now. You can be whoever you want to be."

He closed his eyes. How could someone who decapitates monsters, turns the air blue with her foul mouth, and refers to the male anatomy as a *meatcicle*, be so damned innocent? Oh yeah, right, he grunted to himself, she was a Goddess! He faced her again, loving the lack of guile on her face. "I am not proud of the man I become when I lose control like that. It is not an attractive sight." He guaranteed her.

"I think Diana would disagree with that." She smiled teasingly, her lone dimple hollowing.

He was mortified to feel himself blush. "About that. Max, I apologise for my misconduct. I promise it will never happen ag –"

"Ah! What are you doing?! Don't go putting that shit out in the universe! You were just about to jinx yourself!"

He tilted his head, watching her fan herself from her outburst. He still found her to be a strange little thing sometimes. "Nonetheless, I *am* sorry. I –"

"Do you want to be put back on my Shit List?" She interrupted once more.

Um, that would be a huge, resounding no. "No."

"Then stop insulting me, yourself, and one of my best friends."

"I wasn't!" He was doing the complete opposite! Strange little creature, he thought again, and was glad she couldn't read his thoughts through the Order link. That was another thing he was not willing to examine too closely yet either. He hadn't volunteered to be in her Order again and she hadn't asked. Maybe she didn't want him ...

Max's eyes narrowed, "Trust me. You were being insulting." Her expression softened, "I really am sorry,

Darius. Sometimes I'm just too self-righteous for my own good and I need to be slapped back down to size."

There was no way he was letting her take the blame for his foul mood and his bad decision-making. She was just making him feel more guilt. "And I am sorry too. I will reconcile my thoughts and emotions, I promise you." Sensing the need for levity, he added, "Besides. If anyone were to slap you down to size, there would be nothing left. You are already pocket-sized." He ruffled her thick hair.

"Hey!" She pushed his hand off and then jumped up, landing a kiss to his cheek that had already started to stubble. Like Ryker and Beyden, he had to shave practically morning and night in order to keep the bristles at bay. "Love ya guts!" She spouted before spinning toward the exit. "Oh. One more thing ..."

"Yes?" Infinite patience. He had infinite patience.

"Don't apologise to Diana."

That was not what he had been expecting. "Pardon?"

If he didn't know any better he would swear her eyes held pity right then when she answered, "Don't tell Diana you're sorry. You know – for sleeping with her."

"But I am sorry." Very, very sorry. No matter what the equipment downstairs seemed to think.

Max sighed and the sound resonated with exhaustion. "I know you are. But just trust me. A woman doesn't want to hear that the best sex of her life is a mistake."

"You think it was the best sex of her life? Where did you hear that? Did she tell you that?" His questions were rapid-fire and obviously spoken directly from the afore-mentioned equipment. He wanted to sink into the floor. Had he really just asked Max for pillow talk gossip? Axel would call this a face-palm moment!

Max laughed heartily, practically lighting up his dim room. "Oh, Goddess! You totally just had a man-moment! And I was here to see it! I am honoured." She bowed her head. "But I am also serious. Don't do it, Darius." She shook her finger at him, "It would be very unwise. Especially to a woman who abstained from touching you for eight centuries just because she said she would." She turned and walked from the room.

He stood frowning to himself for a moment, fiddling with the new eyepiece in his telescope. Perhaps Max's advice was sound. Diana was the stubbornest human he had ever met. But then again, Max had also advised a chade to run for its life, so her wisdom was sporadic at best. No – he didn't believe Max was right in this instance. An apology was always wanted and always appropriate ... right?

ELEVEN

Wrong.

Wrong.

Wrong.

How had he been wrong about an apology? Since when was an apology a bad thing? Over the past few days, Diana had taken a leaf from Max's ice-queen-how-to guide and had completely frozen him out. He had reciprocated in kind, regressing into his emotionless, controlled demeanour. There had been no further dramas and no recriminations – formal or otherwise – from Ryker, so he supposed he should be grateful. Too bad his nights were filled with visions of Diana in bright, scanty lace and a fevered lust that complemented his own perfectly.

"I'm coming with you to the Lodge today." Max's announcement was met with silence and covert looks.

Darius glanced around the room. Apparently everyone was extremely busy doing other things. Cowards. He cleared his throat, "Is that wise? There's likely to be a few wardens and paladins there and we are trying to keep you low-key – at least until Ryker can speak privately with the IDC next week." It was strange they still hadn't been to visit yet actually, given their initial excitement over Max's discovery. They still believed she was a Life Warden after all. Diana had actually expressed her concerns that someone was deliberately stalling the meeting. Darius couldn't think of a reason why that would be the case, but it was still curious.

"Well, I can't stay here forever guys. I'm going bat-shit crazy! There are only so many dolphins for me to play with and so many times I can kick all your butts! I need freedom! I need interaction! Let me live, Darius! Why won't you let me live?" She ended, bellowing dramatically.

Darius shook his head at her antics. She hadn't changed much in the weeks since discovering she was a Goddess and forging bonds with her own personal knights. She was still her normal quirky, good-natured self, which meant that she was still going to be just as prone to the harsh realities of their society. She was still going to walk into the Lodge, talk to people who said things she didn't approve of, see behaviours she didn't agree with, and then lecture, yell or throw things in order to show her displeasure. Although he agreed with some of her ideas, now just wasn't the time to put her in the spotlight. It was tricky enough for Ryker and the others that were bonded to hide their new coat of arms whenever they were shifted on at the Lodge. Long sleeves were now an everyday occurrence and none of them could use the showers there anymore after a training session.

"Darius is right, honey." Ryker said. "I'm sorry, but we just can't risk your secret getting out. There are few people outside this camp that I would trust with the information that you are a Custodian. Garrett, the Life Warden on the IDC, is one of them. He assures me the full council will be available for your introduction next week and I really want the opportunity to discuss you and our new Order with him privately."

"I promise I won't tell the world I am somehow the daughter of Mother Nature herself in physical form." She raised her right hand solemnly. At least she was getting the hang of that, Darius thought.

"And what if the local council is there? You didn't exactly leave the best first impression with them." Darius felt the need to point out in their defence.

Max planted her hands on her curvy hips, defiance in every line of her body. "Well, they didn't exactly make a good impression on me either! What a pack of sanctimonious, hypocritical wankers! Angel! They wanted me to change my name to Angel!" Her voice was horrified.

Axel let out a booming laugh. "How hilarious is that? I mean, most wardens are named for their element or their intrinsic natures. Angel?! If they only knew!" He laughed again and Max joined him, not taking offense in the slightest.

"That's our point though, Max. Are you going to be able to appoint yourself properly?"

Max abruptly stopped laughing. "Appoint myself properly? Do I have poor manners, Darius? Do I embarrass you?" Her tone was cold and accusing.

Damn! Now he was on the receiving end of her displeasure again. Did he detect a smirk on the pretty Diana's face? "You know you don't. I just want to protect you."

"I know. And I appreciate it. I even understand your concerns – I honestly do. But I can't live like this. I feel like I had more freedom when I was on the run." Darius heard Ryker suck in a harsh breath as she continued to speak, "I don't want to be a dirty little secret. Or a kept woman!"

Ryker winced. "No. Absolutely not. You are not my kept woman; you're just mine. And you're not a dirty secret; but you are secret." He dragged her close, kissing her mouth. "I'm sorry. We have kind of been harbouring you here. Let's clean up and we'll head to the Lodge for the day. I have a lot to do there anyway and perhaps you could help."

Max's smile practically lit up the sky as she fist-pumped the air and raced upstairs, not allowing anyone time to change their minds. Lark groaned and at first, Darius thought it was because he was picturing all the potential things that could go wrong like he was.

"Maybe she can go in my place. I don't feel so hot today." He murmured instead. That made Darius frown for a different reason. Paladins rarely became ill.

"Actually, I'm not feeling great either." Cali admitted.

"You're not?" Diana asked. Even the sound of her voice got to him these days! "I have a headache as well."

"So, what? We all have a virus or something?" Lark guessed.

Diana eyed the stairs Max had flown up moments ago, a pensive look on her face. "Max!" She yelled abruptly, startling the hell out of him.

"What's up?" Max popped back in, tanto sword in hand. There was no way Darius was telling her she couldn't take that into the Lodge. He knew she had strapped it inside her high boots last time she visited despite the total weapons ban on the premises. The samurai sword was her security blanket. Ry had even told him that she slept with it. That image made Darius acutely sad.

"How do you feel?

Max's expressive eyebrows rose as she shrugged, "I feel good. Better than I have in years. Why?"

"Do you have a headache? Muscle soreness? Eye strain?" Diana pressed.

Max shrugged negligently, "A little, I guess. But it's not bad."

"We're all feeling what Max is feeling? This is the bond? Lark asked, incredulous. Having never been in an Order before, it wasn't surprising that Lark didn't recognise the ebb and flow of energy, emotions, thoughts and sensations through the bond.

Diana nodded. "I believe so."

"But I feel terrible!" Lark exclaimed. He turned to Max with horrified eyes. "This is how you feel every day?"

"No ..." the room seemed to relax at the one syllable, "... like I said, I feel better than ever. This is nothing! What's wrong with you guys?" She enquired, noticing the shocked looks. "I'm sorry my headache is spilling on to you through the bond. I'll dial back the connection."

"We don't want your apology, Max." Lark replied stiffly.

She crossed to Ryker. Perhaps Darius had been mistaken before. The Japanese blade was no longer her security blanket – Ryker was. "Then why are you all so upset?" She wondered.

"It's the fact that you are in pain, Max. It is an affront to everything we are as an Order. And what's worse? You don't even seem to notice how bad you feel or sick you are. This is just normal for you ..." Beyden's deep voice trailed off. He wasn't even bonded yet and looked ill at the thought of Max suffering.

Max laughed. "Guys, seriously! I'm fine! No need for dramatics. I haven't had a seizure in weeks! I'm so very grateful to you all for sharing your vitality. I even wonder myself now how I managed to survive all this time without it."

So did they all, Darius thought. And the IDC was going to wonder the same thing.

TWELVE

Diana was pleased to see the Lodge was filled only half way to capacity as they entered. She spotted Fawn and Ray from the local council but they were actually decent human beings and she knew they wouldn't cause a stir with Max and would even welcome her. There was no sign of Ignatius, thankfully, but he was due to arrive because his paladins were required to undertake their monthly physical review. They were all hoping Max would be outside or otherwise suitably occupied by then. Without conscious thought, her eyes strayed to Darius where he was talking to Fawn and her paladins. His manner was courtly as he listened attentively, nodding and answering her questions flawlessly no doubt. He was clean shaven once again and his short hair was neatly trimmed against his perfectly shaped skull. How could a man have a perfectly shaped skull? She tried not to watch the way his butt muscles tensed as he exited the room, carrying a heavy book of some kind. And she really tried not to remember the way they had flexed as her fingernails dug into them while she payed appropriate homage to the opposite side of his anatomy with her mouth.

"You know, I get it." Max announced, presently.

Diana turned to her. She and Cali had drawn the first 'Max Watch' and they were seated on one of the lounges dotting the large open room. "Get what?"

Max gestured in the direction Darius had taken. "The appeal. I totally get the Darius appeal."

Max had been very close-mouthed over the last few days, to which Diana was forever grateful. She didn't want to invite discussion over the whole debacle.

"I get it too. I mean, he's soooo intellectual but he's also a warrior. It's an irresistible combination." Cali chimed in.

Diana kept her mouth shut. Until Max squealed and clapped her hands, startling the ever-loving shit out of her!

"Oh my God! Indiana Jones! He's Indiana Jones!" Max turned wide, excited eyes her way. "He's educated, smart, a historian, a real life action hero ..."

Damn, Diana thought, *he is Indiana Jones!* She loved Indiana!

"Too bad he's not as playful as Indy though ..." Cali murmured. Once again, Diana didn't say anything. She thought Darius could be *very* playful when he wanted to be – namely when he was naked and horny.

Max smirked, "It's a shame. The potential is there but even the man's soul is rigid. I mean, it moves freely in the air, as if continually captured by the wind, but it's still somehow stiff, as if it's not really free."

She was eyeing Darius through the window across the room and Diana could feel a pulse of power through the bond. She knew Max must be using what they had dubbed her 'Goddess-vision' to look directly into Darius's soul. Even bonded, Diana could not experience what the other woman saw, but she knew it was like a life-size doppelganger, always present next to a person. A couple of the others had secretly expressed concerns that Max could literally look into their souls, but Diana held no such concerns. She was comfortable in who she was and accepted everything about herself; whether it be good or bad.

"If I didn't know any better, I would think Darius had a steel pike up a certain orifice, keeping his soul's spine so straight." Max continued.

"Are you still talking about sticks and butts? Is there something you want to share with the class?" Diana smiled as she heard the voice of the Water Warden behind her. Turning, she saw Caspian and his two bonded paladins approaching, making a very handsome trio. She really liked Cas and the two brothers that formed the Order of Riparian. Not only were they the closest neighbours to them, but they had also become close friends over the years. Diana was a frequent attendee at their poker nights. Max had taken an immediate shine to them too. Diana wasn't surprised – she seemed to have some sort of attraction to the underdogs of the world. First them, as outcast and rejected paladins, and then Caspian as the only publicly gay warden in their society. It didn't endear them to other wardens or paladins as a whole, but Max didn't even blink an eye. She treated everyone the same until they proved themselves or revealed their true natures. Then she acted accordingly.

"Cas! Hi!" Max shouted exuberantly, hugging Caspian tightly. The young warden smiled with genuine warmth and Diana could tell Max's early offer of friendship had well and truly been accepted.

"She was talking about Darius this time, not Ryker. I believe Max has now completed a full cavity search of the Captain and the previously mentioned stick has now been permanently removed." Cali added, helpfully.

Although, the conversation would be considered highly inappropriate in the company of their betters, Diana couldn't help laughing with the rest of them. Cali certainly had no reservations treating Max exactly as she always had and she had never been one to be shy in social situations. Although not as outspoken as Max could afford to be, Cali had often come to the defence of Caspian and his lover Lawson in the past, and frequently took home the pot on poker night.

"You don't say," Caspian smiled, taking a seat. "So you and Ryker ...?"

If any other warden had asked, Diana knew the intent would have been entirely different. Other wardens and even paladins would be trying to pry for information to use against the newest member of their world. But Caspian was after dirty goss, plain and simple.

"Yep. He's all mine." Max confirmed. And although her words sounded flippant the look in her eyes was soft and love-filled.

"I'm happy for you. And Ryker. I knew you would be good for him the moment I met you. Does this mean you're all considering forming an Order?" Caspian asked, lowly. Diana was grateful for his circumspection.

"It is something we are giving due deliberation to." She answered formally but smiled to soften the cool words. Caspian nodded in acknowledgment.

"I'm glad. I think you will all make a good match." The soft voice drifted from behind them and was lightly accented. Fawn was the Beast Warden representative on the local council and Diana actually liked her. Beyden did too if she wasn't mistaken.

All four paladins jumped to their feet to greet the Warden but Fawn merely waved a hand, telling them to sit. "I'm sorry to interrupt. I just wanted to say hello and apologise for our first meeting. I'm sure it was overwhelming for you and it could have gone smoother."

Max grinned. "Thank you. But I'm the one who should probably be apologising. I don't have much of a brain to mouth filter and I was rude. I'm sorry."

Fawn smiled. She really was very pretty, Diana thought. All blonde and feminine looking. "Well, I'm glad you seem to be settling in. You couldn't have found yourself a better group of paladins if you tried."

Diana saw Cali raise her eyebrows at that. Sure, Fawn was nice and always treated them with respect but she had never been overly vocal about their precarious positions in society.

"I feel great. They have all been absolutely wonderful! I've even been able to get some real work done for my graphic novels and I've been able to access all my bank accounts too." Max turned to her then, enquiring, "Do you guys pay a mortgage? Can you tell me the details so I can add my share?"

Uh oh. She was able to share one worried look with Cali before Leo began to laugh. "There's no mortgage on that place. Besides, your share? Max, your share is one hundred percent. That house belongs to you now."

Shit! Diana thought and silently cursed Ryker. He should have been the one to explain this type of thing to Max. Unlike ninety-nine-point-nine percent of all wardens, Diana had a feeling that Max was not going to be happy to find herself an instant millionaire. Sure enough, Diana felt the bond shut down instantly – something Max did whenever she felt she couldn't adequately shield herself.

"What does he mean?"

Double shit! Max's voice had gone ice-princess. "Well, technically ..." She began, "... paladins can't really own their own property. Ryker was an exceptional circumstance because his liege left him the land in his will. It was beyond contestation because Flint had no other living family. But now if Ryker is to be bound to another liege, all his holdings will revert to that liege."

"Revert to that liege ..." Max's voice was low.

Fawn glanced at her four paladins – two women and two men. That was uncommon as well. Women were still not largely embraced as active knights. "Historically, knights were once gifted a benefices, such as land, property or gold. It was granted to them as boons in repayment for their exemplary service. That is what Flint did for Ryker. Unfortunately, such traditions have been considered outdated for a few hundred years now." She explained, appearing to study Max for her reactions.

Max didn't disappoint. "So now wardens just take whatever they want and give nothing in return?" Her tone held obvious disapproval. She turned to Cali, "Do you even get paid?"

"Um, sort of. A paladin is provided everything by their liege, including a salary if they so deem. It's a little different for us though. We are employed by the IDC to run the training centre here so we are actually provided with an income of sorts for equipment, the vehicles and whatnot." Cali explained.

"Wardens get paid though. In fact, you'll find that you are now the new beneficiary of a substantial trust fund." Caspian pointed out. "You will be compensated for the burden you bear in order to maintain your domain."

"Compensated how? And how do they know I'm maintaining anything?" Max's voice was still icy but she was also listening and Diana allowed herself to relax minutely.

"It's almost like a posting in the military. The IDC station wardens all over the world wherever their domains need tending most. Some of the postings are temporary and some are more long term. I was contracted to come here almost five years ago to ensure the local river system and local stretch of beach is maintained. It's a permanent posting." The Water Warden clarified.

"So I'm essentially going to be drafted and sent who knows where?" Max asked in annoyance. She turned to Diana. "And you didn't think this was important for me to know?"

"We're getting there, Max. Little by little we're teaching you about our society. It's no easy task. You can't learn a whole race's history in a matter of weeks."

"Besides, I don't think you need to be too concerned about the International Domain Council sending you anywhere. You are a female Life Warden. Your discovery is a true miracle and you will be embraced as such." Fawn assured her, nodding her head in deference. "Although I am sure, as a Life Warden, you feel the need to help when and where you can. I got the impression you wished to be active in your domain at our last meeting."

That caused Max to close her mouth. Not only did she not want to lie outright by saying she was a Life Warden when she wasn't, Diana knew, but she had also been very vocal about not being passive. "You're right, Fawn. I want to help. I just don't like the idea that our paladins give up everything for us and don't receive any formal acknowledgement for their sacrifice or service."

"I agree." Fawn's brown eyes were direct and Diana knew they had another ally.

"Having a party?"

Diana silently cursed up a storm. That annoying nasally voice belonged to Ignatius. They had gotten distracted by the conversation and she hadn't been keeping an eye on the time. Diana saw Max's eyes brighten in anticipation. Looks like Max thought she now had the perfect outlet for her frustrations over the newest revelations.

"Ignatius. How wonderful to see you again." She said as she stood up. "Your boys delivered my message to you I trust?" She asked sweetly.

Diana saw the red flush begin to make its way up the Fire Warden's neck as he registered the snickers in the room. Several occupants had been at Lonnies two weeks ago. "Threatening an Order is a punishable offense. And threatening a Warden could mean a death sentence."

"Is that right? Well then, I'll be sure to mention your little goon squad assaulting Lark to the IDC when I meet with them next week."

"*Lark*," Ignatius spat as if the name were synonymous with the word *shit*, "is an unbound paladin, with no liege. He instigated the fight and my Order were forced to defend themselves. You have no cause and no right to seek any form of retribution against them."

"Well now, that's just not true. You see, Lark is *my paladin* and I am *his liege*. So I have every right to defend my paladin and every cause to seek retribution because no-one here believes for one minute that Lark started anything!"

Several gasps followed Max's announcement that Lark was now a sworn paladin. Diana did her best not to palm her face; this was not the low profile Ryker and Darius were set on maintaining. And they had been doing so well ...

"You can't do that!" Ignatius actually pointed a finger in Max's face. "Paladins must be vetted by the local council before being formally approved by the international council. The bonding must be acknowledged and witnessed in front of the IDC and the warden community."

Max merely shrugged. "It's already done."

"I'm reporting you to the IDC." Ignatius's voice was excited, almost as if he were a child narking on a sibling. It wasn't a good look on a Warden and Diana could see the uncomfortable stirring in the room and side-glances suggesting that she wasn't alone in that opinion. Not the least being Fawn who was scrutinising Ignatius like a bug under a microscope. Perhaps eyes were truly beginning to open.

"Go ahead. I'll be sure to file my own report about your deplorable behaviour. Who knows, I may even get a petition going." Max looked around them room and appeared to judge the mettle of the occupants. "I bet there are a number of individuals who have righteous complaints where you are concerned."

The Fire Warden crossed his arms over his chest, his five paladins mirroring him. His eyes also surveyed the room, but where Max's were only curious, his held a warning of dire consequence. "Is that so? Well, I'm always open to discussion. Does anyone have anything they would like to address?" His dark eyes focused on Caspian when the Water Warden made a restless movement. "Caspian? Do you have anything you would like to say?"

Caspian actually looked him in the eyes for a full three seconds before he lowered his head and murmured; "No. Nothing to say."

Ignatius smirked, "I didn't think so ... *disgusting!*" He added under his breath but loud enough for the very quiet room to hear.

Diana could see Max was itching to slap the smirk right off his face and although Diana agreed with her whole heartedly, it just wasn't an option. Darius was correct – the wisest course of action was to not create waves and ensure Max's transition into their society was as smooth as possible. The best way to achieve that was to await the arrival of the IDC. If they accepted Max – and they most certainly would, quirks and all – then everyone else would too. The majority of the wardens and paladins were good little sheep. They followed the lead and the proclamations of the seven most powerful wardens alive.

Not wanting the situation to escalate further, Diana tested the link she had with her Captain. Ryker was a potentate and therefore the only one capable of maintaining the link between everyone in the Order – other than Max, that was. They hadn't actively used the link much because they had been more focused on getting Max to understand and control her end of the bond. But now was a good time to get her Captain's attention. Concentrating her thoughts on Ryker, she gave the link a decent pluck, not bothering to waste her time being tentative. Ryker and the rest of the men appeared in the doorway not five seconds later. Seems the link was alive and kicking. Diana tilted her head in the direction of Max and she saw her Captain's eyes narrow as he took in the scene. Five long strides were all it took for him to reach her. He was careful not to touch her and he also remained a respectful distance away from Ignatius and his Order. Darius took his place next to Ryker and Axel, Lark, and Beyden closed in ranks from behind. The sight of them all lined up like a unit almost took her breath away. They looked like a real Order. And judging by the whispered murmurs and widening eyes in the room, they looked like a damn formidable one!

"Ignatius. Your paladins are late." Ryker's voice was brisk and bordering on rude but he was always that way, so no-one could say he was treating the man differently just because of Max.

Ignatius smiled thinly. "My paladins were on their way to you for their monthly fitness test when we were waylaid by your guest here."

Ryker crossed his arms over his impressive chest – not as impressive as Darius's now that she had personally sampled the air paladin's pecks – but Ry never failed to be an inspiration. "You had better all get changed. You're late." He repeated, not rising to the bait.

Ignatius continued to stare at Ryker for a few seconds before nodding to his Order. "Max. Always a pleasure." He bowed regally before he and his paladins moved off.

Diana figured Max would have a few choice words for Ryker or even herself, for spoiling her fun, but she surprised her by turning to Caspian instead;

"Why do you let him treat you that way?" She asked.

Caspian looked startled for a moment before a red flush bathed his cheeks. "It's just easier ..."

Max's gaze was steady as she continued to watch Caspian. "And since when does easy, equal right?"

Lawson placed a comforting hand on his liege's shoulder. Leo and Lawson were always a steady presence for Caspian. Diana knew they wanted to defend Cas overtly with fists and words but they abided by their liege's wishes. Caspian did not want to cause any more issues than his mere presence already wrought. Diana thought him incredibly brave to be an active member of society and to interact socially with their fellow knights rather than becoming a hermit and hiding himself away. Many other homosexual wardens and paladins had been forced to do just that, or felt forced to lie about their sexual orientation. But Caspian didn't do that. Sure, he may not walk around with a rainbow flag or make out with Lawson in public, but he never denied his lover and he worked every day to uphold his domain and maintain the respect of his peers.

Apparently Max intended the question to be rhetorical, for she continued; "You are one of the most powerful wardens in the room. More powerful than Ignatius here, despite only having two paladins in your Order. I can feel it. I can see it. It drips off you. Why do you ignore it? Because this fucked up, antiquated society tells you that you're less because of whom you love?"

Several gasps met Max's speech, not the least of them from Caspian himself. "You're mistaken. I'm not powerful."

"You are." Max's voice rang with authority and a truth no-one would dare deny. Judging by the mutters and scuffling feet in the room, Diana knew that they all must have felt the veracity of those two words as well. "And you! You would just sign over your home to me, your refuge and your place of peace, because some fucked up, antiquated society tells you you're less because you were born a paladin?"

"Uh ..." Ryker was wide-eyed and looking bewildered at the sharp turn in Max's censures. Diana understood how she believed the two issues were linked; they were all about respect.

"Do you really believe that you have no right to earn your pride through your possessions?" She asked, sadness and indignation in her voice. "Let me tell you all something.

Respect is earned, it's true. It can't be forced and it can't be taken. But ... people treat you the way you demand to be treated. If you continue to roll over and show your bellies, you're going to keep getting kicked. You're all worth more than this ..." Max's strange turquoise eyes seemed to glow with an inner light as she focused them on several individuals in the room, including Caspian and Fawn, "... you need to start demanding."

Diana felt tears prick her eyes when Max stormed from the room in righteous temper. Realising she was a Custodian with the potential for true greatness was one thing. Witnessing that greatness was another entirely. Her society was in desperate need of a shake-up. They were a noble race and their role in the world was immense. But they were drowning, sinking slowly back into the habits of the old days and introducing new rules that were even worse in some ways. Diana feared what their declining numbers would mean to the natural wonders of the world. Max truly was going to be their saviour, she just knew it.

"Dammit, this is not going to help. Low-key. She agreed to low-key. That little speech of hers is going to incite gossip among the higher ups and by the time the IDC get here, who knows what they will be believing?" Darius growled from next to her. The majority of the room had dispersed and she was surprised to find herself essentially alone with the man of her dreams.

He had hardly spoken to her in days since the *incident* as Max liked to call it. At least she wasn't referring to it as the *intercourse* like she did after her and Ryker's initial sexcapades. Like Max, Diana was a firm believer in not making issues where they weren't needed. So she listened like a good little soldier when Darius had expressed his sincerest apologies over the *incident* and had left it at that. Well, sort of. She wasn't as adept as Max was at acting casual and normal. Where Max had chatted on as if nothing had ever happened between Ryker and herself – driving Ryker crazy in the process – Diana had frozen Darius out somewhat. She was still professional and courteous with him but she no longer shared her casual affection and friendship with him. She found it a little hard to keep holding the man in high esteem after he had practically said that he had made the biggest mistake of his life.

He had knocked on her door the next day, after first apologising to Max and essentially begging for forgiveness. That had chapped her arse too! He had spoken to Max before her. She shouldn't have been surprised – duty before all else was his creed. He had looked like his usual put-together self in his cargos and dark shirt with the exception of the dark circles. Apparently he'd had a restless night. Well, so had she. But hers had been filled with steamy images of what the man had done to her against the wall of the gym. She had woken up aching and wanting and knowing full well that no other man would be able to compare to the rapture she had felt in his arms.

At first, she could hardly believe the wicked intent she had seen in his eyes; surely under all that smooth sophistication there couldn't truly be a dominant, powerful lover? A lover who sought his own pleasure as forcefully as he did that of his partners? A lover who was unashamed of his desires and who trusted his partner to accept every aspect of him? She was unabashedly assertive in the bedroom and was just as comfortable with a little rough, spontaneous play as she was with slow and premeditated lovemaking. She was unafraid to ask for what she wanted and was more than happy to respond to her lover's desires as well. Darius had been absolutely perfect. But such perfection was not meant to last for he had stood stiffly at attention in her doorway, stating;

"I wanted to express my deepest apologies for the way I treated you yesterday. I know there is likely nothing I can

117

*do to atone for my behaviour, but please know I consider it
one of the worst mistakes of my life."*

Her stomach had dropped so radically that she literally
felt sick. After Max's positive reaction and blessing, she had
briefly entertained the notion that they could perhaps form
some sort of ... *arrangement*. She knew an intimate,
emotional relationship was out, but she thought perhaps
they could enjoy each other's bodies for a time. They were
explosively compatible after all.

"How exactly did you treat me yesterday?" She had
asked.

*"Well ... I took out my frustrations on you. I didn't treat
you like a lady. It's entirely unforgivable."*

"And you suppose I want *to be treated like a lady?"* She
inquired. *"News flash Darius; I like to be treated like a*
woman. *And you certainly did that."*

Her assurances did little to change his mindset however
for he continued to ruin everything about that special
encounter for her by saying;

"I used you, Diana. Do you not have any self-respect?"

The urge to punch him between the eyes had been
monstrous but she had refrained – barely. He was clearly so
far in the closet about his true wants and desires and far too
cowardly to admit to them. Darius and cowardly were words
she thought she would never use in the same sentence. So
just like she had done eight hundred years ago when he had
crushed her feminine pride on the battlefield, she had shut
him down and cut him out.

*"Did you just? Well, did you ever consider that I may
have been using you too, hmm? Perhaps I am the one who
should be begging for forgiveness."* After gaining a sliver of
satisfaction from his widening eyes and gaping mouth, she
had slammed the door in his handsome face. Now here they
were three days later and he had apparently not been using

his time to get his thoughts in order. He was still struggling to reach the point where the rest of them were at.

"You really don't get it, do you?" She questioned him.

He was frowning now, "I don't understand what?"

She shook her head, noting the way his hazel eyes tracked the movement of her errant curls. She knew he had a thing for her hair just as Max knew Ryker had a thing for her boobs. So of course, Max used them to her advantage all the time. Diana wasn't above such small pleasures either, so she gave her coils an extra flip for good measure. "There's a reckoning coming, Darius. A revolution. And Max is the trigger."

She literally heard him swallow and saw the dramatic movement in his throat muscles. Oh, yes, the man knew it. He felt it, just like the rest of them. He just wasn't ready to accept it. Despite being acutely pissed off – and yes, hurt – by the man, she still wanted to help him. "You know the fact that Max is a Custodian is out of your control, right? It has nothing to do with you." She kept her voice low, ensuring they couldn't be overheard.

Darius scowled. "Yes. I am fully aware I have no control over Max's Custodian status." He responded coolly.

"Then why do you insist on trying? You're making this about you; about your insecurities, and your wants. It's exactly what Ryker did when she first arrived. It's why she went so long running on fumes, when the first thing Ryker should have seen was how sick she was. But he was more focused on how her presence affected him – his emotions and his dreams, long thought lost to him. You are doing the exact same thing – albeit not quite as rudely." She acknowledged. "Max challenges everything you thought you knew about the world. Everything you thought you knew about a society where rules and order are paramount. She upsets your sense of self – not just your sense of what you believed possible – and you don't know how to cope."

Darius clenched his teeth. "My duty is first and always to the Wardens of the world. I *always* put them first. Equally, I am putting Max's best interests first. It is my responsibility to do so, just as it is yours. *I* do not factor into the equation at all."

"Uh huh." Diana replied, dryly. "You keep telling yourself that. But you're never going to be comfortable with the whole situation until you begin to accept it."

Diana saw his smooth veneer begin to crack again in the flaring of his nostrils and the agitated hand scrubbing across his scalp. "You are wrong. I not only accept Max as a Custodian and that she is here to stay, but I am trying to ensure her smooth transition into society. Why am I the only one that gets that?" He threw at her, before leaving the room.

Diana sighed as she made her way out front, needing some air. She hoped her little talk with Darius helped. She wasn't anywhere near as good as Max was at putting people in their place, but she was good at psychology. It was why she often took on jobs as a consultant for various law enforcement agencies around the world. As a paladin affiliated with the domain of death, it allowed her a certain sensory compassion she supposed. Where Ryker was empathic – being able to read and sometimes feel emotions from people, Diana was able to analyse those emotions and discover the root of them.

She knew others made the assumption that a Death Warden or paladin were dark or cold and spent their days dealing with ghosts or predicting people's deaths or the like. But that was entirely wrong. As a paladin associated with the elements of loss, grief and pain, she was actually able to bring peace. She was able to analyse the evidence of a crime and all the people involved, while staying completely removed. She could judge the natural reactions of a person. The crux of her domain was acceptance. She understood the cycles of the world better than anyone because death and loss were like family to her, it made her very zen about the shitty things in the world. She was very accepting of the unchangeable things in life. She understood how the world – with all its people and places and things – evolved and changed with time. It was inevitable. But that didn't mean justice shouldn't be served and people could just get away with anything. She was accepting – not forgiving. Big difference. So consulting work had fit her like an old glove and she truly enjoyed it. It had also enabled her to spend large amounts of time away from a certain air paladin. It was a shame she was going to have to stop. She would miss it, and being a trainer too. But there was no way any of them were going to be able to continue with their day jobs now that they were bound to Max as she had earlier thought. There was also no way Diana was going to be in the same room as Ryker when he told Max that. She had a feeling that the feisty female wasn't going to be too impressed.

"Darius is having a real hard time with all this, isn't he?" Max's voice startled her so badly, she actually reached for her sickle before cursing when she remembered she didn't have it on her. No weapons in the Lodge. She wasn't surprised Max had sought her out and she knew Darius was having a huge problem with 'all this'. She was a genuinely caring person and very astute. After the heated discussion about the chades earlier in the week – she still hadn't explained to any of them why she had chosen to let that chade go – Diana knew she had talked with Darius privately and the two had agreed to move past the tension. Darius hadn't revealed why talk of the chades caused him such pain but Max was ensuring he had the time and space he needed to work through it. She was a good friend. Diana found herself nodding in response;

"He is. His whole world is structured around rules and laws. His position in society is dictated to him by how well he follows the rules. Although he has evolved with the times, in many respects he remains an old fashioned guy at heart.

Change is difficult for him. Especially change he cannot quantify in his little books." Max nodded, biting her lip. "Hey, don't worry. He'll come around." She assured her.

Max looked directly at her then, her oceanic eyes piercing and bright. "I hope so. I'm going to need him. He's the final one."

"The final one for what?" Diana questioned quietly, unease filling her. But Max didn't answer her. Her old liege, Verity, had a touch of premonition so she was very good at reading the signs for that particular trait. She sure hoped she was reading Max wrong right now.

"When do you think we can do some more normal stuff?"

Diana had to blink several times in order to clear her mind enough to follow Max's tangents. The woman was going to give her whiplash. "Normal stuff like what?"

"I don't know. Like going shopping the other day. Coming here to work with you guys is okay, but I just figured now that I'm not being hounded by creatures everywhere I go, I might be able to do some more ... normal."

Diana winced. Not only had Max been unable to enjoy the mundane things everyone took for granted due to her being so sick, being stalked constantly, and being afraid of powers she didn't understand, but she also had a restless personality. Diana recognised a woman of action when she saw her. She wasn't going to be content to sit around the camp all day growing daisies and petting the dolphins. Perhaps she had a touch of coward in her like she had accused Darius, because there was no way Diana was going to inform Max that was exactly what the other wardens were going to expect. And as nightmarish as that scenario was likely to be to Max, the other scenario was worse to Diana. And that was that the IDC was going to try to take advantage of Max and they were going to lose her to the Council.

"We don't really do 'normal' Max. This is it. What you see is what you get, I'm afraid." She spoke lightly.

"Don't you find it all a little boring?"

"No." *Yes!*

"Hmm." Max's non-answer was slightly concerning. Perhaps she should talk to the others about ensuring Max's devious brain was kept active. She had the feeling that a bored Max was a dangerous Max.

THIRTEEN

Thus, two days of inactivity later, Diana had managed to talk the rest of the group into doing some more 'normal'. Well, she really only had to convince Ryker and Darius. The others were wholly on board. Later that day they were going to go out for drinks and dancing. She had the strangest feeling that Max would prove exceedingly entertaining under the influence. Wardens didn't encourage their paladins to imbibe often but it wasn't actually a rule that they weren't allowed to drink. That's why Lonnie's was so popular amongst the knights in the area. They could get together and be social in a casual environment. Not that Diana had any intention of taking Max to Lonnie's. After the whole 'dick slit' threat, she figured it was probably wiser to take Max someplace where the male occupants wouldn't be holding onto their genitals in fear all night. She was looking forward to getting dressed up and relaxing as well.

At the moment though, they were all outside watching in amusement as Max finally bonded with Axel and Beyden and added two more members to their eclectic Order. Axel was completely enamoured with his new coat of arms and kept running his hands over it just to watch it writhe. Diana wished he would stop. She could almost feel an echo of it through her own brand. A giggle had her turning her attention to her liege and her mouth dropping open.

"Is she ...?" Diana asked more to herself than anybody. She was standing a distance away from the general chaos and didn't expect anyone to hear her. But Darius had obviously decided to join them, for he was the one who answered;

"Swimming through the air?" Darius sighed, "Yes."

"You don't approve." It was a statement, not a question.

"It's not that I don't approve ..." He began.

"But you don't understand her. You still can't find your answers in your little books and it's freaking you out." She could read him so easily now, and knew he was bristling at her words. They had continued to be polite to each other and she hoped he had given some genuine thought to their conversation at the Lodge the other day.

"I am *not* freaking out." He disputed but didn't rise any further to her taunt. He continued to watch Max as she did breaststroke through the air. Diana had only ever seen Air Wardens with the ability to float. It was wicked cool.

"She'll calm down. This is still just all so new to her. With six of us sharing our vitality, she's got energy and power in droves."

"Yes. That is what concerns me." He admitted.

"You think she can't handle it?" Although her tone was level, she could hear the underlying tension in it. Because she was bound to Max, it was hard for her to fight the instinctual need to defend her liege against any form of criticism – no matter how veiled or minor. But Darius just shook his head;

"It is not Max I am worried about. I think Max can handle anything. I think her powers have always scared her because she didn't have the knowledge to understand them or harness them. And because, even in her weakened state, they were always so strong." They watched her laughing now, both feet firmly planted back on the ground, and he was satisfied to see the healthy blush in her face. "Anyone else would have tried to cultivate all that barely-restrained power. Regardless of whether or not they understood it." Darius continued, seemingly contemplatively, "But not Max ..."

"No, not Max." She agreed. "But others might take it upon themselves to exploit all that power – and all that natural goodness." She added, testing to see which direction Darius was taking the conversation.

"Our society is inherently good, as are its citizens, but ... I feel as though the International Domain Council is running on fumes. The chades are increasing in numbers again, warden births are continuing to decline, the local councils are being given more and more power, and the few wardens we have left are becoming more reclusive and passive with their domains."

And yep, Diana thought, his feelings were heading in the same direction as hers. Perhaps he had taken the last few days to consider things. Or perhaps she had been unkind and not given him enough credit. Perhaps his deep understanding of the politics in their world was the crux of his reservations and concerns for Max.

"So what will happen when we present a Custodian – a daughter of the Creator herself?" Diana questioned.

"Exactly. That much power?" He shook his head. "If you were suddenly handed a magic wand that could fix all your problems, wouldn't you be tempted to accept it?"

"She isn't a magic wand." She was quick to point out.

"Not to us. No. Never. But to those who would do anything to see their species survive ..." He trailed off, not needing to finish and likely not wanting to finish.

She actually felt a little bad now. Seems he was on the same page as the rest of them in all that was important. She was going to respond but he had already moved off to congratulate Beyden and Axel. Later. She would talk to him again later. But for now she could give Max the good news of their plans for the rest of the evening. It might also serve to help Max burn off some of her new energy.

"We should start getting ready for tonight." She announced.

Max turned to her from Ryker's arms where she was securely snuggled. "Tonight? What's happening tonight?"

"We're hitting the town! Karaoke baby!" Lark crowed.

Max's initial full wattage smile dimmed and froze in place as the colour leached out of her face. "What did you just say?"

Lark paused, eyeing Max warily. "Um ... karaoke?"

"Why do you hate me?" Max looked so forlorn it was almost comical.

"What? We don't hate you! What are you talking about?" Poor Lark.

"Why else would you want to take me to such dens of torture? Why else would you want to punish me in such cruel, horrific ways?" She spouted dramatically. Diana could see Ryker rolling his eyes from behind his small love.

"I take it you're not a fan of karaoke ..." Diana took a stab in the dark.

"Absolutely not! Lucifer himself dreamt up that little peach of a nightmare. And it won't die! It just won't die I tell you!"

"Lucifer isn't real, Max." Darius argued, rationally. As if that was going to help.

"Oh yes he is! I've met him. And do you know where I met him?" She pointed an accusing finger to the sky. "That's right! It was in a karaoke bar! Never again! Oh no, never again ..." She muttered, shuddering from head to foot.

Axel was eyeing Max, deep in thought. "Does this have something to do with the donkey and the train thing?"

"Hush! Quiet you! We do not speak of such things!"

As amusing as this was – and it was *very* amusing – Diana was keen to get the show on the road. "Fine. No karaoke bar. But we are still going out." She could do with a few stiff drinks herself.

"Definitely! Let's go to Dave's Dive." She offered with enthusiasm.

Ryker grimaced, "Dave's? Max that place is filled with degenerate humans and smells like body odour, sweat and failed dreams."

"I know! Perfect right?" She smiled cheekily, "Besides, it's where I first met you guys. It has sentimental value."

Diana looked around at everybody and received various nods and shrugs. Looked like they were going to Dave's Dive.

"Oh, and ..." Max added, "... let's invite Caspian, Leo and Lawson. And maybe Fawn and her paladins – they seemed nice too – a little reserved, but that's nothing a bottle of tequila wouldn't cure. Oh, and the triplets! We're definitely inviting the triplets!"

Uh oh, Diana thought. What had she done?

FOURTEEN

"Dance with me." Max demanded to her lover. They were about hour four into their evening at Dave's. The human bar owner had raised his scarily hairy monobrow when he saw them enter but hadn't said anything and had continued to serve them drinks as the night progressed. He had even plugged in the sad excuse for a jukebox in the corner. Diana couldn't believe the thing even worked, it was so old. But it did have a great mix of old school tunes on it. Ryker seemed to have some kind of relationship with the owner, if she wasn't mistaken, so she was sure that helped too.

"I don't dance." Her captain responded flatly to Max. He wasn't drinking – half of them weren't. Some of them had to ensure they were protected.

"Not even sexy dancing?" Max cajoled.

Although his brown eyes lit up at the word *sexy* – typical male – he still shook his head. "Not even."

"I'll dance with you, honey." Beyden volunteered. He had been drinking, but only a little and was a far cry from tipsy. It was good to see him so relaxed. He jumped up and steered Max towards the dance floor. The beast paladin then proceeded to lead Max in an intricate series of steps, his hips and shoulders moving with a fluid grace as they glided across the 'dance' floor.

Ryker raised his eyebrows, "I didn't know he could dance!"

Diana rolled her eyes, watching her fellow knight's hips move appreciatively. "The man is Spanish, Ryker. He could Pasa Doble before he could walk."

"I'd be careful, Captain." Cali smirked, cheekily. "You know what they say; a man who can move his hips on the dance floor, can move them *off* the dance floor."

"Dip me! Dip me!" They all watched as Max's thick, long red locks brushed against the floor before Beyden righted her again, leaving her breathless and flushed.

Diana was really enjoying herself. It was nice to see everyone relaxed and enjoying each other's company. As promised, Caspian, Leo and Lawson had been invited as well as Fawn and her paladins. The latter had declined due to duties, she assured them, not because she hadn't wanted to come. But the triplets were here, much to Ryker's displeasure. The three identical gorgeous specimens were proof there was in fact a God or a Goddess in Diana's opinion. She watched as they talked with Leo and Lawson and saw the appreciative gleam in Caspian's eyes. Sure he was very much in love with his partner, Lawson, but he wasn't dead. He gave her a wink when Lawson wrapped an arm around him, pulling him closer to his side. Diana winked back, appreciating the playfulness of the Warden of Water.

Ten minutes later, a breathless Max and a flushed Beyden re-joined them. Their numbers at the table had dwindled to Axel, Lark and Cali. Ryker and Darius had begun talking shop and Cali had firmly moved them along with Leo and the triplets, saying; *'This is the fun table!'*

"Thanks, Bey. If you could set it up, that would be great." Max was saying as she took her seat and picked up a waiting shot of vodka. Diana shuddered as Max downed it in one healthy swallow.

"Set what up?" She asked, curious. She hoped Max wasn't up to anything too bad.

"Bey is going to introduce me to his sister."

"Ivy?" Diana asked, a little surprised. Beyden didn't talk about his sister too often. She thought maybe he was worried mentioning the Ranger would make them uncomfortable.

Max nodded her head. "Uh huh. She's a Ranger so I expect she is one of the leading experts on the chades."

Diana felt the others go still at the same time she did. Max frowned at them and gave them a serious look despite the bright blue drink she was now currently holding. "Did you think I was just going to let it go? I can be circumspect when I need to be. I have been giving Darius time but this is not an issue I am willing to drop. I will be conducting my own investigations – beginning with Ivy." She stated.

Cali patted her arm. "Good for you. But not tonight. This is the fun table." She reminded her and took the blue drink from Max, shotting it back. Cali was also drinking.

"Does that mean I'm not allowed to ask something about the bond?" Beyden queried.

"After that dancing, you can ask me anything you want, you sexy beast!" Max guaranteed him, causing heat to flush his cheeks.

"It's just something I've felt through the bond today ..." Beyden began a little tentatively.

Max gave her full attention to the man with the smooth dance moves. "What have I done now?"

"No, no! It's nothing you've done!" He was quick to reassure her, "It's just something I noticed with Ryker ..."

"What about him?" She asked with a head tilt.

"Well ..." Beyden looked at them but Diana could offer no assistance for she had no idea where this was heading. "Have you actually told Ryker you love him yet?" He finally blurted out. Ah, she thought. So she wasn't the only one to notice their Captains insecurities.

Max's head snapped back. "What? Of course! I tell him all the time!" She insisted.

Cali rolled her eyes, tipping back her Corona and draining half the bottle. "It doesn't count if you say it when you're orgasming."

"Why? That's when I mean it the most." Max pointed out logically.

Axel snorted once, then chuckled, then laughed so hard he had tears seeping from his eyes. "Oh, Max. If only I'd have snagged you first. You're the perfect woman."

She blew him a kiss and a wink. "See, Axel's on my side. Besides, it's not like he doesn't know. He can feel it through the bond."

They all could, actually. And it was genuinely lovely. A pure, non-selfish emotion given and taken freely without reserve or fear. She often had to reprimand herself when a tiny green-eyed monster reared its ugly head. "Men need to hear the words, Hon." She enlightened Max.

"Och! Men are *so* needy!" Max slapped her palm on the table as she rolled her eyes in exasperation. "I'll fix it." She assured the table in general, holding up a placating hand. She cruised her eyes around the room for a moment, before seeming to latch onto Darius;

"You know, if you wanted to take sleazy advantage of Darius while he's under the influence of good 'ole Jack, now would be the time." She said, nudging her with an unsteady hand. Diana couldn't help but eye her liege with amusement; Max was the one leaning heavily on Cali as she downed yet another shot of vodka. For a small thing, she sure could put 'em away! She had been consuming an impressive array of alcoholic beverages for the past few hours and had proved to be a highly entertaining and good natured drunk. But Darius on the other hand, seemed to be by no means intoxicated as

Max's statement implied. That was despite consuming almost an entire bottle of whiskey – Diana may have been watching. She turned to Max;

"Even if I wanted to take advantage of Darius –"

"Dirty, dirty, sweaty, messy, dirty advantage!" Cali interrupted, ostensibly being helpful. The water paladin was just as drunk as their liege.

Diana rolled her eyes, "Sure. All of that. Even if I wanted all of that ..." *Which I totally do! I want it bad!* She acknowledged, silently praising the vocabulary skills of her fellow knight, "... I doubt he would be receptive. Besides, it wouldn't be taking advantage – the man isn't drunk."

Diana was forced to lean back to avoid a face full of Max as she pitched forward, laughing so hard Diana was concerned she was going to rupture something internally. "My sweet, sweet Di ..." Max placed a comforting hand on her forearm, "... that man is completely and utterly wasted!"

All of them turned to watch Darius as he sat straight in his chair, deep in conversation with Ryker. He was nodding, listening intently and responding appropriately as they discussed training techniques and schedules. His short hair was still neatly styled and his clothes unrumpled. He was – as usual – completely put together. And by no means *wasted*.

"Sorry, Max. But I think you're seeing the world through the bottom of a tequila bottle. Darius is not moving; you are." She said, figuring Max was probably seeing a very wavy Darius by now.

"Bup-Barm!" Max made an obnoxious buzzer-sound as if Diana had answered incorrectly on a gameshow. "Trust me – if you could see what I can see ... then you would see what I can see." Max stated seriously, as if that sentence made complete sense. Cali – the drunk idiot, was nodding sagely as if in agreement.

"I'll prove it to you. Hey Dare!" Max shouted. Diana saw Darius wince from across the room at the nickname Max had taken to calling the air paladin after her sixth vodka shot.

"Yes?" Darius asked, courteously.

"The song is almost up. Will you please put on another? Your choice." She smiled.

He frowned slightly but immediately excused himself from the conversation and walked, straight as an arrow, to the jukebox. Diana was surprised when he seemed to give the contents a genuine perusal, eyeing it critically as if searching for a particular tune. He never really showed much interest in music, unless it was Axel on the piano of course. He preferred to spend his recreation time with his books or his darn *Star Trek*. Finally, he grunted and stabbed his finger decisively at his selection. Max's grin widened as the first four beats of the music began – a quick four-count loop of the first note – *boom, boom, boom, boom.*

Diana's mouth dropped open and the entire room stopped what they were doing to stare at the oldest and most respected paladin in the room as he began to rock his hips in time to the music and mouth the words silently.

'My milkshake brings all the boys to the yard,
And they're like, it's better than yours,
Damn right, it's better than yours,
I can teach you, but I have to charge.'

Milkshake. Darius was singing *Milkshake* and shaking his arse all over the place as he made his way back to his seat. Diana was yet to close her mouth and the room was yet to regain activity.

Milkshake. Darius was singing *Milkshake.*

Max's giggle had Diana tearing her avid attention away for a brief second. "I told you. That man is *plastered,* my friend!" And giving her a hearty slap on the back, Max shimmied and shook her own butt over to the now very clearly inebriated Darius.

*****

Darius was actually enjoying himself. He wasn't a big fan of drinking and parties but it was nice to just stop thinking for a while. He thought he might need to have a word with the owner of the bar about his alcohol though. He had been drinking all night and didn't feel a thing! He bopped himself over to a free table, feeling the beat of the music pumping through his body. What a great song!

"Good song choice."

Darius nodded his head, of course it was a good song choice – he had chosen it. "Thank you." He answered politely.

"May we?" Kane asked, indicating to the empty seats. Darius shrugged. He didn't mind if the pretty boys joined him. Maybe it would do them some good. They were just so ... *pretty*. Darius understood Ryker's aversion to them as he felt the same way. Pretty people couldn't be trusted.

"Dare!" A short spitfire of a woman shouted in joy before seating herself firmly in his lap. "What are you going to do about Diana?" She asked without preamble.

Screw her into the wall again? His inner voice suggested. "Nothing." His outer voice answered.

"You and Diana?" Kellan asked. At least he thought it was Kellan. They really did all look the same.

"No."

"Yes." Max answered at the same time. "He blew it – apologised for not treating her like a *lady*."

The three walking cover models winced and eyed him in sympathy. "You didn't?! Man, poor form."

"I am not discussing this ... But even if I was – which I am not – I would not require advice from pups such as yourselves." He assured them firmly. He was a thousand years old and these youngsters thought they knew more about women than him? The notion was laughable!

"Sure, man. I'm just saying, a woman like Diana? She needs a firm hand. She wants to know her partner can give as good as he takes. That's what she respects."

Darius glared dangerously at one of the men with the identical faces. Pretty boys! The lot of them! What would they know about how to treat a woman with a firm hand? *Hey ... wait a minute.* His brain was moving at a slower rate than normal and it wasn't able to process the conversation as rapidly as usual. What did the pretty boy know about Diana in particular wanting a firm hand?! Max apparently had no trouble following the conversation for she gasped loudly;

"You and Diana? No way! She never said anything to me, that skank! Which one of you was it?"

Which one was what? Darius's sluggish brain asked.

Max had her eyes narrowed on the three pretty boys and the three identical expressions of smug. Darius wanted to push their faces into the brick wall behind him just on principle.

"Was it all of you?" Max asked in stunned disbelief. "Oh, my dear friend, Di. I have underestimated you horribly. Will you ever forgive me?"

Darius looked around. Diana wasn't even here. Max sure must be drunk, he thought to himself.

Kai laughed, a horribly grating sound in Darius's opinion. "A gentleman never kisses and tells."

That was very true, Darius acknowledged. At least they had some semblance of manners ... wait ... kissing and telling ... Diana ... triplets ... Diana and triplets and kissing and telling ... "You have *not* slept with Diana!" He growled, lunging across the small space to grab a handful of pretty boy.

"Whoa, tiger!" Max grappled him back to his seat, which was pathetically easy given he couldn't seem to stand straight. Was he drunk or something?

"Yes. You are drunk. Very, very drunk." Max assured him. "So it's the perfect time to use some of that liquid courage and wipe out the memory of the gorgeous triplets from Diana's orgasm memory bank."

He growled. "My Diana! Mine! Not for pretty boys!"

"That's the spirit!" Max cheered.

Yeah, that was *the spirit.* He thought, pinning Diana with his eyes across the room. He saw her breath hitch and her grey eyes darken as they gazed steadily back.

A firm hand, huh? It just so happened he had two.

FIFTEEN

After her little talk with Darius, Max found herself outside in the cool night air. She leaned back against the wall, pretending not to be concerned about the thick layer of filth she knew must be coating it. She also pretended she didn't notice two stealthy silhouettes leaving the back door, one with a slender hand firmly lodged down the front of the other's pants! Smiling in satisfaction, she closed her eyes, inhaling the fresh sea air. Her family was inside that bar, laughing, drinking and just being merry. *Her family* – how weird was that? She was desperately praying this wasn't some sort of post head injury dream and she was going to wake up in a hospital somewhere being fed by a tube and shitting in a bag. Good things like this just didn't happen to her. But here she was, a freaking minor Goddess, with a crew of knights devoted to her health and happiness. And on top of that, she also had a Ryker. She loved every little thing about him. Her soul literally reached out for his. They were now so deeply intertwined that she knew she wouldn't be able to survive without him. But really, why would she want to? The man was panty-melting gorgeous, a God in the bedroom, loved her, respected her, and accepted her. Where the camp had been Ryker's refuge, Max knew that he was now hers.

The earth beneath her feet gave off a small vibration, alerting her to the appearance of another presence. Max opened her eyes to see Ignatius striding toward her, arrogance in his every step. *What did that tool want now?* She couldn't see his knights anywhere but they must be nearby somewhere.

"I know what you're up to and you won't get away with it." He snarled without preamble.

Max raised her eyebrows, "Having a party? It's not exactly hard to figure out, what with the noise and all." She smiled sweetly, "I would have invited you and your goon squad but there's a 'no wanker' policy."

"I can see what you're up to. You think everyone is buying your whole 'lost warden' act? You expect us to believe you just showed up from nowhere, like a lost little lamb and we're all going to embrace you and bow down to you? You're a fraud and a fake and I am not going to let you get away with tarnishing our society."

Hmm, Max thought. *Interesting notion.* She wondered how many others had the same idea? She would have to mention it to Ryker and the others. Rumours and suppositions could bring about unrest and she didn't want to cause any more trouble than she already had. "I have no idea what you're talking about. I assure you, I am what I say I am." *Other than being a Custodian*, Max thought. But she sure as shit was not going to tell Ignatius that! "And I have no desire to tarnish anything."

"Bullshit! You're trying to turn the others against me – against the local council even! Well, listen up bitch; you better watch yourself, otherwise what happened to your pathetic Earth paladin will seem like a walk in the park." He threatened.

Max was careful to keep the flow between her and her Order shut tight. The whole situation would likely become out of control if they were alerted to her predicament and she wasn't about to pull them into trouble. Besides, she'd been handling despots like Ignatius for years and Joy was securely in her boot as usual. "Be very careful, Ignatius. I don't take kindly to threats. And you need to stop reminding me about how you hurt my new brother – I may just follow through on my earlier warning."

Ignatius snorted rudely, "I'm not afraid of you."

Something in his tone had her pausing before responding. Focusing her powers, she decided to let her extra sight free – not something she would usually do because of the invasion of privacy. But she needed to get a clearer picture of this guy. What she saw had her eyes widening in awareness. He was lying big time. He wasn't just afraid of her; he was bone-deep, piss-his-pants terrified. And he had no idea why ... but she did, so she decided to clue him in;

"Oh yes, you are. You are terrified of me and you don't know why, so it makes you – a normally arrogant and entitled man – even more hostile. It's a defence mechanism, you see." She pointed out, helpfully. She cocked her head to the side, giving him another study before continuing, "Would you like me to tell you why I disturb you so?"

"I –" Ignatius began, but she wasn't interested in his opinion. After perusing his soul, she now had a very clear view on exactly who and what he was; he wasn't just a spoiled a-hole like she had originally thought. No, his rot went to the very core of his being and there was no redemption to be found there. She would have to warn Ryker about him, but for now a few home truths would have to suffice.

"You fear me instinctively – like prey fears a predator. You haven't seen my powers but you can feel how strong they are. You fear the fact that I have managed to garner the love and loyalty of the strongest and most feared paladins ever to be born in a matter of weeks. You've seen how some of the other paladins and wardens have received me into your little world and you fear the impact I may have. You're afraid of the changes I'm going to bring. And you know what, Ignatius?" She asked, leaning in close, "You are right to fear me. I *am* a predator. You *are* my prey. And I *will* bring about changes to this once-proud, but now sadly-outdated society."

Max watched impassively as his face turned beet-red. She could feel the temperature begin to rise in the air around her and knew he was calling upon his element to retaliate. Silly, silly boy. Careful to show no outward signs, she simply cooled the air along with his internal body temperature, effectively making his ability to control fire impotent. Feeling as though she had given him enough of her valuable time and pissed that he had effectively sobered her up, she turned and began strolling back inside to the warmth and laughter, speaking as she went;

"This is your last warning: stop pissing me off because you are at the top of my Shit List ... And it is not a fun place to be, trust me!"

Annnnd, that was when the spit landed on the back of her neck.

SIXTEEN

Diana wasn't sure what the tiny evil Custodian had said to the man but Darius was now staring at her with hungry eyes and she found herself instantly hypnotised by the raw desire burning in their depths. Standing up and marching purposefully from the room, she felt helpless against his magnetic pull and followed him outside, careless of what anyone might think of their abrupt departure. The second she exited the building, she found herself pushed up against the rough brick as a wicked mouth laid siege to hers. A hard thigh pressed hers open as two large hands encouraged her to move freely. Darius broke the kiss, panting roughly and leaned down, burying his face in her hair.

"I love this hair; you know that right?"

Oh yes. She knew that.

"Do you know what I dream of every night? What I've dreamed of every night for the last eight hundred years?" His voice was low and raspy as he twined the inky coils around and around his fingers. He gave a small tug. Oh, apparently she was supposed to answer.

"What?" She hardly recognised her own voice, it was so low and husky.

"I've dreamed of this hair wrapped around my cock; caressing and sliding, soft silk over my hardness, driving me insane as eyes the colour of thunderclouds stare up at me with raw want."

Oh, holy Gods! Diana couldn't contain her whimper if she tried. Who knew the man had such a wicked mouth? And such a wicked brain? He had planted the image in her head and now all she could think of was giving it to him. Still, she felt the need to at least try to be the voice of reason here.

"You're going to regret this in the morning." She warned.

"What's your point?" His teeth were latched onto her sensitive earlobe now and his growled reply sent shivers coursing through her body. Her point? What was her point? There was something about regrets and mornings … Darius took advantage of her lust induced fog to shove his hand inside her tight black pants, pull aside her silk underwear, and push a finger in deep. She moaned sharply as he set up a swift advance and retreat with the thick digit. The man truly had talented fingers!

"Come back with me to the house. Stay with me tonight." His words seduced just as much as his hands did and her answer came in the form of an intense orgasm mere seconds later. Arching and bucking against the hand in her pants, she hummed and sighed her way through the delicious aftershocks, murmuring the word *yes* over and over again. His hazel eyes appeared to watch the show in adoration and sobriety, even though she knew he had to be acting severely under the influence of all that whiskey. Was she going to let that stop her? She allowed her gaze to rake over his hard, strong body, stopping at the sight of the large bulge in front. Reaching out, she forced her hand between the tightness of the waistband to touch the perfect maleness beneath. *Hell no!* She thought. There was no way she was going to allow a bottle of whiskey and potential morning-after regrets to ruin another shot at what she held in her palm.

"Take me home."

*****

Back at the house, she allowed Darius to drag her up the stairs to his third floor bedroom. She had rarely entered his domain, knowing he needed his sanctuary with his telescope just as much as she needed her own refuge. The room was filled with muted colours, largely greys and blacks. It somehow worked but she would love to add a pop of colour here and there. As soon as they crossed the threshold, Darius began removing her clothes, sucking in a harsh breath when her silk blue underwear was exposed.

"Do you really wear this stuff every day?" He asked, reaching out a reverent hand to cup her breasts.

She pushed herself more fully into his palms. "Yes. I like pretty things against my skin."

"*Mercy.*" She thought she heard him mutter before he unhooked the powder blue bra and shaped his hands over her now bare skin. The callouses on his palms were rough against her nipples and added an extra friction that was very stimulating. He pushed her gently but surely backwards and she allowed herself to be turned around, welcoming the cool wood of the wall against her overheated cheeks. Darius's mouth made its way leisurely down her spine and over the flare of her right butt cheek, still encased in silk. She moaned at the sensation and reached back to stroke her palms over his thighs but found her hands captured and pinned to the wall above her head.

"Keep them there." Darius's dark growl sent another spark of lust directly to her clit and she felt it throb in anticipation. She appreciated a man who knew what he wanted. But she was also a woman with wants of her own and

Darius had had his wicked way with her last time. It was her turn to play. Besides, ever since he had whispered his erotic fantasy involving her hair, she had thought of nothing else besides making it come true. Breaking his hold and ducking under his arm, she spun around and sidestepped out of his reach.

His chest rumbled as he spoke warningly, "Diana ..."

She raised an eyebrow at his grumpy expression. He thought she was playing with him. "Easy there, Sir Darius. Don't you want your dreams to come true?"

That seemed to give him pause and his disgruntled look cleared only to be replaced by a sexy leer. Crossing his arms in front of himself, he gripped the bottom of his shirt and pulled it off in a slow controlled motion. His abdominal muscles flexed along with his biceps as the cotton was removed, revealing smoothly tanned skin. He toed off his boots one by one, taking his time and it wasn't until the second one hit the floor that Diana realised the man was giving her a strip tease! He turned around before bending over to take off his socks. His pants pulled taught over his tight arse and his back muscles bunched.

Socks. He was making socks sexy.

He winked at her over his shoulder before running both palms down his chest and stomach. The rasp of a zipper sounded loud in the quiet room as it was lowered slowly. Darius finally turned around but didn't remove his pants, instead he gripped his own length and began to stroke it. Her mouth watered at the sight – she wanted to touch. Taking a step forward, she was stopped when Darius tsked at her, shaking a finger in reproach. He then shook and shimmied his hips until the material of his slacks pooled at his feet. Apparently he was set on finishing his little show. He even turned around again to shake his money-maker at her! And this was the man Cali was concerned had no playfulness in him? Darius was seriously confident in the bedroom! It was sexy as hell!

Stripped to the skin, Diana now had a completely unfettered view of his entire body. He looked like the statue of *David*, she thought. Smooth, strong and sculpted. She prowled closer, adding an extra swing and fluidity to her steps, before standing directly in front of him. He didn't reach for her and she smiled; he was going to let her play. She smoothed her hands over his shoulders and chest, noting the tickle of fine hairs over his pecks and treasure trail. He grunted when she gripped him firmly, not wasting time claiming her prize. Keeping her grip sure, she stood on her toes to outline his lips with her tongue before delving in and exploring the spicy depths more thoroughly. He tasted like sin and goodness at the same time.

Breaking the kiss, she maintained eye contact as she lowered herself to her knees. But unlike last time when she had latched her greedy mouth onto him, this time she spiked her fingers through her own hair, shaking the locks out over her bare shoulders and breasts. His breath hitched and his dick jerked in front of her. Smiling seductively, she uncoiled a long lock of her black hair and proceeded to wrap it around the warm steel length in front of her. Darius was panting harshly and swearing explicitly before the she even had him half encased.

Over the next few minutes, she continued to add coils to her 'hair job' as she rolled the silky strands over his dick repeatedly. His gaze never once left hers and she found herself just as worked up by the act as he so obviously was. Sensing his eminent explosion, she pulled away. It may be sexy as hell watching him writhe and curse from her ministrations but it would be decidedly unsexy if he were to make a mess in her hair! Besides, she wanted him inside of her again.

Rising, she shook out her hair and pushed her now very damp panties down her shaking thighs. She then found herself airborne as she was tossed into the centre of Darius's king bed. Luckily she was on birth control for the man didn't seem to be interested in wasting time with it on his end. He hadn't last time either and if that didn't demonstrate his sheer breakdown in control, she didn't know what did! She opened her thighs wide and sighed in bliss as he settled his weight on top of her, kissing her over and over again. She felt the hard head of his erection nudge at her opening so she raised her hips up, welcoming him inside her body. His groan was rough and she found herself spellbound by the raw pleasure captured on his face; his eyes were closed, head thrown back, revealing a strong neck and muscled shoulders. He was a thing of beauty. Her own body was also caught in a web of tangled pleasure. She was breathing rapidly, sweat was causing her now infamous curls to stick to her face and neck, and her lower body was stretching to accommodate the hard length of the man above her. She was in Heaven, pure and simple.

Darius finally began to move, his control appearing to snap as he braced his arms beside her head and thrust. The pace was furious now, a race to the finish line, as they rolled and plundered, chasing the elusive mutual orgasm. It wasn't the longest sex session she had ever had but it was by far the most intense, she thought, as her orgasm hit. It caused her to arch high off the bed and into the strong grip of the air paladin who was also bellowing out his release.

How was it possible for two people to create such overwhelming pleasure together? And how was she ever supposed to give it up?

SEVENTEEN

Darius woke up feeling surprisingly refreshed the next morning. His limbs felt loose and limber and his head was clear. He must have slept deeply and peacefully for the first time in weeks, he thought as he made his way downstairs for breakfast. He had even gone for a long run before enjoying a hot leisurely shower. Although the latter part of the evening was a bit foggy to him, the night out must have done him the world of good. He was a little concerned about that fog, but it wasn't unusual for him to experience memory loss when he was drinking. And given that he had woken up safe and sound in his own bed, feeling like a million bucks – he must not have gotten into too much strife. He trusted his fellow knights to keep him on the straight and narrow anyway.

Entering the kitchen, he inhaled the smell of a hot breakfast into his lungs. He was positively starving! Axel, Bey, and Lark were the only occupants in the room and they gave him bright expectant smiles as he walked in. It was a little strange, but they were often a little strange, so he chose to ignore them as he lifted the lid on the platter of scrambled eggs.

"Good morning, Sunshine!" Axel greeted, merrily.

"Morning." He smiled back.

"Good day?" Axel asked.

"So far ..." Okay, so maybe Axel was acting somewhat stranger than usual.

"That's great! Oh, here man. I made you something." Axel said, passing him a tall glass with a straw in it.

Darius was surprised. Whoever was on breakfast duty typically cooked enough to feed everybody but drinks were their own responsibility. He sniffed the concoction experimentally, "Is this a milkshake?"

"Yep."

Darius frowned at the snickers from the peanut gallery. "Why would I want a milkshake?" He asked, perplexed.

"Why indeed? Why ... indeed ..." Axel repeated slowly.

What the hell?

"Morning!" Max sang as she breezed in, Cali and Diana in tow.

The sight of the paladin of death caused a shiver of awareness to spread through his body. Her presence always sparked a gut-deep reaction in him but this time there was something more. Almost like a hint of danger. Her grey eyes met his directly and the stormy depths looked like they were challenging him. But challenging him for what? He honestly had no clue. He also had no idea why he suddenly felt a raging need to feel his fingers tangled in the disarray that was her hair, nor why his dick had sprung to such hard and adamant life.

"Is that a milkshake?" Max asked, pointing toward the glass still in his hand.

"Yes," He answered, "Axel made it for me." Laughter met his innocent statement. Just what the hell was going on here? "Why is that funny?" He was genuinely confused.

Beyden patted his shoulder as he passed. "It's not funny. It's actually sad; very, very sad!"

He was beginning to get annoyed, his strange euphoric mood he had awoken with was vanishing rapidly under the haze of ambiguous comments.

"You don't drink much, do you?" Max asked, looking sympathetic.

What did that have to do with anything? Still he responded; "No, I don't. I don't get hangovers but I experience terrible blackouts. I can never remember what happened the next day so I don't drink much anymore and certainly never alone."

Max was nodding even as she cringed, "That explains a lot."

He narrowed his eyes in concentration. Had he done something untoward last night? Before he could question anyone, Diana brushed past him, her scent stirring in the air. He saw a flash of a semi-naked gypsy woman kneeling in front of him as he cursed and begged and he felt himself go stone-still. He was worried his brain was short circuiting or something because that little fantasy felt darn real! But it wasn't. No way. Surely, if it was real Diana wouldn't be calmly eating her breakfast and discussing Beyden's dance moves from the night before? She would be slapping his face or more likely, punching his face – she wasn't really a slapper. Besides, there wasn't enough alcohol in the world to make him forget sex with Diana. There just wasn't.

*****

He didn't remember.

He didn't freaking remember the series of deviant acts they had mutually participated in last night. The 'hair job' had been the first of many and Diana had woken slightly sore but very smug this morning. She had left him alone in his bed in the wee hours of the morning, not wanting to be subjected to the inevitable morning after regrets. But this was worse than regrets. The most wonderfully sexually charged night of her life … and the man didn't even remember enough to have regrets! She didn't know which urge she wanted to follow more; the urge to throat-punch him, or the urge to curl up and cry like a little baby.

"I'm sorry, Di."

"Hmm?" She answered absently, turning to Max, only to wish she hadn't when she saw the look of piteous knowledge in her turquoise depths.

"I didn't know drinking would cause memory loss."

Diana considered playing dumb for all of one second before deciding it made little difference. Max already knew – or thought she did. So she attempted a casualness she didn't really feel. "It's fine. I didn't expect anything different anyway."

"Did you even get a chance to talk? I figured after that hand shandy you gave him last night, you would maybe hash things out."

Diana sputtered "The what?"

"Hand shandy. You know, a hand job? You had your hand down his pants when you left Dave's last night."

"Oh, right. Hand down pants. Hand shandy means *hand job*." She fanned a hand in front of her flushed face.

"What did you think I meant?" She asked, curiously.

"Nothing! Nothing at all." Diana was quick to assure her.

"Uh huh … It was more than just a hand shandy wasn't it?"

Diana wanted to hit her head against the table … repetitively. "Firstly; stop saying *hand shandy*. Secondly; … Yes. It was much more."

Max's eyes lit with glee for a moment before dimming somewhat. Her gaze then moved about the room, judging the positions of the occupants. Ryker had walked in about a minute ago and all the men were currently at the island bench, along with Cali. "I'm sorry, Diana. I'm being incredibly insensitive. You're in love with him and he's being a typical male."

"Who says I'm in love with him?" Diana managed to ask around the lump in her throat.

Max threw her small hand out as if to say; *'Girl, please!'* and that's when Diana saw it; her way out of this nightmarish discussion. "What's this?" She asked, inspecting the bruised knuckles on her liege's right hand.

Max curled her hand up protectively. "It's nothing."

Nothing my arse! "You look like you slugged someone."

Max shrugged, focusing on her cup of Milo. The non-response made Diana suspicious as well as the lack of feedback through the bond. Max was getting very adept at censoring her thoughts and feelings through their bond. It was a little unnerving, given the whole point of the bond was so they were in tune with their liege at all times in order to anticipate their needs.

"Max ..." She queried, mildly.

"Yes, Diana?" Max returned, just as mildly.

"Who exactly did you punch last night?" She asked, getting more specific. That seem to attract the attention of everyone in the room, including their Captain.

"What? What are you talking about, Diana? Max hasn't been punching anyone." He stated.

Diana narrowed her eyes on Max. Nope, she didn't believe Ryker's statement for a second. "Come on, fess up."

She watched as Max stuck out her bottom lip in a pout as she raised seemingly innocent blue-green eyes to hers. Diana merely arched her own eyebrows. That bottom lip might work on the men, but not on her. Max must have clued in to that for she sighed;

"You're all going to make a big deal out of nothing."

"What exactly isn't a big deal, Max? If it isn't a big deal, then there is no reason not to tell us."

"It's nothing really. Last night, Ignatius showed up and I may have, accidently, beaned him in the nose."

Max's comment naturally garnered an array of 'you what's?' from the entire crew. "Ignatius was there last night?" Diana asked for clarification.

Max sighed, "Yes. When I went outside to get some air."

"Why didn't you come get us? Or call us through the bond?" Ryker demanded, angrily.

"Because it wasn't a big deal. And I can take care of myself. I've been doing it for years." Max's response was stern, bordering on defensive.

"It's not that we think you can't handle yourself, Max." Diana was quick to assure her, before the men could cause any damage with their big, testosterone-driven mouths, "But that is what your Order is for. To support you. That's what friends do."

Some of the tension left Max's body. "I know. Thank you. But I honestly didn't even think to. I wasn't in any danger – he was just posturing."

"What did he say?" Ryker's voice was dark with barely repressed anger and Diana knew most of it was directed at the fact that Max may have been in danger – not at Max herself. Although, she was sure Ry was gearing up for a Max-lecture as well.

"Just some insults. I tried to walk away – really – but his manner displeased me, so I decided to break his nose instead." Max shrugged. "No biggie."

"It is a *biggie*, Max." Darius assured her. "You can't go around breaking warden's noses. Especially without provocation. He has it in for you as it is, this is just giving him more ammunition."

"I had provocation! I was totally provoked!" Max assured him.

"What did he do? Did he hurt you?" Ryker's voice was low and ominous.

"No, he didn't hurt me." She answered, hurriedly.

"Then it wasn't self-defence. Max, if he reports you, you could get into real trouble with the Rangers." Lark's voice was worried.

"I don't think so." Max's voice was confident. "After all, he kind of touched me first."

Ryker's brown eyes darkened as they narrowed, "You said he didn't hurt you."

"And he didn't ... but he did spit on me."

Diana felt the snarl on her own lips as anger and insult flared to life within the entire Order. Her coat of arms even began to writhe in response to the burst of power in the room. None of them could contain their emotions at the thought of their liege – a *Custodian* – being spit on. The idea was absolutely abhorrent. Without conscious thought, Diana sought out Darius. Such an act would be intolerable to one such as him, who held his 'betters' in such high esteem. Sure enough, Darius's hazel eyes sparked with contained fury. His clenched jaw demonstrated his iron will at keeping his emotions and reactions hidden, but the air seemed to writhe around him – a warning of the animal crouching within. Diana shuddered, so turned on by his dangerous bearing that she had to clench her legs together to repress the ache throbbing there.

"Shit! Ryker!" Max's shriek returned Diana's focus to the room. Her Captain was striding purposely from the room, murder in every line of his body. Before he could reach the door, Max flung herself at him and proceeded to wrap herself around his body like an octopus. Her tiny five-foot-three frame looked so insignificant compared to his six-foot-four one that she resembled a barnacle on a submarine, more than an octopus. And she was about as effective as a barnacle too, Diana mused, watching impassively as she hung on to his leg as he dragged her across the room.

"Guys! A little help here!" Max yelled.

PALADIN

"Of course." Beyden replied. "I assume you are going to kill Ignatius?" He inquired to Ryker.

"Fuckin' A!" Ry growled.

"Let me help you with the door." Beyden returned, courteously opening the back door for Ryker to exit.

"Beyden! You're supposed to be helping me *stop* him!" Max screamed, gripping Ryker's leg ineffectually. Her butt was now on the kitchen floor with her arms and legs wrapped around Ryker's left leg. All she was doing was polishing the floor with her arse with every step Ryker took.

"No." Beyden said.

"No?" Max's voice was incredulous.

The giant Spaniard crossed his arms, as immovable as a mountain. "No." He repeated again. Max seemed surprised by his refusal to assist her. Beyden was the gentlemen, practically tripping over himself to do her bidding – not that Max ever took advantage of his generous nature. But not now. Diana wasn't surprised in the least. Max was Beyden's liege. That was the beginning and end of it as far as they were all concerned. She didn't know how else to make Max understand what being a paladin was all about. They had all told her, numerous times, that a paladin's purpose was to serve their liege; her health and happiness came before all else. Serving her was now their whole reason for being. Looking around the room, Diana saw the same resolved purpose on each and every face.

"Ryker, please! Will you stop?!" Max asked, rather beseechingly this time.

Ryker inhaled deeply, coming to a halt. He looked down and their eyes met. Diana knew they were communicating through their private thread, for after several tension-thick seconds, he exhaled and stroked her messy hair.

"He spat on you." He stated.

"Yes." Max acknowledged. "And I broke his nose. We're even."

"No, you're not!" Axel snarled.

"Now don't you start, Axel!" Max shook her finger at him. "I'm fine. It was just a little saliva. I'm not saying we let this go," Max continued before anyone could jump in, "... we can't. He's not ... *right* on the inside. But I am saying we go through the proper channels. You're always saying I need to follow the rules, well, let's play this one by the book. I want to report him to the council. Will you help me?" She asked, looking up at Ryker from her perch on the floor.

At first, Diana didn't think Ryker was going to respond, that maybe he was going to let go of his control again, but in the end he nodded. "Of course. I'll show you how to fill out the forms and we'll send it off today." He eyed her critically for a second before smiling, his brown eyes lightening, "But you may want to get up off the floor first."

EIGHTEEN

After hanging up the phone with the secretary of the Rangers, Ryker made his way outside to find his miracle. He paused, absolutely stupidly smitten by the way the sun reflected the deep crimson strands in her hair. Max was rocking contentedly in the hammock strung up where the lawn met the sand. His hand went to touch the atrocious scar on his cheek where a chade had literally tried to claw his face off, but all he felt was the scratchy evidence of his day-old growth. Max, the short but mighty Goddess, had healed his scar – as well as the tattered remains of his soul. Damn, but he'd been a miserable bastard for years before Max had fallen into his life. Bitter, resentful, and filled with hate and guilt over the loss of his liege and Order. He had lived when his whole family had died; they had been his responsibility. He never dreamed he would be a Captain again, regardless of his innate potentate status. But he was – Captain of an Order with paladins from all seven elements and a liege who was a Custodian. She was also the love of his freaking life.

Fuck, he was a lucky bastard, he thought as he watched her rock back and forth lazily in the cool morning air. But a tremble of unease made its way through the bond as he saw her reach up and rub her forehead. She had a headache. She pretty much always had a headache, he knew. Although her health had improved by leaps and bounds since being able to recharge with vitality, she still wasn't what he considered in top form. He was forced to hold onto her every night as she tossed and turned, trapped in nightmares that were not solely her own. She lost too much energy just being passive and minor aches and pains were a persistent daily nuisance. He didn't like it.

"Are you going to stand there and stare at me all day?" The lazy humour threaded with warmth in her voice caused his dick to twitch. *Stupid dick.*

"I was just enjoying the view."

"Uh huh. You were clucking like a mother hen ... again. I'm fine."

He just grunted. Her version of fine and his version were lightyears apart. Her beautifully strange eyes rolled in their sockets as she said;

"Join me?"

Ryker eyed the flimsy looking piece of coloured cloth and the ropes tying it to the two supporting trees dubiously. Max may be tiny at five foot three but he was six foot four. No way was his giant arse going to fit in that little hammock.

"You'll fit. Snuggle time."

Snuggle time with his girl? It took some manoeuvring – and swearing on his part, giggling on Max's – but he managed to find a comfortable position with his front to Max's back and her body nestled snuggly between his legs. He wrapped his arms securely around her and watched as she smoothed her hands over her Heraldry on his forearm. He shivered when it seemed to leap into her touch. It was very odd. But he kind of liked odd these days.

"How's your head?"

She huffed, "It's fine."

"It's not fine, Max. You get headaches every day and your nightmares ..."

"Are better. Being bound to all of you really helps. And the constant renewal of vitality? It's amazing!"

"But still not perfect." He pointed out, rubbing his palm in a circular motion over her stomach. He loved touching her.

"No. Not perfect." She acknowledged. "Something's missing."

"Darius. Air." He stated.

She sighed, "Yes, I believe so. Darius, as air, is the final element."

"I'll talk to him." His patience with his second in command was beginning to run thin. He had been acting out of character for weeks now. Ryker was the first to admit that a person was entitled to have a bad day, or week ... or even years, as was the case with himself. He also believed people should be left the hell alone to sort through their shit. But when it started to affect the integrity and harmony of the Order? Then it was time to intervene.

"You'll do no such thing." Max's voice was strident. "I won't force him to be in my Order, Ryker."

"It's hurting you." And he wasn't referring to the headaches either. The thought that one of her new friends didn't want to be on her team anymore hurt her feelings. He could feel it and it pissed him the hell off. Nobody had the right to hurt her; nobody!

Max tilted her head back and smiled at him softly, "My fierce knight. I'm a big girl. I can take it. He needs to come to me, not the other way around. It's important, Ry."

He scowled even as he listened. He could do no other than obey her wishes. It didn't mean he had to like it though.

"You're such a hard-arse." She poked him in the chest.

He felt his chest puff up in pride. *Damn right he was a hard-arse!*

She chuckled, "I love you."

Say what now?

Max rolled over onto her stomach, causing the hammock to sway precariously for a moment. "I love you. Everything about you. Everything you are. I'm so glad you're mine. I'm so grateful I get to keep you. I love you."

Ryker swallowed the very unmanly lump in his throat. Although he could feel the love and affection flowing through the bond, he had been desperate to hear those words, spoken just like that. He told her constantly – like every single damn time he saw her – so he had no doubt she knew how he felt. So how to respond now? Thinking back to when he had first told her he loved her, he smiled, and said simply;

"Okay."

*****

Diana was beating the hell out of a punching bag when her Captain walked into the gym. He was dressed for a workout in tracksuit pants and an old shirt, but he had a dopey look on his face that was anything but ferocious. She barely refrained from growling out loud; clearly the loved up man had just had some quality time with his equally loved up woman. Well, bully for them, she thought as she hammered the poor innocent sandbag. Three hours! It had been three hours since breakfast and Darius still hadn't had any memory revelations! How could he forget the feel of her hair across his groin? How could he forget the feel of her mouth across his strong chest? How could he forget the feel of her fingernails digging into his arse? *Bastard!* She snarled as she killed the Darius replacement in front of her.

"Want to go a round?" Spinning on instinct, she punched out with her fist, only to find it caught in a much larger one. "Sorry." She panted.

Ryker just raised his eyebrows. "Want to talk about it?"

"Not really." She answered. *Not at all!* She thought.

"Fair enough." He shrugged and made his way to the free weights. Bending down he picked up a thirty kilo weight in each hand and began doing bicep curls.

Eternally grateful that her Captain was a man of few words, she decided to head to the bikes and peddle out her remaining frustrations. She tripped and nearly fell flat on her face when Ryker spoke, however;

"I had a major crush on you, you know."

She turned slowly, apprehensively, unsure she had heard him correctly. "I'm sorry?"

"A crush." He put down the weights. "I used to have the hots for you."

She was gaping, she knew she was but she couldn't seem to stop. She'd actually had a crush on him too for a while. What girl wouldn't? He was tall, built, broody ... and that scar? No matter what he thought, scars were just plain sexy. Especially scars on a warrior. But she would never have imagined he would admit to a crush! "I had a crush on you too." She confessed.

He laughed and she couldn't help admiring the way his chocolate eyes filled with warmth – he really was a gorgeous specimen. "I never knew."

She arched her eyebrow, "You weren't supposed to. I'm adept at hiding my feelings."

His grin dimmed. "I noticed."

And we're done. She thought, turning to exit the room now.

"Do you want me to talk to him?"

She stumbled again, "No. Hell no!"

He crossed his arms and planted his feet wide. "But he's hurting you."

"I'm fine."

Ryker scowled viciously. "What is it with women and saying they're fine when they so obviously are not?"

"It's a DNA thing, I guess." She shrugged, negligently.

He grunted in typical man fashion, gazing steadily at her before finally remarking, "He's hurting Max too."

She sighed now, feeling terribly exhausted. She knew it; she could feel it. But she also knew Max would sooner go to her own grave than to confront the man. It was an innate stubbornness that Diana could relate to, and even approved; no begging. They were strong, independent women – they didn't need to beg for anything.

"It's not intentional." Why she felt the need to defend the man, she had no clue. But she didn't want Ryker to think badly of Darius. He was a noble paladin with a long and rich history.

"I know that. He's not like me. When I'm a dick, it's on purpose."

Despite the circumstances, Diana felt herself smiling. You gotta love a self-aware man. "Just give him time."

"I've given him time."

"More time." She clarified.

"How much more?"

Well, that was the million-dollar question wasn't it? And going by the look on Ry's face, she wasn't certain she had convinced him to wait.

NINETEEN

Crap, crap, crap, crap, crap! There was nothing else going through Darius's head other than, *crap, crap, crap, crap, crap!* He had done it again! He had fucked Diana! *All ... Night ... Long!* In the bed, on the floor, against the wall. Hell, maybe even upside down! And he had forgotten every single extraordinary, bliss-filled moment until Axel had sat down at his piano in the front room and began to play a pop song. It was unusual, given the fire paladin was classically trained and played classic masterpieces like a maestro. But the beat had drawn him down the stairs and he had found himself humming words he didn't even know he knew. A series of flashes from the night before had reverberated in his brain and he had nearly broken his neck falling down the stairs. *Milkshake!* He had been dancing to *Milkshake* last night!

But that wasn't the worst of it. He remembered wanting to throttle one of the triplets at the implication they had touched Diana in any way. He had then practically dragged her back to his room where they had proceeded to debauch each other for the rest of the night. He groaned as he thumped a hard fist against the side of his head. How could he forget such a thing? And how was Diana ever going to forgive him? How had she even been able to keep a straight face in the kitchen this morning, for that matter? By the Great Mother, he was one messed up, miserable bastard at the moment.

"Darius."

Darius closed his eyes and prayed with everything in him that the sound of Ryker's voice was a hallucination. The plain spoken Ryker was probably the last person he wanted to talk to at the moment – well, second last – Diana was probably the last.

"Darius. I want to talk to you."

Okay, so that deep, intimidating voice wasn't an illusion. Nor was the dark, intimidating shadow that fell over the top of him where he was sitting on the front step. Taking a deep breath in the hopes of calming his wildly fluctuating emotions, he stood to face the Captain of the household. And what do you know? The Captain looked pissed; this was not going to be pleasant. Although not a true empath like Max or the Life Wardens, Ryker did have a touch of empathic abilities – he was attuned to life itself after all. So Darius was pretty sure he knew where this conversation was headed.

"What is it?" Darius asked, feigning ignorance.

"I think it's time you told me what the fuck is going on with you lately."

Oh, yeah. Ryker was nothing if not blunt. "What do you mean?"

"Don't fuck with me Darius. You've been moody for weeks, bordering on disrespect and insubordination with me and even with Max. You've been treating Diana like an arsehole, and you drank two litres of whiskey last night. So, I ask you again; what's going on?"

Darius felt his hands clench and unclench spasmodically. Hearing his twisted thoughts and actions of the past few weeks summed up so eloquently was a real prick to his pride.

"I apologise. I know I have been acting out of character. You know I like to process things. I've been processing."

Ryker snorted rudely, "Processing how to be an arsehole maybe. If you're having second thoughts about Max being your liege, then just say so. You know she would never force you."

"I'm not having second thoughts." *Much*, he added silently as he paced back and forth.

"You're hurting her."

Darius stopped in his track and squeezed his eyes shut upon hearing those three words. "I'm sorry. I'm sorry, Ry. I don't mean to. I love her." He added, gruffly. And he did.

Ryker cleared his throat at that and lost some of the attitude. "I know you do. And I get it – at least some of it. I know all the talk about the chades must have brought up bad memories about your brother –"

"Stop! Don't go there, Ry." His voice sounded guttural even to his own ears. His brother was *not* up for discussion. "I mean it. This has nothing to do with him."

"You don't want to talk about Charlie? That's fine." Ryker raised his hands in surrender even though he had just said his brother's name. Didn't Darius just say he didn't want to talk about his brother? What was Ry trying to pull? Was he purposefully trying to piss him off?

"*Don't* say his name." He warned.

His tone had Ryker crossing his arms over his chest and narrowing his eyes, searching Darius's face. "Fine. What about Diana, then? What are you planning to do about that mess?"

Darius felt a tick in his jaw. "That is not up for discussion either."

"Oh, isn't it? Well, I'm sorry Sir Darius. Why don't you tell me what we can talk about?" Ryker's voice was heavy with sarcasm and he could tell he was beginning to lose patience. Well, so was Darius. He felt like his entire world had been turned upside down in the past few weeks. First, Max had waltzed into a bar and decapitated a chade with a samurai sword. Then she turned out to be a Goddess. Then she had flattened him in order to save a chade. A chade! And then Diana had pushed his buttons, using his years of percolating lust to ram through his iron-fisted control.

"She's not just any old lay, Darius! She is a fellow knight, in this Order. She's a friend, more than a friend – she's family!" Ryker continued, heatedly.

Darius was starting to feel the tenuous thread on his control getting thinner and thinner as each of Ryker's words lashed at him. He was feeling real anger towards Ryker like he hadn't in a long time. When he had first moved in, Ryker had been practically impossible to live with. If not for the fact that Darius owed him a blood debt – or rather, multiple blood debts – he would have given up on him in those early days, despite the fact that Darius had nowhere else to go and nothing else to do but latch onto the lifeline that was the Lodge. Ryker had mellowed somewhat over the years so that he was at least civil but he was still far from the noble paladin leader Darius had first met over a hundred years ago. And now he had the nerve to spank him because he was being a little moody?

"Need I remind you of your behaviour where Max was concerned not two months ago?"

"As I recall, you raked my arse over the coals."

Darius kept his mouth studiously shut. He didn't want to dig himself into a deeper hole.

"Come on, man! I'm trying to help you here. You know you can't lie to me, right? I can taste a lie."

Darius narrowed his eyes. Just as he suspected; Ryker was admitting he had used his empath abilities on him. It was definitely not what he wanted to hear. "I haven't lied."

"Maybe not. But you're sure as hell omitting a lot. Do you want to know what you're omitting?"

"No!" The one syllable was a growl but the stubborn bastard continued on as if he hadn't spoken;

"I see the way you look at her when you think nobody's watching; like a precious treasure made just for you. I see the way your eyes track the movements of her hair; daring the wind to tease those wild locks. I can feel the longing coming from you in waves; the need to feel, the need to touch, the need to *have*. And you have had her, haven't you Darius? *Twice* now ..."

CRACK!

*****

Fuck, damn, shit! Darius swore silently as he shook the pain from his fist. Ryker always did have a hard head. Darius hadn't meant to hit him. He didn't even realise he'd moved until he felt the pain arrowing up his arm but now here he was, staring down at the unconscious form of one of his best friends ... and his Captain ... *and* a Goddess's lover. Of course Ryker knew what would hit him the hardest and his aim had been perfect. Hearing his most secret desires aired out like that had pushed him over the edge – because they had all been true.

Darius looked down at Ryker. The big man had yet to move so he bent down and started slapping him, not so gently, in an attempt to wake him. Ryker began to come around a full two minutes later; *must have been a damned good punch*, Darius couldn't help thinking with pride. But he didn't think Max was going to feel the same way if her screech was any indication;

"Oh, my God! What the hell happened?" She charged out the front door and knelt by Ryker's prone form, all five of her paladins in her wake.

"Ah ..." Not quite willing to confess, he looked everywhere but at Max. Unfortunately, his gaze was ensnared by eyes that resembled storm clouds. Diana's eyes were condemning and made him feel about two feet tall.

"You hit him?" Max's voice was tremulous and there were tears in her eyes as she gazed up at him.

He felt sick. "Max, I ..."

She sniffed as she stroked Ryker's cheek soothingly, "Please just go away for a while."

Looking around, he saw that everyone was on the same wavelength. So away he went.

TWENTY

"Lucky you have such a hard head, babe. Are you okay?" Max asked, stroking Ryker's already bruised jaw.

Ryker grunted. "Fucking big bastard. He always did have a good right hook." He shook his head ruefully and Diana thought she could see a hint of pride in his eyes. *Men!* She thought, *always with the testosterone.* But her levity was short lived as Ryker continued;

"Darius has been teetering on the brink of insubordination for weeks. I can't let this go. He's going to have to be punished." Ryker's brown stare was intense as he looked directly into Diana's eyes.

Diana swallowed hard, "I know." She said. And she did know. Paladins and Wardens both functioned under a set of strict rules for a reason and underwent rigorous training regimes and education from the time they were very young. Wardens, because they were so powerful, all ran the risk of abusing all that power, hence the need for the Rangers. The same was true of paladins; they were strong and produced a life-giving energy. Such strength of body and mind could not be free to roam the world without discipline. It was why their training was so intensive before they were allowed to bond to a liege. They not only had to prove themselves in battle but they also had to prove they had the temperament, the control, and the loyalty to serve. They also followed a strict chain of command – and one simply did not punch their commanding officer. Although Darius was not yet bound to Max, and Ryker was not officially his Captain, Ryker was a potentate and the most senior paladin in the house. What's more, Darius had agreed to living under Ryker's roof and had therefore submitted to being under his rule for the duration.

"Punishment? What do you mean by punishment?" Max asked. She was frowning in confusion and Diana could detect the unease in her body. Max had been upset initially, but had perked up as soon as Ryker opened his eyes. She was a big softy under all that steel.

"Darius struck a superior, Max. That simply cannot be tolerated. Darius will have to be disciplined." Beyden's deep voice was sombre as he answered.

They were all seated around the dining table as was their usual location for a pow wow. Diana could see that Cali, Axel and Lark were apprehensive about discussing the punishment of a fellow soldier and friend, but she also saw the disappointment in their eyes over his actions. They had been very patient with Darius's erratic and uncharacteristic mood swings over the past couple of weeks and any one of them would do anything to help. Just as they had been when Ryker first met Max and had made a complete dick of himself with that mouth of his. But Darius kept pushing all of them away, his pride and sense of duty was far too ingrained to allow any sign of weakness. The only time she had managed to strip away some of those defences was when he was buried deep inside of her and even then, the regret that hung heavy in the air afterwards was clear evidence that their attraction was only a contributor to his mixed up emotions, not a help.

"I don't like the sound of that, disciplined how?" Max's eyes were narrowed now and focused solely on her partner.

Ryker sighed, "In the past, such insubordination would be punished by a public flogging or beating."

"WHAT?!" Max exclaimed, her chair falling to the floor as she jumped up. "That's barbaric! You are *not* whipping Darius! I don't care what he did!" Max's chest was rising and falling rapidly and her glaring eyes were a little panicked.

"Easy, sweetheart." Ryker soothed, immediately wrapping his big arms around her and chafing her arms. "I'm not suggesting that. I would never do that. I don't believe in corporal punishment – although, a good solid arse-kicking never hurt anyone ... much."

Max's breathing calmed somewhat but Diana could still detect the fine shaking in her limbs and Ryker, for all his gentleness with Max, had a hard look in his eyes. What was going on here? It was like Max had a personal aversion to physical discipline or ... Diana's thoughts trailed off as she realised that was *exactly* what was going on here; someone had hurt Max. Looking around she could see the dawning realisation on the faces of the others. Lark in particular looked a little green. Given his own past, Diana couldn't blame the poor guy.

"Ry's right, sweet Max." Axel said, tweaking her nose playfully. Max batted it away much like a kitten would and Ryker bared his teeth. Axel was going to flirt with Max one too many times. Axel continued on, uncaring of the testosterone-fuelled Captain. "A beating is too old school, but he will still need to be disciplined. He will be expecting it and I don't think he would be able to move forward without it." Axel said, tone level and devoid of the playfulness present a few seconds prior.

Diana focused her grey eyes more fully on the jokester of the group. His own blue eyes were serious and held an intuitive awareness that Diana hadn't acknowledged he was capable of. He was always so flirty and laidback, it was easy to forget he was also very intelligent and had lived and served a Warden under trying circumstances. As he continued to gaze at her, she believed Axel might be the only other person in the room who truly understood what made Darius tick.

"So I'll send him to his room or something." Max said, shrugging casually now, her eyes still defiant.

Diana tugged on a curl, unconsciously revealing her anxiety, as she shook her head. "That won't be enough, Max. Axel is right. Darius must atone for his actions. He must be penalised."

Something in her demeanour must have stopped Max from her immediate rebuttal again, for she tilted her head, narrowing her clear eyes, "Why?" She asked simply this time.

Diana answered just as simply. "Because his nature demands it." It was true; Darius was a soldier, a warrior, a man of duty and fidelity. It wasn't his last one thousand years of service that made him that way either. It's what flowed in his veins, what pulsed in his heart, what kept him going all these long years. Darius was a knight, soul-deep.

"His heart beats with his sense of duty and loyalty. He is a knight down to his bones – down to his very soul. His penance is essential for him to heal." Max stated, her eyes flashing with that beautiful but strange inner light.

Diana barely refrained from wincing as Max seemed to repeat her own words back to her, as if she was reading her mind ... or her soul. She still found it a little unnerving. "That's right." She acknowledged, even though it wasn't really necessary.

"What do you suggest?" Max asked.

"What?" Diana was startled.

"What do you suggest his punishment be, Lady Diana?" Max asked, her formality unsettling her even more. She looked to Ryker for guidance but her Captain wasn't giving anything away. Apparently he was deferring to his liege on this one. She swallowed hard; she knew what she *wished* could happen, what she *hoped* could happen. Dare she ask?

She looked at Cali and her best friend gave her a smile and an encouraging nod. Axel's sensual lips also quirked on one side in a small smile, as if he also knew what she was thinking. Diana took a deep breath. *No guts no glory, right?* She thought to herself. And this could very well bring Darius back from a precipice nobody wanted him to be near, so she opened her mouth ... and asked.

TWENTY-ONE

What was wrong with him? Darius thought in agitation, gripping the steering wheel as the car sped along the coast line. He was the calm paladin, the one always in control. He was thirteen hundred years old, so he'd had plenty of time to cultivate patience. But lately he had been easily distracted, easily riled to temper, and easily tempted by his lusts. He had been disrespectful to Max – not just a Custodian, but also a friend and a sister he never had. He had been rude and temperamental to his fellow knights. He had thrown Diana against a few walls and had his fill of her. And now he had struck an immediate superior. He actually felt a little bit sick – he had *punched* Ryker! Ryker was going to hand him his arse and Darius was going to let him. There was a time when such an offense would earn him a public whipping. Such practices were no longer the norm but he wouldn't blame Ryker in the slightest if he chose to beat him bloody.

He was so distracted, he barely managed to swerve in time to miss the small animal that darted out in front of him. He slammed on his brakes and veered to the left, grateful it was a quiet road and there were no cars behind him. Not hearing any sickening thump, he figured the little critter had escaped his tyres. Knowing he had to double check to be sure, he undid his seat belt and stepped out into the cooling afternoon air. At first, he couldn't see anything in the dense bush that lined the road but then a rustle of leaves caught his attention. He looked to his right where the sound had come from, still not seeing anything. He wished Bey was with him. Being affiliated with the beasts meant animals were naturally calm around him; Beyden was great with animals.

"Hey, little buddy. It's okay, you're okay. I'm not going to hurt you. I just want to make sure you're alright." He pitched his voice low and sat down on his haunches making himself smaller. A few seconds ticked by before a small furry head poked up from behind a prickly shrub. A scrawny body followed and Darius couldn't help but wince in sympathy at how hungry the poor little thing looked. Its fur was still baby-fuzz and was mottled with an array of browns, blacks, sands and greys. Its eyes were two different colours – blue and brown – and it had one straight ear and one floppy one. He had no idea what breed the small pup was and Darius figured the dog had no idea either. It was clearly a mutt. But it was also clearly a baby and too young to be on its own.

"What are you doing all the way out here? And where's your mother?" He kept his tone soft and held out a hand so the little guy could give him a sniff. The pup cocked its head much the same way Max did when she was considering something or puzzling her way through a conundrum. He was patient, keeping his hand out and non-threatening. Apparently he now had patience to spare, he thought, annoyed with himself all over again. He was rewarded though, when the little ball of fluff gave quite a happy yip and bounded over to him. Darius caught it up and couldn't help laughing as the little bugger proceeded to deliver puppy-kisses all over his face.

"Okay, okay little guy," he paused and lifted it up, "yep, little guy is right." He said, noting he had all the right equipment. "Now, are you hurt?" He ran gentle hands over the pup and besides being too skinny and covered in prickles and burs, he didn't seem to be injured. "What am I supposed to do with you, huh?" He asked.

The pup cocked its head to the left, right ear flopping at the tip as he regarded him seriously for a moment. He yipped again before scrambling out of his arms and racing toward the car. His short, uncoordinated legs tripped a bit as he turned almost immediately and ran back to him. Darius felt his eyebrow raise; "You want to come with me? Well, I'm really sorry little man but I don't think that's a good idea. I'm in trouble you see and bringing back a stray mutt like yourself probably won't help matters."

To his surprise, the fur ball gave a small growl, his sharp little puppy teeth latching onto his pants. If he didn't know any better, he would think the dog could actually understand him and didn't want to take no for an answer. Although he knew Beast Wardens could communicate with animals and even paladins associated with the beast domain had a strong connection, he didn't really think animals could understand English. Besides, he had no affiliation with the animals whatsoever. The pup was still tugging on his pant leg, growling with his little butt in the air, sable tail wagging madly. Darius sighed, rocking back on his haunches and letting himself sit back on the ground, uncaring of the dirt and leaves. The pup immediately let go of its prize and climbed into his lap.

"You can't suck up to me, you know. I can't take you home with me." His hand paused mid-pat as he realised what he said. He had called Ryker's camp his home. Twenty years he had been living under Ryker's roof in that glorious log house by the sea and not once had he been tempted to call it home. He always figured he would be moving on at some point but he just hadn't gotten around to it yet. He had been humbled and ever so grateful when Ryker had offered him a place to stay and then a position as a trainer at the Lodge. Losing his brother and his paladin status had nearly destroyed him and he had been terrified that his life would never hold meaning again. Ryker had given him a lifeline and a sense of purpose but the camp had never really been a home. No, Max had given him that – had given them all that, he acknowledged. And how had he repaid her? By punching her soul-mate in the face. *Damn! I'm such a mess!*

He continued to sit in the quiet, finding comfort in the company of the little mutt in his lap. He allowed the rough edges of his anger and self-disgust to be soothed as he stroked the dog's back repetitively. After an hour, the pup was sound asleep and Darius had reached the inevitable conclusion that he needed to head back to camp and accept the repercussions of his actions. But what the hell was he going to do with the hairy mass in his lap? He couldn't in good conscience leave him on the side of the road but he couldn't afford to take him to the animal shelter in town. Sighing, he stood, rousing the animal;

"One night. I may be able to get you a reprieve for one night and then tomorrow morning we can see about finding you a home." He told the pup sternly as it blinked sleepily up at him. Its tongue lolled out in a happy grin as if it knew Darius would cave all along. He pointed his finger at it;

"Now, don't go getting too cocky. Ryker is probably waiting to kick my butt the second I walk through the door. Even a puppy won't stop him from doing his duty. But he does have one weakness." He told the stray, "Max. You had better flash those strange, bi-coloured puppy-dog eyes at her. She's a bit of a sucker for strange eyes. If you do that, you might just have a chance at staying the night."

The pup yipped again as if in agreement and Darius exhaled heavily. Looks like it was time to face the music. He only hoped Ryker would allow him to maintain his honour and dole out his punishment in private. He wasn't sure he could stand looking into the eyes of his fellow knights if they saw him take a beating from their Captain. And he was positive Diana would never again give him the time of day.

TWENTY-TWO

Darius parked the black Dodge Durango out the front of the house instead of putting it away with the other one in the garage. The car was nice and sturdy and was supplied to them by the IDC because they worked at the Lodge. He wasn't much of a car man, so it didn't bother him what they drove but Darius knew Beyden and Lark were both rev-heads and they dreamed of owning Lamborghinis or Aston Martins or some such fancy car. But just like paladins were not supposed to own their own property or land, the same was true for cars. They typically used whatever their lieges had. Darius knew Max held issue with them not being able to own property but that's just the way it was. It's not like they ever wanted for anything – their lieges provided everything for them and most did gift their knights with various items anyway. His old liege used to indulge Darius's hobby of astronomy. No matter where they were in the world, his liege would always buy him a new telescope – the top of the line. Ever since the first official telescope had been invented in the 1600s, Darius had been absorbed with the universe revealed by the lenses. What he wouldn't give to crawl up to his third floor suite and plaster himself to his eyepiece right now, he thought.

Tiny growls drew his attention to his new passenger. The puppy was attempting to chew on the handle of his sickle. "Hell!" He picked up the sickle, moving it out of reach. He wasn't worried about the pup hurting himself – the weapon was sheathed – but he didn't want those pointy milk teeth to leave dents in his leather. The little mutt promptly began to chew on the side of the leather seat and Darius winced, scrubbing rough hands over his close-cropped scalp. Yeah, no way was the little fur ball going to help his situation.

"Come on." He said, scooping him up and placing him immediately on the ground outside the car. He walked up the winding stone-paved pathway and took the fork to the right, heading toward the back kitchen doors. They rarely used the massive front double doors. "Now. I want you stay out here until I can recon the area. Only if I give you the all clear, may you then enter. Do you understand?" The animal plopped its little butt on the ground in answer. Giving him one final warning look, Darius turned the handle.

And as he opened the door, his worst fears were realised. The combined kitchen-dining room was filled with paladins and five heads swung his way. For the first time in centuries, Darius felt his face go hot. He couldn't remember being this embarrassed or ashamed before but he refused to tuck tail, so he kept his head up and made eye contact with everyone. There was a mixture of pity and censure in their eyes but the biggest emotion he saw was ... relief. They had been worried about him. Him – the pathetic knight who had KO'd his superior officer. Could he feel any more like a worm? The only person who didn't look at him was Diana and he felt his balls shrivel up – had his actions caused her to lose all respect for him?

"You okay, man?" Lark asked, holding out a strong palm for him to grasp.

Darius swallowed the sudden lump in his throat as he took the offered hand in a sure grip, "Yeah. Thanks. I –" But before he could get any further a small fuzzy missile hit his leg. The room stilled as all eyes focused on the miniature terrorist attacking his shoelaces.

"Ah, dude. You know you have a little something attached to your left leg, right?" Axel asked, rocking back on his chair.

"Don't do that, Axel. You're going to break it." He said automatically, before replying, "And yes. I do know. He ... um ..."

"Oh my God, is that a puppy?" The breathless hope-filled voice came from the doorway leading into the main living room. Max was standing there, bare-foot as was the norm, but in clothes that actually fit her. The shopping trip had been successful in that regard.

Darius reached down, detaching the killer teeth from his laces and receiving a nip in retaliation from the disgruntled animal. He picked him up and tucked him under his arm. "Ah, yes. It's a puppy ..."

As Darius watched, Max took a couple of tentative steps into the room, her turquoise eyes shining and never leaving the squirming bundle in his arms. "What's it doing here?" She asked.

Darius frowned. Although he couldn't feel what she was feeling because he wasn't linked in the Order, there was no missing the fragile hope in her eyes and her query. Glancing around, he saw the soft looks on the faces of the others and the uncomfortable shuffling of feet as if they were invading a private moment. No doubt they could all feel the emotions surging through the bond. Max finally pulled her gaze away from the pup – who had been just as transfixed with her as she was of him – and Darius nearly staggered from the naked emotion on her face. He was such an idiot. Of course Max would have an intense reaction to having a dog in the house. A dog had been her first friend, her family and the only creature in the world to ever show her any warmth or affection when she had been all alone on the streets as a teenager. Hell, she had even named herself after that first friend.

He was so insensitive. He never used to be, he prided himself on being a gentleman. They all knew Max talked the talk and even walked one hell of a good walk, but underneath it all she was still quite vulnerable. She was yet to fully trust them, this house and even her relationship with Ry. So many years of being alone and relying only on herself had made her wary of good fortune and also desperate for the comfort of home and family. He thought they were all slowly providing her with those things and as Max looked up at him with a question in her eyes, he thought – maybe, just maybe, he might be able to offer her something a little more. Although Ryker may not see it that way, he thought silently. Oh well, he was already up to his neck with the potentate anyway. He cleared his throat and held out his arms, "He's for you."

Max stilled. "For me?" She whispered.

Darius nodded, smiling gently at the little Custodian. "Yes. I found him on the side of the road. He looks like he's been on his own for a while but he's too young to be without a mother. I thought you would make the perfect replacement."

Rude snorts met his declaration and he frowned darkly at Axel and Cali, who merely mouthed back, *'bullshit'* at him. Cali even went so far as to make a crude hand gesture as if she were tugging on something. If he had been any other type of man he would have flipped them both the finger. Instead he chose to ignore the miscreants and focus on Max instead who had yet to come any closer. "Here, Max. Take him." He said, all but thrusting the animal into her arms.

"I can really keep him?" She asked again, not even looking at the puppy who was surprisingly still and quiet in her arms.

Darius felt his heart break a little. How desperately must she have wanted a dog all these years for her to be so dismayed over the prospect of keeping one, mangy mongrel pup? "Of course. He's yours. No-one will take him away from you." His voice was firm and brooked no argument. He glared at the others, daring them to say anything that would oppose him. Beyden was grinning, Lark was smiling indulgently, Cali shrugged, Axel held up his hands in surrender, and Diana was staring at him rather than Max with a look of gratitude and ... pride? Maybe there was hope for him yet.

*****

Diana found herself swallowing around the lump in her throat as she watched Max squeal happily and launch herself, puppy and all, at Darius. "Thank you, thank you, thank you!" was interspersed between kisses and puppy licks to his once more flushed face. No way had Darius found that pup and brought it back here with the intention of giving it to Max. No way! But nobody was foolish enough to call him out on it though. He looked like he would rip out the voice box of anyone who dared. Besides, the unadulterated joy pouring through the bond from Max was enough to stay anyone's comments – sarcastic or not.

"He is so freakin' cute! Oh, look at those eyes! You are so special, yes you are!" Max rubbed her nose against the small black one.

Diana cringed and noted that all the others, save Beyden, did too. Baby talk. The most powerful creature to walk the earth had resorted to baby talk. She really hoped Max wasn't going to revert to it every time she spoke to the animal. But seeing the hint of moisture in Max's eyes, Diana knew that she would gladly listen to the idiotic dialogue if it meant her liege was this happy.

189

"Max? What's going on?" Ryker's voice boomed through the room as he entered briskly, no doubt drawn by the intense emotions surging through the Order. Diana saw Darius stiffen and come to attention, his face becoming remote and controlled once more as Ryker stopped in his tracks, eyes narrowing on the knight before turning to Max and the new addition.

"What is that?" He asked the room at large.

"It's my new puppy! Darius gave him to me." Max smiled, lone dimple flashing as she held the young dog up for Ryker's inspection.

Ryker's left eyebrow winged up. "Darius gave him to you, did he?" The question was clearly directed at Darius, not Max. For Darius's part, he just continued to stand in stoic silence.

"Uh huh." Max giggled when the dog attempted to lick every square inch of her face but she did push the little guy's head back, tempering his slobbery enthusiasm. Diana was relieved. She liked dogs as much as the next person, but she wasn't a fan of face-lickers. And she was *so* glad she hadn't just said that out loud. Axel would have had a field day with it. A cheeky grin and a wink from her liege though, let her know that she had heard enough through the bond. No doubt she would bring it up again later. "Isn't he handsome?" Max asked Ryker.

Diana watched as her Captain's eyes roved over the stray dog. The skinny little guy was a strange mish-mosh of colours ranging from beige to black and everything in between. He was stripy and spotty at the same time and had two different coloured eyes. The dog was the very definition of a mongrel. Ryker clearly thought so too, for he didn't answer immediately. Max and the pup were waiting for his answer, both silent and peering up at him through unique irises.

"He's ... different." Ryker finally answered.

Max nodded her head. "Different is good."

Ryker smiled. "Yeah. Different is good."

"I can keep him, right?" Max bit her lip.

"Max, this is your home. You don't have to ask. If you want to give this little guy a home, then you can." Ryker told her softly.

"Yay! Thank you! Now say hello to your new son!" She demanded passing the puppy over.

Ryker caught the small bundle but frowned ferociously. "No. No way are you going to start calling him that. I mean it Max." He said over the many snickers.

The next few minutes were spent oohing and ahhing over the latest stray to take refuge in the large log house by the ocean. Darius remained by the door, unmoving and silent, no doubt tense waiting for his presence to be formally recognised. For his part, Ryker blatantly ignored his second in command. It was rude and disrespectful and definitely a pointed statement to the older man. Ryker was deliberately keeping Darius hanging, drawing out the tension and playing on his apprehension. Diana was a little pissed at Ry – there was no need to torture him. Ryker must have felt her glare on him for he raised an eyebrow at her in challenge; *'got something to say?'* it seemed to ask. She wisely shook her head and lowered her eyes. No, she had nothing to say. Ryker was her Captain and the wronged party; he had every right to deal with the situation as he saw fit. Besides – he was a hard-arse – always had been and it was somewhat reassuring to know that falling in love hadn't turned him soft. He must have figured Darius had sufficient time to stew in the juices of his own making for he finally turned to him;

"Do you have anything to say, soldier?"

The room fell silent and Diana felt her heart clench in pity again for Darius. This would be one of his greatest fears and greatest shames – standing in front of his fellow knights and admitting to an offense. She saw him nod his head jerkily before he spoke formally;

"I have harmed you in anger. I submit myself to you in reparation for my slight so that justice may be served and balance restored."

Ryker crossed his arms over his thick chest. "And what punishment do you believe would achieve this?"

"I will accept anything you deem appropriate."

"And if I wanted to strip you down, tie you to the railing out front, and give you ten lashes with my belt? What if I deem that appropriate?"

Damn, Diana thought silently. Even though he had agreed with Diana's suggestion earlier and was willing to follow Max's lead and allow her to dole out Darius's punishment, the man was still very clearly pissed. And also very clearly reasserting himself as alpha. *Men!*

Darius didn't so much as twitch. "I will accept anything you deem appropriate." He repeated.

Ryker grunted and shook his head. "Fuck, man! Would you take that stick out of your arse?! At ease." He shook his head again. "You're forgiven. And after Max delivers your sentence, it will also be forgotten." He stalked over and leaned in close, "But don't ever do it again."

Darius nodded once. "No, Sir. Never again."

Ryker reached up and squeezed his shoulder, jostling him slightly. "Now. You go with Max ... and be polite!" He jabbed a finger in Darius's face. "You may think this is a punishment at first, but trust me; it is a great gift." Ryker rubbed his chest directly over his heart as he spoke as if remembering the moment when Max had placed curative hands on him – healing more than any of them knew was possible.

Diana saw the exact moment Darius understood what Ryker was alluding to. His piercing hazel eyes widened and his face paled beneath his usual healthy tan. Diana couldn't really blame him for his trepidation. If she was told someone was about to look inside her and see her deepest wounds and her most traumatic scars, she would be feeling a little pale too.

TWENTY-THREE

They walked in silence across the sand, close to the water so their feet didn't sink too far into the golden softness. Max seemed quite content to enjoy the walk as if it were nothing more than an evening stroll along the beach rather than a death march. That's how Darius perceived it anyway. His hands were sweating and his stomach was in knots at the prospect of Max having access to his soul. As far as punishments went, it sure was a doozy.

"Are you okay with this?"

Her voice startled him so much he almost tripped. "Do I have a choice?" He demanded, regaining his footing.

"Of course you do. In fact, I don't think it will work if you're not open to it." Max's response was pleasant, containing none of the heat Darius's had. It made him feel foolish ... again! She stopped abruptly, plonking her tush in the sand. Looks like they were sitting, Darius thought, taking a seat beside her.

"Open to what exactly? What are you going to do?" He asked with more control.

Max snorted, a decidedly unfeminine sound, "Fucked if I know." She answered bluntly. "All I know, is that Ryker was able to reconcile his past and present, giving him a chance at a better future. At the time, I just had this undeniable urge to take away his hurt; to reward him for his years of unending, loyal service. I've had that same feeling with you for weeks now and as soon as it was mentioned for your penance, I felt the rightness of it. If you let me, I think I could help you."

Max's voice was soft and she didn't look up from where she was playing in the sand. Darius realised she was giving him the chance to choose his ultimate fate here, despite what she wanted the outcome to be. No doubt all of the others were hoping Max could magically stop him from acting like a moron the same way she had with Ryker. Darius didn't really believe the same thing would happen here, although he was more than willing to subject himself to anything she wanted. He owed penance and deserved to be punished for his actions against his Captain, and by proxy, his Order and liege. Although ... that still wasn't official, and that grated too, he acknowledged. All the others had now bonded with Max and were exceedingly happy and proud to be in her service. Darius wanted that too, truly he did, but something was still holding him back. He had reservations about Max and what her presence in their world meant in the grand scheme of things. He couldn't reconcile where all the clues were pointing to. That one word Diana had uttered with such hope and reverence; *revolution*. Could he really be a party to a revolution? Did he *want* to be a party to it? He just didn't know. In addition to that, he felt like he was betraying his old liege. If he bound himself to another, did that mean he was forgetting his brother? Or maybe even forgiving his brother? He didn't know if he was ready for any of that ... he just didn't know.

"This was Diana's idea, you know." Max told him presently.

"What – my punishment?" Max nodded her head and Darius found himself smiling sardonically, "Of course it was.

She's pissed off at me." Not that he really blamed her. He hadn't exactly been treating her well.

Max shook her head, the sun reflecting the deep red of her hair, "No ... she's in love with you."

Darius felt himself go stone-still. Diana was in love with him? He burst into laughter; full, unrestrained, genuine laughter. There was no way Diana was in love with him. Max waited patiently for him to get all the hysteria out of his system, saying nothing as she ran sand through her fingers. "You are so very wrong, My Lady." He finally said.

"I'm not." She said simply and with surety. "I also know you are in love with her."

This time he didn't laugh. "Max ..."

She held up a stalling hand, "You know, this will go a lot easier if you don't lie to me ... or yourself. The biggest sin you can commit is lying to yourself."

Darius felt himself shiver as goose bumps popped up over his arms. Almost those exact same words had been uttered to him eight hundred years ago on a bloody battlefield in Portugal by Verity, Diana's liege. *Revolution*, his mind whispered, but Darius pushed the whimsical voice aside. Max could see a lie as easily as she could see the ocean in front of them. That's why she had said those words – there was no other reason or agenda. Given she could see a lie, he decided to go with the truth;

"Yes. I do love her. But it's not the same love you and Ryker share." He was quick to point out.

"Of course it's not." Max agreed. "Nobody loves the same."

"That's not what I meant." He shook his head, "Besides, the feelings are not reciprocated." He assured her.

"They are too." Max argued, much like a ten-year-old would. "I can see your souls remember? Not to mention the threads holding everyone and everything together."

Darius frowned, a strange fluttering in his belly that was definitely *not* hope, he assured himself. "And you can see a thread between Diana and I?"

"Absolutely." Max's voice was clear and confident.

"So you can see my thread fruitlessly chasing after Diana, huh? Wonderful. That's not embarrassing or anything." He ran his hands over his face, cursing when sand got in his eyes.

"Not exactly." Max hedged.

He rubbed his eyes, squinting at Max and trying to decipher the look on her face. "What do you mean *'not exactly'*?"

"Well, I think it's pretty much the opposite. Diana's soul reaches for you."

He swallowed when the butterflies made an appearance again. "I don't believe you." He would know if Diana had feelings for him like that ... right? He had slept with her twice now!

"Then why is the thread gold and not grey? The thread sustaining the bond, sustaining the emotion, is gold. Gold is the colour of Diana's soul; grey is the colour of yours. It is *her* soul that reaches out to *you*. *Her* soul forming a bridge with *yours*. Not the other way around. Trust me, she is in love with you and has been for a long time. The strength of the thread is like a bridge, connecting you two together even across countries. It's one of the strongest I have ever seen."

He was flabbergasted ... and humbled ... and flabbergasted. They had been connected by an unbreakable gold thread for eight centuries?

"Now." Max pushed up onto her knees. "I would deliver your punishment ... and your reward on the Great Mother's behalf."

Darius felt the Adam's apple in his throat bob up and down as he swallowed. He stared into Max's eyes and they seemed to challenge him; *'you game?'* they appeared to say.

He narrowed his own eyes. He was an ancient knight, wasn't he?

TWENTY-FOUR

Diana stood next to Ryker and watched as Max planted a solid lip-lock on Darius in the distance. She wiped her hands on her pants – her palms were sweaty. She had been so nervous that this wouldn't work, that she had pushed for this and it was going to backfire. She was terrified Darius would never forgive her for breaking his trust and revealing his past to Max. But Max was his liege – or would be, as soon as he pulled his finger out – and she had every right to know her paladin's histories. After putting in the request for Max to attempt to help Darius the same way she had helped Ryker only a couple of months before, she had shared some of Darius's history.

She had explained how Darius had been bound to his previous liege for over a thousand years in the Order of Magne. The Magne Order and its Warden were one of the most famous in all of their history. He had been a staunch supporter of regular humans and had thrown his lot in with them multiple times over the years, participating in battles and wars, including the Battle of Lisbon where Diana had first met Darius. Partaking in the trials of non-wardens was not commonplace, even back then and not typically well received by the higher-ups. But even they could find no fault in the way the Magne liege conducted himself; he was a hero in every society, a true man of honour, paying tribute to his domain. He had been an Air Warden just as Darius was a paladin of air. But that was to be expected, she supposed, given they were brothers. She had then gone on to explain that Darius was the younger brother by a hundred years or so and had actually been raised by his soon-to-be liege after the death of their parents. They were close, very close. But around forty years ago, a good decade after The Great Massacre, Darius's brother began to change. The deterioration was swift and he had withdrawn from society and his brother mere days before becoming a chade.

Darius had never forgiven him. His sense of abandonment from the person who had raised him, from the person he had laid his life on the line for, for the person he literally gave his life force to ...? Well, it was immense and all consuming. Hence, the deep-seated hate and disgust he felt for the chades. Darius believed his hero brother and liege had chosen to betray everything he stood and fought for and had become a creature with no morals who preyed on his own kind. Diana wanted Max to understand how her continued defence of the chades would impact Darius and how difficult it was for all of them, let alone for Darius who had a very personal history, to contemplate her theories. Diana was actually on Max's side and felt her ideas held merit. Max was innately in tune with nature, people and the world, it stood to reason that she may feel something nobody else could. She was also unbiased, having no pre-conceived notions about the chades. Darius was an extremely intelligent and rational man. She knew that if he could just clear his head and accept some of his past, he might be able to move forward and see the potential too.

That was another reason for her racing heart and the swirling butterflies in her stomach. What if Darius wasn't open to Max and the soul-deep healing she knew the Custodian could bestow? What if he wasn't ready to begin the healing process? Ryker had practically needed to be dragged into it by the tiny redhead. Diana hadn't attempted to follow them nor listen in, even though she had been horribly tempted to do so. But about thirty minutes after they had walked down the beach, she and the others had felt a strange stirring of power through the Order. Max had well and truly closed down the link but clearly power of that nature was unable to be fully contained and their Heraldry's had writhed on their forearms, pulsing with power. Diana would be lying if she didn't admit it was a little disconcerting to have a moving tattoo on her arm. Ryker had stood up from where he had been playing with the new pup on the ground – grumbling the entire time about having to keep the 'mongrel thing' – and walked outside. Unable to contain her impatience any longer, she had followed and was now able to breathe deeply for the first time in what felt like hours; the kiss she was witnessing boded well.

"Why is Darius kissing my woman?" Ryker grumbled, wriggling his jaw. No doubt he was picturing returning the bruised favour to his second in command. He hadn't allowed Max to heal the evidence of the punch. Some kind of man thing, no doubt.

Diana narrowed her eyes at the picture they both made; the sun was setting behind them and cast their bodies in a romantic silhouette as Max's much smaller body arched into the wide, muscled frame of Darius. They looked darn good together. For the first time *ever* Diana felt a twinge of jealousy. Over the years she knew Darius had been with other women, just has she had been with other men. She wasn't going to live a life of celibacy just because the man she considered perfect in every way was too dense to make a move. But right now, after having been intimate with the man, Diana felt the first stirrings of possessiveness.

"I think it's more like Max is kissing *my* man." She stated forcefully. Diana winced, *shit!* Had she really just said that out loud to her Captain? She was bound to serve Max for as long as she walked the earth now. An emotional attachment with another was no longer an option for her and a relationship with a fellow paladin? There was just no way – no matter what Max seemed to think. Diana felt her heart break a little. She had been fine living and working with Darius all these years – at least she could be close to him and their relationship, though not an intimate one, was comfortable. But now? Well, now Diana wanted more. And she was never going to get it. "I'm sorry, Ryker. I didn't mean –"

But Ryker held up a silencing hand. "You know I cannot tolerate any sort of distraction that would endanger Max. And not just because she is my everything either. She is a Custodian, a daughter of Mother Nature and the most powerful entity on the planet. I believe she's here for a reason. A much bigger reason than to make my sorry arse complete."

Diana nodded her head, "I know. I agree." And she did.

"Having said that. I will give you this one opportunity to be completely honest with me." Ryker paused, his chocolate eyes intense and searching hard for something. "Is Darius your Max?" He asked.

She swallowed convulsively. That was *not* what she was expecting him to ask. As strange as the question may have sounded to anyone else, she knew exactly what he was asking and it wouldn't have had the same depth, the same intensity had he asked; are you in love with Darius? Max was his everything, he had literally just admitted to that. Was Darius hers? She cast her eyes back toward the couple, now picking their way carefully through the sand in their direction.

Darius had his arm around the little Goddess's shoulders and she seemed to be leaning a little heavily against his side. His broad shoulders cast a magnificent shadow along the waterline and his straight, noble back held an almost royal bearing. Was he hers?

"He is. Darius is my Max." She answered, a little embarrassed to feel the sting of tears trying to escape the confines of her eyes.

Ryker gave a decisive nod of his head, "Then we'll make this work. We'll figure it out, I promise. To hell with the council and their rules. To hell with tradition. Max is mine and not even the Great Mother herself would have the balls to try and take her away from me. If Darius is that for you … then we'll figure it out."

Diana felt one rebellious tear track a hot path down her cheek. She knew Ryker was a man of his word; not only was he her Captain and a born potentate, but he was also her friend. If he said they would figure it out, then they would. Her Boss-man would never let her down. Throwing decorum to the wind, she launched herself at the huge paladin of life, snaking her arms around his neck;

"Thank you, Ry … just … thank you."

He cleared his throat and patted her back roughly in that awkward manly way that all males did when a female cried around them, "Yeah, yeah. You're welcome. Just don't let me down."

Taking a step back, she shook her head, sending her hair flying in all directions. "Never. I give you my word." She paused, considered not asking her next question, but then couldn't resist. "You really are a romantic at heart aren't you? All those flowery words and sporadic fits of poetry you spout at Max? That's the real you, isn't it?"

He winced and blushed – a real rosy blush that worked its way from neck to forehead. "Damn, Diana! Didn't I just do you a huge favour? Don't go spreading that shit, okay?"

Her laugh was still a little watery as she replied, "Whatever you say, Boss-man."

"And stop calling me that!" He snapped.

Diana grinned, "Sure thing." *Not!* She added silently.

"Hey! Handsy!" She turned and saw Darius helping Max up the three stairs. She was definitely leaning on him heavily and her face looked pinched and pale. Diana didn't really understand what kind energy or power it required to heal a person's soul but it was obviously taxing. Max was going to need to recharge her vitality before the evening ahead. Her mouth though? It didn't seem to be lacking in energy, for she continued;

"Handsy woman! I saw you throwing yourself at my man. Get your own six-plus-foot mountain of muscle!" Her grin assured Diana her words were in jest and likely designed to break the ice of her and Darius's return.

"I intend to." Diana muttered softly as Ryker moved quickly to intercept the duo, picking up a protesting Max. The stress lines on Darius's face now looked non-existent and he looked relaxed and happy. And although his hazel eyes held questions when they met hers, they were yet to hold the same resolved look she knew hers did. "Oh, I intend to." She repeated.

TWENTY-FIVE

Holy crap, Max sure packed a punch! Darius thought, the morning after his 'punishment' as he basked under the pelting hot spray of his shower. On the beach, when Max had placed her hands on him, he had thought for sure he was going to die for a few seconds. The agony from where she had touched him had been gut wrenching; loud, cold, hot, slicing and ripping away at his insides until he thought he would pass out. It had felt like his brother had abandoned him all over again – like he had been thrown aside and was left with nothing and no-one. He had no sense of self, no duty, no purpose. How was a man of fidelity supposed to survive something like that? But then, like some kind of shining star, a feeling of warmth, of peace, of *hope* had filled him and he had felt something ... more. He could have sworn he felt another presence; a presence of great power, both magnificent and malevolent. The perfect balance of light and dark. Opening his eyes, he had been momentarily blinded by the colourful display of lights and sounds, that he could have sworn he saw something other than Max. But then he blinked and all that was in front of him was a tiny redhead, smiling up at him.

The tingling warmth that had passed through his body appears to have chased away the cold and the resentment of the last forty years. Darius really did feel like Max had healed his soul. He only hoped it was permanent. But then, he supposed that was probably up to him. Max had given him a hand up but it was his choice what he was going to do with it now. The fact that he could actually take a deep breath and think rationally about his past and his brother was a miracle in and of itself.

Stepping out of the shower, he dressed and prepared for the day ahead of him. He figured it was going to be a big one. But he had slept the best he had in years, so he felt fully charged to meet it head on. He was also going to be meeting Diana head on, he resolved. Last evening, as he had made his way back up the beach with Max, there had been a look in Diana's grey eyes that hadn't been there previously. He didn't understand what the look meant but for some reason, it made his gut tighten in anticipation. He had to talk to her – if she would let him.

Making his way downstairs, he counted off his to-do list; number one: make amends to his comrades; number two: make amends to Diana; number three: accept the fact that his brother was never coming back and a new liege was literally staring him in the face. He paused when he heard the commotion in the kitchen. The sound of clanging pots and plates hitting the table, raised voices and laughter, suggested that the kitchen was already full with the other members of the household. He was a little scared to go in now. After all, he had disgraced himself yesterday by physically assaulting his Captain and then had been forced to accept penance in front of everyone. Even though none of them had actually witnessed the act, he knew they were all aware of what Max had subjected him to – gifted to him, he amended – although none but Ryker could fully understand what he had gone through on that beach. Because he now felt like he was back in the headspace he had been before all the drama forty years ago, he now felt extra embarrassed and ashamed to walk into that room, filled with comrades and friends and family. He had been a miserable excuse of all three of those things recently and he knew he was going to have to eat a little crow this morning. This was going to be awkward.

A hearty slap on his back had him hastily palming the wall in order to steady himself. "Hey man. You going to stand there all day?" The deep voice belonged to Axel and Darius braced himself for the imminent ribbing sure to follow.

"No. I'm coming in." He answered.

"Good." Axel smiled, a genuine smile filled with warmth and none of the teasing Darius assumed would be there. "I was on breakfast duty and I made omelettes; bacon, mushroom, cheese and capsicum." He continued.

Darius frowned. "Those are my favourite."

"I know." He stated simply.

Darius swallowed around the sudden lump in his throat. This was Axel's way of saying he forgave Darius, that he accepted him, and that he supported him no matter what. Darius felt some more shame trickle through when he remembered his unkind thoughts about the younger knight. Maybe he had been wrong when he had thought Axel had some growing up to do, that he was never serious in his duties. The light, the laughter and the banter? That was Axel's nature, just as much as the control and rigidity was Darius's. Now that he thought about it, he realised that Axel always acted like a knight even when he hadn't been bound in an Order, despite his irreverent attitude. He had also been the one to take on the role of protector and defender of Max's fragile heart in the beginning too; standing up to Ryker and even asserting himself physically in her defence.

Damn, Darius thought, *he's going to give me a run for my money when he gets older.* Axel of the surfer boy good looks and the brash manner could one day quite easily become, '*Sir Axel*'.

"Thank you." He replied, dipping his head slightly in gratitude.

Axel returned the nod, "You are most welcome. Now come on, before they get cold."

*****

His arrival heralded no real spark of interest other than the habitual 'good mornings' thrown his way. He sat down and Axel placed a plate in front of him, overflowing with a huge omelette complete with all his favourite fixings. A mug of black tea was added next and he looked up to see Cali smiling at him as she added his usual two spoons of sugar. They were spoiling him and it made him feel even worse. But not bad enough to ignore the generous offerings, so he dug into his food and drank his drink, listening to the casual banter of the voices around him. Diana was at the opposite side of the table and her eyes were the only ones he had yet to meet. A wake up call and a fresh outlook he may have. But his balls? They were still growing back.

A low growl and insistent tugging on his cargos had him glancing down. Looks like the pup had survived the night in his new home. "Hey buddy. You're still here I see."

"Yes. He is." Ryker's words were low. "He slept on the bed all night."

Max laughed, reaching over to scratch the mutt behind the ears. "He's just cranky because he didn't get any this morning. He thinks the dog was watching him."

"He was!" Ryker yelled. "Watching me with his weird eyes, judging me for defiling his new mother."

Everybody laughed, including Max – although it was a bit evil on her part. "Zombie just needs a little time to get used to you. In time, I'm sure he'll realise that you're not trying to hurt me with that thing swinging between your legs."

"Max ..." Ry blushed but Max just laughed again.

Darius cleared his throat, "Um ... did you just call the pup, Zombie?"

"Yep! That's his name. Cool huh?"

Darius peered around the table – all eyes were on him. No doubt they were waiting for him to put his foot in his mouth again. Well, no dice. Today was a new day and he was his old self; sophisticated, wise, controlled and logical. "It's unique. How did you come up with it?"

Max shrugged, watching indulgently as the dog attempted to chew his thumb off. "It just suits him. Besides, he chose it himself. You should have seen him sitting on my drawings for my graphic novels. He was completely fixated on Gage, the hero zombie in book number nine."

"So why didn't you call him Gage then?"

"Because that's Gage's name." She looked at him with wide eyes as if that answer was obvious. And to her, he supposed it was.

"Okay. So Zombie, huh?"

"Yep."

Zombie apparently already knew his new moniker for he yipped happily at the name, demanding to be put down and loping clumsily around the room like a lunatic; he was going to be a handful. He didn't dare look at Ryker in case the man was shooting him a death stare for introducing the dog into the house.

"I'm glad you're up and looking so fresh this morning, Darius." Max said, presently, "As much as I don't want to rock the boat, I need to tell you something." She added, looking him in the eye.

Damn! She sounded serious again, like this was something he wasn't going to like hearing. "Oh?" He responded, keeping his voice light.

"Ivy will be arriving soon and I expect everyone to be here and welcome her." Max stated.

Darius was a little confused, a lot surprised, and very alarmed. What was a Ranger coming here for? Had Max and Ryker changed their minds and decided to dole out a punishment in the old ways? "Why is a Ranger coming here?"

Max's clear eyes remained steady on his as she answered, "As a Ranger she is likely the most knowledgeable person in regards to chades that we can talk to. She deals with them every day and it is my understanding that she is very good at her job. I'm hoping she'll be able to answer some of my questions."

Darius sucked in a breath; Max was very clearly *never* going to give up on her notion that something could be done about the chades. Yesterday, any mention of those creatures would have sent him flying off the handle. His wound where they were concerned was an open, seeping mess of pain and infection. But now, he was able to react more rationally and on the off chance that Max was actually onto something? Well, he owed her the chance to prove or disprove her theory.

He felt the stillness of the room around him and realised everyone was essentially holding their breath, awaiting his reaction. Like he was a bloody ticking time bomb or something! The thought mortified him and made him thankful once again that Max had performed her little voodoo and he was able to think and react like a true knight once more.

"That is a smart idea. Other than the members of the IDC, I believe a Ranger would be the best person to talk to. And as Beyden's sister, I'm sure we can trust her." He answered steadily, deciding to keep cutting into his omelette casually. *Nothing to see here – nope – nothing to see,* he thought.

The tension immediately seemed to dissipate because of his casualness and everyone returned to their own breakfasts. The mention of chades had left a bad taste in his mouth but he was willing to follow Max's lead in the matter. He owed her that much at least. Unfortunately, it now meant the rest of his day would be spent mentally preparing for the arrival of a Ranger into their midst, rather than the pathetic grovelling to a certain grey-eyed paladin of death.

TWENTY-SIX

Darius had been in better spirits that morning and the new light in his eyes gave Diana hope that perhaps they had a chance at some kind of future. Unfortunately, he had retreated to his room, no doubt to consider all the recent changes and prepare for the arrival of Ivy, who was due any moment now. The doorbell ringing had Diana thinking of that old saying; speak of the devil. The Rangers were the boogeymen of their society, after all.

"I'll get it." Beyden yelled as he made his way to the door.

Diana followed closely and watched as Bey enveloped a tiny woman in his huge arms until she almost disappeared completely. The Ranger was probably only a couple of inches taller than Max and her straight black hair and dark, almond-shaped eyes reflected her Asian heritage. She couldn't look any more different to Beyden if she tried! The two murmured lowly to each other for a moment before Beyden spun her around and introduced her to the Order who had accumulated in the hallway to greet their guest.

Max stepped forward and offered her hand. "Hi. I'm Max. Thank you so much for coming. I really appreciate it."

Ivy eyed Max's hand for a moment before gripping it and replying, "Hello. It's not a problem. It's nice to be able to see Beyden."

"Oh, of course it would be! Feel free to come over whenever you want. Right, Ry?"

Ryker cleared his throat. "Of course." He sounded a little strained. Max clearly thought so too because she peered up at him critically for a moment before shrugging it off and ushering everyone into the kitchen. She offered Ivy a seat and watched as everybody else sat at the table. Everyone except Ryker, that is.

"What is wrong with you? You're acting very strange," Max pointed out as Ryker continued to stay over the other side of the room.

Diana could not believe he hadn't told Max he and Ivy shared a past. Max's eyes continued to rove back and forth between Ryker and Ivy and it wasn't long before Max clued onto what type of tension was in the air;

"You two had sex!"

Ryker winced and Ivy's face became even more remote, apparently expecting a bad reaction from Max. This was why Ryker had been hesitant to allow Bey to call his sister.

"It was a long time ago ..." Ryker began, obviously trying to placate his woman.

"Only last year – not that long ago." Ivy pointed out unhelpfully. What was wrong with the woman? Was she trying to force a wedge between the two lovebirds? Diana didn't know her well, but she knew she was an honourable soldier.

"It seems like a long time ago to me!" Ryker snapped at Ivy. "And I don't even remember it. I was drunk out of my mind."

Diana scowled darkly in Darius's direction at that. There was another individual in this room that conveniently seemed to think alcohol was a satisfactory excuse for not remembering orgasms. Darius squirmed uncomfortably in his seat and avoided eye contact. *Men!*

Max's eyes narrowed dangerously, as she asked for clarification, "You don't remember having sex with her?"

"Not at all." Ryker was quick to assure her. Ivy's expressionless face was yet to change but Diana could tell she was watching the proceedings carefully.

Max gasped in outrage; "That is so fucking insulting! Apologise to Ivy this instant!"

Ryker managed to look confused, shocked and strained at the same time, "What?"

Max jammed her hands on her hips, "Apologise to Ivy for not remembering having sex with her."

"You want me to apologise to another woman because I don't recall being intimate with her?" Ryker's voice was incredulous.

"Yes, Ryker, I do. And it had better be sincere!" Max warned.

Diana was careful to hide her amusement from her Captain as he sputtered in disbelief. She noticed that the other occupants of the room were in various states of amusement – all except for Beyden of course – nobody wanted to be reminded that their best friend had slept with their sister in a drunken haze. Max's eyes began to take on a luminous hue and Ryker must have realised she was serious for he turned to Ivy;

"I apologise for not remembering our brief encounter. I am sure my behaviour was not ideal and I am sorry for insulting you just now." He bowed his head briefly before quickly looking to Max for her reaction.

Max nodded her head. "Good. Ivy, do you accept his apology?"

Diana thought she saw the Ranger's lips twitch for a moment before she replied, "I do. Thank you, Ryker."

Beyden let out a strangled sound, "Can we please not discuss this anymore? And also, like, never again?!"

"Dammit, Bey. I apologise. I didn't mean any disrespect. I –"

"It's fine. We covered this a long time ago." He assured his Captain

"Why exactly are you apologising to him? He has no say about who I do and do not sleep with!" Ivy pointed out indignantly.

"I'm your brother!" Beyden yelled.

"What does that have to do with anything?" Max asked, causing Ivy's lips to twitch again.

Beyden's cheeks began to turn red as he looked from one woman to the other. "Why am I suddenly in trouble here? I haven't done anything."

Cali patted his hand, "You're not in trouble, sweetie. You just happen to have the wrong equipment for this conversation."

"Well, now that is settled, maybe we should move on?" Max suggested, seating herself across from Ivy at the table.

"Thank the Goddess." Beyden muttered, wiping his hand across his sweaty forehead. Diana noticed he pointedly ignored the snickering from Lark and Axel.

Ryker finally joined her, picking up her hand and nipping the back of it. "You are hell on my ego, woman."

Diana smirked. No doubt he had been expecting fireworks in the form of jealousy – which of course, would pander to his inflated male self-esteem. Max's easy going nature was damn good for him, Diana believed.

"Chades; how many of them talk?" Max asked without preamble.

"Chades don't talk." Ivy's voice was unequivocal.

Max sighed, "And here I thought we were going to be friends."

Ivy's expression didn't change. "I don't have friends."

Diana winced. That was the wrong thing to say to a woman who collected strays. Sure enough, Max responded as predicted;

"Well, now you do. Zombie likes you and everybody knows dogs have great instincts." She pointed to the new pup who was sprawled at Ivy's feet, contentedly chewing on the ears of his new stuffed bunny. He had barely left the Ranger's side since she walked in. It would seem that Zombie did in fact like Ivy.

Ivy's face didn't change but her eyes did flick down to the offending beast. "I suppose you can see a lie?" She asked Max.

"Yep. And I take exception to it, so don't bother."

Ivy leaned back in her chair, "I wasn't lying – exactly. Chades *do not* talk. But –" She held up a slender hand to forestall Max's arguments, "But, I believe there are different types of chades, different levels if you will. Some that are not as far gone as their brethren. And those? Yes, they talk."

Diana saw the way Darius stiffened upon hearing those words. His fingers gripped the edge of the table so tightly, she could hear his knuckles crack. She felt some pity work its way through her. Although Max had healed that horrible open wound inside of him, this must still be hell for him.

"There are no different levels of chades. You either choose to become one, or you don't." His voice held authority and it was indeed what they had always been told. Diana herself, had certainly never encountered a chade that hadn't been trying to kill her or a warden. And never one that could talk. They were wholly voiceless. But those eyes ... she shivered. They always looked so accusing, like they were blaming her for not understanding.

Ivy flicked her dark gaze Darius's way. "I'm not prepared to argue with you. You asked for information; I'm giving it to you. Wardens don't just wake up one day and are suddenly chades. It's a process – a fast process for most, but a gradual process for some."

"And those who convert much slower, they retain their human sides longer? Like their ability to communicate?" Max asked.

"That's correct."

"How does the IDC not know about this?" Ryker asked, incredulous.

Ivy's look was direct, "They do know. They have always known."

Darius stood up and began to pace and Diana was worried he was going to blow a gasket again. Max shook her head at her, indicating she should remain in her seat. "They know?" Darius asked.

Ivy nodded. "Yes. How could they not? It's why us Rangers are needed so much. So we can detect and stop the ones who are in the process of turning."

"Why is this a secret, Ivy?" Beyden asked his sister.

Her eyes softened somewhat when she looked at her brother, "It's not really. We're are all told in basic training and it is discussed openly at every meeting we ever have with the IDC. They don't disseminate the information because they are afraid people would panic and anyone showing any signs of aberrant behaviour would be targeted – whether affected or not."

"So they're just keeping important information from everyone?" Darius demanded, angrily.

"How important is it?" Ivy asked. "What difference does it make? The ones that change slowly, still change and become creatures of darkness, bastardising their natural gifts. There is no stopping it. Their course is set. I haven't said anything here that changes anything." She sat back in her chair and addressed Max once again, "What's with all the questions anyway?"

Max shrugged, seemingly negligent. "Some of them have spoken to me but I understand that isn't normal. I just wanted to learn more."

Ivy's eyes sharpened. "Some have spoken to you? Where? When?"

"Oh, all over the place really and a long time ago. What causes them to change?"

"We don't really know. We know certain wardens start requiring more vitality to recharge and start abusing their powers. One day they just ... change. They don't feel anymore, eat, sleep, talk. They cease being guardians of nature and instead choose to hunt their own kind, draining them of their vitality and killing them. They are soulless."

"You think it's a choice?" Max tilted her head to the side.

"Of course. What else would it be?"

"A sickness; a disease." Beyden's voice was soft as he answered on Max's behalf. Diana found it very interesting that Ivy didn't act surprised by the theory. She just continued to regard them all with those dark, exotic eyes of hers in silence.

"Besides," Max added, "why would someone *choose* to lose their soul? It doesn't make sense."

Darius finally halted his incessant pacing. "Max. You are too sweet, too good to understand what true evil is really like. For many, being evil is its own reward."

Max eyed him speculatively as she gripped Ryker's hand tightly. Diana saw Ivy note the action with little to no interest, "I used to have sex for money when I was sixteen years old. Do you know the type of humans that would offer a child of sixteen payment for the use of their body? Don't patronise me, Darius. I know what true evil is; I've seen it, touched it. Don't think me ignorant or innocent just because I ask questions."

Diana felt the blood drain from her face and saw most of the others pale at the thought of their liege selling her body when she was so young. Max still didn't talk much about all those years she was alone but every now and then she would dole out these little snippets – like she spent time in a mental institution, or had undergone physical abuse, or prostituted herself – as though it were nothing. It made her feel sick to her stomach and also extremely sad that Max didn't seem too bothered by those facts. She also found it nothing short of a miracle that Max had turned into a generous, kind, compassionate and affectionate woman. The Order link was suspiciously quiet and she knew Max must have dialled it back. Ryker was running his thumb back and forth over Max's hand; he seemed unsurprised by the information. Apparently, Max didn't keep secrets from the love of her life.

"Max, I –"

But she held up a quieting hand to Darius, instead focusing on their guest again. "Is it possible that they are going after Wardens because they are starving and sick and they are just trying to recharge? To cure themselves by attaining vitality?"

"You don't think they do it out of malicious intent." It wasn't a question, but a statement from the Ranger.

"Not all of them, no. I'm sure some do, don't get me wrong. But a minority of them? I think they're still aware. I think they're sick. And I think they're just trying to help themselves the way their instincts demand."

Ivy regarded Max steadily, face blank, eyes dark and mysterious. Damn, the woman would be a killer at poker – which coincidentally, is where they were headed after this little meeting. "Why do you believe that?" She asked.

"I can see it. Sometimes their souls are intact; sometimes they're not."

Diana whipped her head towards Max at that, as did all of the others. Max could see their souls? She looked at Ryker but he didn't seem surprised by the news – Max had no doubt already told him. Was that why she had let that chade go last week? Because she could see its soul? Diana thought back, remembering what Max had said; '*not that one*' as if that one had been special, as if it had been different. And perhaps it had been – Max had seen that it had a soul.

Ivy frowned, one of the first expressions Diana had observed on the face of the Asian beauty. "What do you mean, you can see their souls? That's not possible."

"She is referring to their auras. She can see the colours." Ryker explained. It was partly true at least. Max did indeed see colours.

"I see. I suppose it is possible – in theory. But I would imagine the IDC have already considered it. I appreciate you are trying to find answers and a way to help. But if there were such a thing as a cure, the IDC would have figured it out by now."

"I guess." Max's reply was non-committal and Diana sensed she wasn't convinced. The strange thing was; she didn't think Ivy was convinced either. They continued to talk back and forth, a little more casually and Diana saw Darius relax back into his seat. No doubt he had a lot on his mind. After a couple of hours, Max abruptly jumped up, startling Zombie awake and causing him to yip in agitation. Ivy actually reached down, petting him into quietness. Perhaps the Ranger really did feel emotions.

"Shoot! We're late for poker night!" Max said, after glancing up at the clock. "You should come with us." Max extended the invitation to Ivy.

Ivy looked startled at the abrupt shift of focus. "Come with you, where?"

"To poker! Apparently this lot play poker with Caspian and his paladins every month or so. I have a great poker face. I'm totally going to kick their big paladin butts!" Max crowed.

Ivy raised her eyebrows and looked at Beyden, silently asking his opinion. Beyden just shrugged and smiled, "Cas won't mind. The more the merrier. I'd love for you to hang around a while longer. I haven't seen you in over a year."

Diana saw Ivy's eyes soften with affection; she clearly cared for her brother even though they were lightyears apart in personality and temperament. She cast a quick look in Ryker's direction, who was studiously looking the other way, and nodded her head once. "Okay. I'll just check in with my Commander – make sure I'm not needed back before tomorrow." She stood, pulling her phone out as she left the room.

"Great!" Max said before turning to her man. "Well? Chop chop! Get moving gentlemen. It's rude to be late."

Ryker looked like he was going to say something but decided it wasn't worth the effort. "Sure. We'll get changed and be back in five." He planted a long kiss on Max's lips, leaving the room with all the males following behind. Diana and Cali stayed, with Diana halting Max before she could go to the corner and grab her shoes.

"Um, Max. Maybe Ivy doesn't want to hang out at Caspian's tonight ..." Diana's words were tentative, a subtle hint for Max to consider Ivy's feelings.

"Why wouldn't she?" Max asked, genuinely puzzled. She paused for a moment thinking, and Diana was glad she wouldn't have to explain the potential awkwardness of the situation. But that hope soon died a fiery death as Max gasped; "Do you think she doesn't like me?" She asked, aghast.

"What? No!" Diana responded, immediately. Although the female Ranger never revealed much about what she was thinking, Diana could tell that she was warming to Max – most people did. Max just had a way about her. Unless you were outdated, prejudiced, misogynistic arseholes of course, she amended. "I just think, maybe ... well, you know ..." How did she explain this in a way that wouldn't bring up the elephant in the room again?

Cali clearly was more interested in expediency over subtlety for she interrupted, saying flatly; "What dear Diana is trying to say is, that Ivy might not want to hang out with a man she had sex with and his new girlfriend."

Max frowned, that adorably confused look on her face she got when she didn't understand social cues. "Why? Who cares?" She asked, sincerely perplexed.

Movement behind Max caught Diana's eye and she saw the Ranger in question had returned and was listening intently. Diana sighed, "*She* might care, Max."

"Huh." Max pulled a face like; 'whatdoyaknow?' – as if she truly couldn't fathom why someone would care about a little casual, drunken sex. "Do you think Ivy wants to have sex with Ryker again?" Max asked, as if trying to figure out a brainteaser.

Cali choked on a laugh, looking between the doorway that held Ivy and back to their liege, before saying; "No. I don't think that's the problem."

Max nodded, "Do you think Ryker wants to have sex with her again?" She asked.

Diana actually felt her own eyes bug a little at the lunacy of that question, "No. I definitely do not think Ryker wants to have sex with anyone other than you ... ever again."

Max bobbed her head in agreement. "Then what's the problem?"

Cali laughed again, apparently finding the whole conversation hysterical. Diana was amused as well, but another part of her kind of wanted to pick up the tiny female and shake her like a broken toy. Before she could try and explain further, Ivy obviously decided she had heard enough, for she walked back in, showing more expression on her face than Diana had ever seen. She was smiling slightly and her dark eyes were definitely amused.

"Turns out I don't have to hurry back tonight. I would love to come to poker night with you." She even inclined her head respectfully.

Max beamed. "Awesome! I know Beyden would love to spend more time with you. He misses you." She narrowed her eyes in thought, cocking her head to the side and Diana knew she was gearing up to ask Ivy point-blank whether or not Ivy cared that she'd had sex with Ryker in the past, and if she did, why was that? Diana could practically see the little wheels turning. Cutting her off before she could make the attempt, Diana clapped her hands;

"Okay. We're running late as it is. Let's round up the boys and be off, shall we?"

Max snapped her mouth shut and nodded before turning and making her way outside, Zombie following close behind. She spun back around in the doorway however, and opened her mouth again.

"The men, Max." Diana reminded her loudly, feeling the drum of curiosity through the bond. Max was dying to question Ivy.

Max scrunched up her nose, aiming it in her direction, "Fine!"

Diana already felt exhausted and the night was young as far as their social obligations were concerned. She was going to tag-out on Max-etiquette duty as soon as they arrived at Cas's. A snickering Cali drew her attention. "You were real helpful."

Cali laughed again, "What? I didn't do anything."

"Exactly." Diana muttered. "I'm sorry about that. Max is ..." Well, what could she say really? Max was Max and Diana adored her just the way she was. But she also valued a certain decorum with guests in social settings – her age showing, no doubt.

Ivy surprised her by gifting them with a genuine smile that reached her eyes. Her dark, almond-shaped eyes really were quite lovely when they were animated like that and her features were dainty and very pretty. Diana bet she would be a real man-killer if she chose to be.

"She's the real deal, isn't she?" Ivy asked, although it was more of a statement.

Now Diana grinned widely in return, no doubt showing off her crooked front tooth, "That she is, my friend. That she is."

TWENTY-SEVEN

Darius was riding shotgun in the car with Axel driving and Ryker, Cali and Max in the back seat. Lark, Beyden, Diana and Ivy were following closely in the second vehicle. His mind was a swirling mess of thoughts and emotions as he tried to process the revelations and the potential repercussions if Max was indeed correct about the chades. At least he could now make an attempt at a rational and methodical approach to the possibility, thanks to Max's little 'punishment'. Was it possible she could indeed determine which chades had intact souls and which didn't? He didn't know for sure, but as a Custodian she was the only being on the planet gifted with the ability to see a person's true depth, a person's true being. It followed that she would also be the only person in existence to have the ability to heal a soul. Darius had no doubt that is exactly what she had achieved with himself and Ryker. Could she accomplish the same miracle with a chade?

He was brought out of his inner revelations by a gasping Max, who doubled over as if she were suddenly in pain.

"Max!" Ryker yelled, panic infusing his voice. "Max, what is it? Are you hurt?"

Max continued to breathe shallowly, gripping her stomach, as her eyes went opaque. "Max! You slammed down the bond! I don't know what's going on. You have to talk to me!" Ryker's voice was a mixture of demand and plea as he practically dragged her onto his lap.

"Perversion. Perversion. Someone is corrupting their element." Max muttered quickly, rocking back and forth.

Axel's grip on the wheel tightened to the point where Darius could hear the leather creaking. "Fire." He said. "Someone is using fire."

"And water." Cali added, her blue eyes wide in fear. "Lots of water."

Understanding dawned in an instant, and Ryker shouted out the name at the same moment as himself; "Ignatius!"

Darius felt the car speed up, taking the dips and bends of the road recklessly. Although it wasn't very late, it was dark out and the roads were thankfully quiet. They were still at least ten minutes from Caspian's house but at the rate Axel was driving, they would likely get there in five. Darius just hoped it would be in time. Ignatius had to be attacking Caspian in some way for Max to be having such a severe reaction and for Axel and Cali to be able to feel the disruption in their domains. Darius knew the man was no good and Max had warned them his soul was far from pure, but he never would have believed he resort to such extremes. Even after what he did to Lark; Lark was a paladin but Caspian was a Warden. Ignatius must truly be unhinged. Perhaps it was some strange twist of fate that they had a Ranger in the car following dangerously close behind them. No-one would be a better judge of the Warden's state of mind than a Ranger. Max let out a tiny squeak and Darius revised that last thought; a Custodian would undoubtedly be better.

He cursed out loud – why hadn't they taken Max more seriously? She had expressed her concerns and although he had acknowledged them, he had still thought her overly dramatic. When was he going to stop questioning her and her abilities and start accepting that she was indeed a daughter of Mother Nature ... and a Goddess in her own right? He had been so caught up in how Max was affecting his cosy little world and his cosy little traditions, that he hadn't given much thought to the fact that his opinion – his feelings – didn't matter worth a damn. His acceptance, or lack thereof, didn't change a thing about who and what Max was.

Damn. He was a real grade-A prick, he thought.

"Max ... sweetheart. You have to open the bond back up. Your Order needs to be able to feel what you're feeling. We need to be able to communicate with you."

Ryker's tone was as gentle as Darius figured he could make it. Max didn't answer, just kept staring into space with her milky white eyes. When his Captain made eye contact with him, Darius figured it was a miracle his skin didn't peel off.

Ryker was pissed.

"After Max told me what she saw that night, I reported him to the council. Part of the reason Ivy is here, is to check on him and see if the accusations have grounds."

"You did? It is?" Darius was surprised. Usually Ryker would ask Darius to do that sort of thing.

"Of course I did. Do you think I haven't learned to always take Max seriously? I believe in her without reservation. I just hope it's not as bad as it seems when we get there." Ryker stated, a hint of condemnation in his tone.

Damn, Darius thought again. Looks like he was the only arsehole in the car now.

*****

The scene that greeted them as they all piled out of their cars was like a nightmare. Caspian's quaint little cottage was awash in flames so hot Darius could feel his arm hairs singeing from metres away. Yelling, cursing and metal ringing on metal could be heard but he couldn't see where it was coming from, thanks to the huge ring of fire encircling the property. Caspian, Leo and Lawson must be inside surrounded by Ignatius and his paladins. The Warden of Fire had well and truly gone off the reservation. No warden in their right mind would stoop to attacking another this way.

"Axel." Max said the fire paladin's name softly but he somehow heard over the roaring blaze for he joined Max, placing his hand in Max's outstretched one and offering his vitality without hesitation. A few seconds is all it took before Max released him and raised a hand toward the inferno. The whole blaze seemed to falter for a moment before igniting again even hotter than before. Max narrowed her eyes and Darius saw the others wince and grit their teeth. Max must be pulling on the bond in order to gather more energy. Darius felt a pang of loneliness, not being included in such an intimate moment. He also cursed himself for his foolishness in not bonding with Max before now. He could be contributing his own vitality, strengthening the Order and boosting Max. Instead, all he could do was watch as the others served their born purpose and shake his head in wonder as he saw the ring of fire snuff out like it was a giant candle being blown out.

With no more heat or fire in the way, he took in the scene and was immediately filled with rage. Ignatius and his five paladins had Caspian and his two knights completely surrounded and were engaged in hand to hand combat. Leo and Lawson were vastly outnumbered and overpowered by the five other knights, but they somehow managed to keep Caspian between them at all times. For his part, Caspian looked to be fighting valiantly using his own domain of water.

For every fire bomb Ignatius hurled his way, Caspian would block it with a ball of water. There was no way he was going to be able to sustain that, Darius knew. He only had two paladins to recharge with; Ignatius had five. Darius processed all this in a matter of seconds and was off and moving along with his fellow knights in the direction of the battle. Casting a quick glance, he saw that Max was manoeuvred behind Ryker and between Diana and Beyden. Diana looked like a true knight of old – just as he had first seen her in the Crusades all those years ago. And now, just as he had then, he felt his heart take a tumble and his lungs stop working.

Love at first sight; that's what it must have been all those years ago ... and love it must still be now. He only prayed he hadn't left it too late to man up and take what was rightfully his. He met her eyes and wasn't surprised to see the thunderstorm roiling within them ... or the look of death. She was deeply entrenched in her domain, charging the Order and relishing the thought of crucifying the wrong doers.

Stay safe. Please stay safe. He begged her with his own eyes. And even though they couldn't share emotions or thoughts through the Order, some part of his meaning must have gotten through, for she nodded grimly and mouthed back; *"You too."*

The abrupt loss of the fiery heat had the desired result of drawing the attention of everyone in the field. Darius noted the grim relief on Caspian's face and saw him sag ever so slightly against his partner, Lawson – who looked like he wanted to rip Ignatius apart with his bare hands. The piece of filth in question spun around and literally snarled at Max, shaking his weapon – which was on fire! Darius figured Max would make good with one her famous one-liners, throw in a few insults and the like. But she did none of those things. Instead, she looked around the clearing that had once been Caspian's front yard and Darius could see the pain in her eyes. *Damn!* For someone so sensitive, with such strong empathic abilities and a direct link to nature, the damage to the landscape must be like a physical blow. She was likely feeling every burn, every tear, and every rent in the earth as though the injuries were her own. She turned luminous eyes to Ryker for a heartbeat as he grabbed her hand and he saw the entire Order shudder. She was sharing the load – filtering her pain and emotions through the link and her bonded paladins just like she was born to. And they were shouldering the burden – standing tall as was their purpose. He could also make out Max's Heraldry writhing like living tapestries on their forearms. After this mess was dealt with, Darius was definitely getting himself one of those, he vowed.

A sad shake of Max's head and a penetrating look of disappointment apparently was enough to send Ignatius off the handle once more. He charged, blade raised ... and met Ryker in a clash of steel. Satisfied that not so much as an ant could get through their Captain and touch Max, he shifted his attention to the Captain of the offending Order. He watched as Marco made a bee line directly for Lark. Marco was a skilled fighter, top of his class in hand-to-hand, most often using brute strength to overthrow his opponent. And he'd had a hard-on for Lark since the moment he first saw him for some strange reason. Insults and veiled threats had been commonplace for years, with the abuse culminating recently in the assault just weeks ago. Darius was tempted to intervene, relishing the opportunity to kick the living crap out of him, but the raw determination in Lark's eyes had him pausing. A resolute nod from the auburn-haired paladin had him turning and focusing on Chad instead – the Order's second in command. Lark deserved a little retribution and Darius had no doubt that his speed, strength and skill would best the strongarm tactics of the Captain of Vulcan.

Chad was moving with great speed, looking to join the fray between Lark and Marco. And outnumber his fellow knight once more? *I don't think so!* Darius moved with equal speed, the wind at his back a driving force of strength and partnership. Chad was also a skilled soldier and detected his approach, turning and launching a high round-house kick in one smooth motion. The other paladin was slightly out of breath and was caked in sweat – he was an earth paladin and the destruction to so much of his associated element must be taking a toll. Darius easily dodged the size eleven boot, catching it in his fist and delivering a swift punch to Chad's inner thigh. The hard strike had the desired effect, deadening the large muscle and causing him to hobble back a step, off-balance. Not allowing him a chance to recover and not concerned with a fair fight – Chad was an honourless cretin, after all – Darius swept his foot out and tumbled him to the ground. Two steps were all it took to deliver a hard kick to the fallen soldier's temple. Chad gave a garbled grunt before his eyes rolled back in his head. He didn't get back up.

Looking around he saw Lark had Marco in much the same predicament; he was standing over the disgraced Captain, his sickle pointed low and warningly against his throat. Marco appeared to be goading Lark, pushing into the steel and drawing his own blood as he no doubt uttered obscenities. Lark spared him one disgusted look before drawing back his left arm and punching Marco directly in the middle of his forehead. That sure shut him up. Lark was by far the bigger man, not allowing himself to be provoked into further confrontation while his liege and family were still in danger. Darius was mighty proud of the young paladin.

"Bitch, please!" An aggrieved sounding Cali yelled. Darius didn't need to see the stunning blonde's face to know she was rolling those ice-blue eyes of hers. Dan, another of Ignatius's paladins was gripping her long locks in his fist – talk about fighting dirty! Cali clearly thought so too, for her disdainful comment was quickly followed by an elbow into the underside of Dan's chin. The snap of teeth clashing together was loud enough to be heard across the yard. A spurt of blood flew from Dan's mouth as he landed, dead-weight, on the hard ground. No doubt, he had also bitten his tongue.

A caress of air drew his attention to art in motion – the sexiest damn moving artwork Darius had ever seen! Diana's shirt was ripped down one arm, leaving her right side bare and displaying tanned, smooth skin to its best advantage. Subtle muscles flexed as she executed a perfect roll, tucking herself under a huge outstretched male fist. The springs on her head – which she affectionately referred to as hair – flew in complete disregard to gravity, whipping crazily in a cloud of black chaos. Darius remembered the feel of those curls twisted around his hands as she screamed his name in ecstasy. She shifted quickly, moving to the balls of her feet and ramming the butt of her own sickle forcefully into Ricky's kidney. He gave a loud howl, dropping his blade as he reached for the area and Darius figured it must not have been the first time Diana had scored a hit to that location. But she was like that – stubborn as the day was long, willing to press an issue until the wound under pressure was lanced.

Darius watched her turbulent grey eyes as they narrowed in calculation. She swung her sickle directly at Ricky's head, smiling a little evilly as his eyes squeezed tightly together – no doubt not wanting to see the killing blow coming. But Diana twisted her hand at the last second and the handle hit his temple at the last minute. Back when he had first met her, she would never have shown such mercy. But then, neither would he. Both had moved with the times, he supposed and he couldn't wait to move with something else as soon as they finished dealing with the scum. Speaking of which, Darius forced his eyes away from the promise of heat in Diana's grey depths and sought out his Captain.

Ryker was actually partnered up with Axel and they were fighting Ignatius in tandem. It was more than a fair fight considering Ignatius kept drawing on his domain to send bites of flame licking at the two knights. Ryker had his dual sickles out – they were his pride and joy and he was one of the only paladins Darius had ever met to use two weapons simultaneously. The two of them fought in harmony as if they had been fighting together for years. And although they had been training together for a handful of years now, they rarely had the occasion to battle anything but chades. A Warden was by no means a chade, but the two were holding their own, ducking and weaving, delivering well-timed and well-placed blows. Darius noticed that all of them were non-lethal.

A rush of air warned him once again of impending danger. A spinning sickle was winging its way directly toward Max but before it could reach her, a large bronzed hand snatched it out of the air – blade first – and sent it whizzing back to its owner in one smooth motion. Goddamn but Beyden was good with blades! His aim was as true as it always was and a dull thud followed by a thin scream provided evidence that the weapon had embedded deeply into the shoulder of Clint. Darius figured there would be no removing that blade without surgery; Beyden was a big, strong bastard on a normal day. But on a day when he was protecting his liege and his family? Clint was lucky Bey hadn't severed that arm.

The raw sound of pain from one of his paladin's finally had Ignatius wavering and Ryker took immediate advantage, incapacitating him with several swift blows to the solar plexus. Gasping for air, Ignatius staggered back to where Axel kicked out one of his ankles, hiking his right arm up and … *POP!* … dislocating his shoulder. Now it was the warden's turn to scream. Ignatius landed hard, his knee caps echoing loudly as they banged against the earth. He swore colourfully, threatening them all with vile acts of vengeance. The obscenest threats were directed at Max, who for her part, had not even raised her tanto sword. She had watched the proceedings with an almost eerie calm, almost as if she had been judging the spectacle and all of its participants. It wasn't hard to tell who she had deemed unworthy.

Although it made him feel a twinge of guilt, he was just a tiny bit glad that Max had witnessed the contemptible actions of Ignatius and his Order. After listening to Max and Ivy, and receiving a soul-cleanse of sorts, he was at a point where he could admit he may be wrong in some instances regarding the intentions of the chades. The admission twisted his gut and he actually had to force back bile as it rushed up his oesophagus. The thought of maiming and killing true guardians of nature all these years, when he should have been helping them? It made him sick to the stomach. And he still wasn't able to touch on any memories of his brother. He had believed his brother had abandoned him, but what if it had been the other way around? His brother's thin voice on the day he had become a chade haunted him to this day; *help me!* But Darius had convinced himself he had imagined the strangled plea – chades did not talk. That gut-wrenching nightmare aside, clearly there were some Wardens out there who *chose* to betray their birthright, who *chose* to turn their backs on everything they were sworn to uphold. The cursing, snarling, pitiful excuse for a Warden in front of them was obvious proof of that and he hoped Max recognised it also.

Much as Lark had done with Marco, Max refused to be drawn into the indignity of sparring with Ignatius, despite his continued and colourful vocabulary; she turned her back on him and made her way to where Lawson was cradling a clearly very depleted Caspian. Darius could see that Ivy was over there with Leo as well, helping as best she could to stem the flow of blood rushing from a leg wound high on his thigh. Max rushed over and immediately placed an open palm over the long gash. Darius couldn't make out what was going on but judging from the surprised gasps and the lessening of pinched lines on Leo's face, Darius figured Max was doing her healing thing. He ran a tired hand over his soot-streaked face. They were going to have some explaining to do to Caspian and his paladins. Even if the small display of power Max was now exhibiting wasn't enough, they had surely seen a few of their coats of arms by now too. Darius wasn't all that concerned – Caspian would be a staunch ally.

Max was preoccupied attending to Caspian now, obviously figuring the battle won, so couldn't see what Darius did; Ignatius gaining his feet, a look of mad hate contorting his once handsome features into a mask of malevolence. If only Darius was bonded to Max and their Order, he would have been able to gain her attention through the bond. But his pride and stubbornness had cost him that lifeline, so he did the only thing he could when Ignatius raised a palm of flame in Max's direction.

He leaped in front of her.

TWENTY-EIGHT

"NO!" Diana shouted as she saw Ignatius release his spear of fire directly at Max's exposed back. There was no way any of them could get to her in time, but just as she was certain she was going to watch a second liege be killed in front of her, a blur of movement intercepted the spear before bursting into flames. An inhuman cry shrieked into the night air and Diana realised the sound came from her own throat.

Darius. That thing that was on fire was Darius.

The shocked stillness of the yard was bolstered into life by Diana's scream as she charged to Darius, desperately patting at him and rolling him along the ground in a fruitless attempt to smother the flames. She hardly felt her own skin burning as she sobbed, knowing extinguishing the unnatural flame was impossible. Ignatius had tainted his element, corrupting it in order to do his bidding against his fellow warriors, it would not be so easily tamed. The rancid smell of burning hair and flesh met her nose, even as weak pitiful mewls of pain, wrenched from a scorched throat, met her ears. Darius was burning alive right in front of her and she couldn't stop it.

A feminine hand entered her field of view and reached directly through the crackling flames as though they held no heat. Immediately the fire was gone but only to be replaced with the horrific image of a blackened Darius; his skin was practically melted to his bones in places and his hair was completely singed off. His eyelids had been burnt away and she had to turn her head in order to retch as she saw his beautiful hazel eyes wheel crazily inside his oozing, charred head.

"Diana! We need you! She's going to kill him." Cali shouted. Diana spared a brief glance up, seeing Ignatius clutching his throat and choking as if he couldn't draw breath.

Suffer! She thought. *Suffer long and suffer hard before death takes you.* The others were trying desperately to talk Max down but none could get near her. Energy seemed to crackle around her in palpable waves as she stood still and silent, glowing eyes focused on Ignatius. Her hair was whipping in the wind and her fingers were twitching spastically, but that was all. They were insane if they thought she was going to help them stop Max exact revenge.

Ignatius had killed her Darius.

"Diana!" A loud, hard voice was suddenly in front of her. "He's not dead yet and the only person who can save him is Max! If she kills Ignatius – if she crosses that line – we won't be able to get her back and who will help Darius then?" Axel shook her so hard she swore she could hear her neck crack. It had the desired effect though. Could Max really save Darius? She had healed Ryker's scar, Lark's bruises and lightened the burden in Darius's heart. If there was any chance ...

Glancing at the love of her life one last time, she stood on unsteady legs and allowed Axel to help her over to Max. The frenetic energy grew stronger with every step she took and she didn't think there was any way she was going to be able to reach Max. But suddenly, Diana could feel a wealth of grief and loss and pain surging through the bond and she realised she was feeling Max's anguish. As a paladin affiliated with the domain of death, she was naturally attuned to the darker emotions. She dealt with these kinds of emotions all the time – it was what made her so good as a consultant. Taking a deep breath to steady herself, she reached for her years of experience. She had been able to talk Max out of a power-fuelled storm before and she would do it again.

Anything to save Darius.

"Max." She said softly – a raised voice was never useful in these circumstances – but there was no response.

"Max. Look at me." She tried again. Still no response. Diana could see Ryker prowling helplessly in her peripheral vision and she knew this must be killing him as surely as Darius laying on the ground was killing her.

"Okay. You don't have to look at me. But I want you to listen. I need your help Max. *Darius* needs your help."

Upon hearing Darius's name, Max swung her head in her direction. Diana's breath caught – Max's eyes were a spectrum of colour, dancing and swirling as if in a tempest. They held an ancient arrogance that bespoke great power and although there was an eerie awareness in them, it wasn't wholly Max. At least, not the Max they had all become accustomed to. No, this was the Goddess. Instead of the healthy dose of fear and reverence that would normally accompany such a realisation, Diana instead felt hope. Surely this being in front of her would be able to save Darius.

A rustle of movement caught her attention from the corner of her eye but in the next second Ignatius's two remaining conscious paladins were frozen in place ... and looked to be having the same difficulty breathing as their liege. Max hadn't even glanced in their direction.

"Darius." The Custodian's voice filled Diana's ears even though her lips didn't move. "This *filth* hurt Darius."

"I know. But you can help him. You are the only one who can help him. But you need to let them go."

"After ..." Again, Max didn't open her mouth and the words were a chilling tone of powerful intent. Diana shivered under the intensity of that God-like stare. Max had every intention of killing them all. Gods were just as vengeful as they were loving. The others looked to be at their wits end; they all knew what it would mean if Max killed Ignatius. Their Max – the Max that walked around bare foot, consumed chocolate like air and had the mouth of a sailor – would be no more. Diana took a deep breath and steeled herself to chastise the most powerful element on the planet.

"No, Max." Her voice was firm and brooked no argument. "Not after. Now. You will release Ignatius and his paladins and you will help Darius now." Diana knew she portrayed a calm, in control presence – a direct contrast to the pulsing energy and tension. She continued to say Max's name, hoping the familiarity would remind her that Diana knew her and was on her side ... but that she also wasn't going to take her crap.

Max tilted her head and Diana felt a flicker of hope – Max always did that when she was trying to figure something out. "*After ...*"

This time Max's lips formed the words and the tone was almost a pout, like Diana was taking away a favourite toy. Although Diana wholly agreed with the sentiment of killing the miserable Fire Warden, she wanted Darius to live more and time was of the essence. Ignatius was no longer gasping and was literally blue. Diana didn't even know if he was still alive.

"No. Now, Max. Look at him." It took everything in her to turn and look at her knight, lying completely still and silent save for the horrendous rattling sounds coming from his scorched throat. She had to force down bile ... and the urge to break down and cry until the end of time.

Max's technicolour irises peered over ... and just like that, the world went still again. The energy storm ceased raging, the two paladins fell to their knees gasping and gagging, and Ignatius's dead weight crumpled to the ground in a heap. Max let out a keening sound when she took in Darius's unrecognisable form as she rushed over and knelt beside him. Diana was peripherally aware of Ivy, Caspian, Leo and Lawson hurrying over to the downed traitors but her focus and that of her Order were on Max and their fallen comrade. Diana practically collapsed at Darius's side. She saw Max's hand hover over Darius and she thought Max must be scared to touch him at first, but then she realised she was doing some kind of scan or something. Under her palms, blackened skin began to turn pink and Diana choked on a sob – she was healing him. But mere seconds later, Max shook her head and sat back on her knees. She ran a trembling hand over a face that was obscured by the mass of messy red hair. It came away bloody.

Ryker cursed and knelt beside them, pushing Max's hair out of the way and revealing a face pasty white and a nose that was dripping blood. "I need more vitality." Max's voice was thin – nothing like the voice of supremacy from minutes ago – and Diana realised that all the fighting and the little show she had just put on had depleted all of her vitality.

No. Please, no. She begged, knowing she had little to no vitality stores to recharge her.

"We're all running on fumes, Max. I'm sorry. The fight and the ... *strangulation* used up all of our reserves." Ryker's voice wasn't condemning although his words definitely were ... to Darius. No vitality equalled no powers equalled no healing.

"Use me."

Diana sniffed and saw Ivy offer a slender hand to Max. Max didn't question her or even hesitate, she only dipped her head briefly in thanks and acknowledgment before grasping it tightly. Diana had forgotten the Ranger was even there. She felt the earth vibrate beneath her feet and hoped that was a good sign that the earth paladin was able to recharge Max's diminished stores. She felt a tug on the threads holding the Order together and knew Max was taking what they all had left as well. Diana didn't care if she took it all and felt the same sentiment mirrored by her fellow knights. They shared her desperation for Darius too.

Max released Ivy's hand and placed them over the top of Darius again. Warmth spread across Diana's skin and a tingling sensation began to permeate her pores. Once more, power filled the air. But this display of power was a complete juxtaposition to that which Max had wielded on their enemy. This was filled with warmth and love and healing. It was soothing and it was mighty and it was awe-inspiring. This was the loving Goddess, somehow even more vital than the vengeful one. Max's whole body glowed – it just lit right up like a Christmas tree. Colours Diana didn't even know the names of seemed to radiate around her like a whole-body halo. Her hair lifted gently in the air and danced around her head almost lazily. Diana couldn't make out her eyes but she didn't need to see them to know they were a living rainbow.

"What is she?" Diana registered Ivy's demand. "What the hell is she, Beyden?"

She didn't bother listening to Beyden's response for Max suddenly stopped with the glow worm routine and slumped back against Ryker. Diana cried out in pure happiness and relief; Darius was whole once more. He was naked – very naked – what with all of his clothes being burnt off, but his skin was back and it was a healthy tan colour. Her eyes feasted upon him greedily, checking every inch of him. He was perfect, from his close-cropped hair to the soles of his size twelve feet. The only issue she could think of now was that he was still unconscious and she wasn't able to kiss him senseless! That was until she heard Ryker cry out and saw Max begin to seize painfully on the hard ground.

TWENTY-NINE

Zombie was sprawled across the threshold to his master's doorway. As Darius approached, he raised his head and gazed at him mournfully with his bi-coloured eyes. His tail gave one desolate wag as he let out a huge doggy sigh. Darius smiled; the mutt sure was cute.

"What are you doing out here? You look like the world is about to come to an end." He bent down to scratch him behind his spotty, stripy ears and was rewarded by a happy doggy grin and a bared belly. "You're easy, you know that? You should at least make a man work for it a little."

"Is that right? No wonder you're so into Diana."

He nearly fell on his butt when Ryker's voice sounded from above him. Straightening, he saw that Ryker had opened the door to his room and was smirking at him. "Ry, hey ..." He trailed off, suddenly at a loss for words. Yesterday had been intense. He didn't really remember too much after the point where he had been engulfed in flames. A fact he was eternally grateful for, after listening to the recounting from first Axel, then Beyden, then Lark and finally Cali when they had all shown up one by one at his door this morning.

He had awoken feeling refreshed and energised – better than he had felt in years. And that was including after Max's mind meld thing. It taken a few minutes for the previous evening to come rushing back to him and he had exploded out of bed, patting himself down. But all he had found was unblemished skin. Unable to believe what he was feeling, he rushed to the bathroom and had indeed seen unblemished skin. He remembered Ignatius lining up to throw a palm of fire at Max, his abject fear that he wouldn't be in time, and then a flash of pure, blinding agony, before waking up in his bed this morning. If he thought hard enough, he imagined he could see Diana kneeling above him, her storm-cloud eyes filled with tears as she begged and cursed. He didn't know if it was reality or fantasy and he really didn't want to. Especially since Axel had told him his eyelids had been burnt off. His eyelids! That must have hurt. All of his fellow paladins had brought thanks, watery pride-filled eyes and hugs … or manly slaps on the back. The only people not to visit had been Diana, Max and Ryker. Cali – as the last person to visit – had explained the shape Max was in last night and that she was still recovering. Ryker had ordered her to stay in bed for the rest of the day. Which is why he was standing in the doorway facing a now very awkward Ryker as well.

"Oompf!" The wind was knocked out of him as the huge paladin Captain wrapped his arms around him in something that could by no means be considered a manly slap on the back. He could barely breathe from the tight squeeze the other man was giving him. Perhaps Ryker wasn't feeling so awkward after all …

"Thank you, thank you, thank you!" Ryker stepped back but didn't release his hold. "My brother, I … just, thank you."

"You don't need to thank me. It is my duty." He stated. And it was. A paladin rarely got thanked for doing their duty; it was their honour to serve.

"But it's not really, is it? Max isn't your liege." The words were gentle but they still felt like a blow to Darius.

"That is something I intend to rectify immediately. If she'll have me." He guaranteed Ryker.

Ryker snorted at that and released him – after giving him the requisite slap on the back that pushed him forward a step. "Are you kidding?" He asked. "All she's been talking about all morning is; *Darius this* and *Darius that!* You're a sure thing. So I wouldn't play hard to get anymore if I were you. She's not into that."

By the stern tone, Darius figured Ryker was most likely the one who didn't appreciate it, but was wise enough not to say so. Zombie chose that moment to give a yip before charging through the open door.

Ryker grimaced. "I had to put the damn thing outside earlier so I could get a little, you know –" He gestured vaguely. "I swear he watches me with death in his eyes every time I touch Max."

Darius chuckled at that. Ryker looked sincerely put out and also sincerely concerned. He was glad to see Zombie had made himself at home.

"Is that Darius?" He recognised the tenor of Max's voice but not the sound. It was reed thin and held a quavering note.

He stepped into the room, only to stop short when he caught his first glimpse of Max propped up on the bed, Zombie now in her arms. She looked like hell! She was so white, she was practically translucent; she had dark circles under her eyes; her cheeks looked hollowed out; and even her vibrant red hair appeared dull and limp. He rushed to the bed and took her frail hand in his, "Max. What ...?"

She waved her hand casually like she always did when she felt they were all being silly, "I'm fine. Just a little tired."

"This is not tired. This is ..." *Death*, he thought silently. He turned accusing eyes on Ryker. "She needs vitality! Why haven't you been recharging her? The others – what are they thinking?"

Ryker's brown eyes were grim as he answered, "I know. We all know. But apparently it's not as simple as that. We've all shared our renewed vitality – multiple times. But it's taking longer to replenish her stores."

"Yeah, Ry's been *sharing* all night long." Max gave him a salacious wink, causing Ryker to blush and clear his throat. "I'll be fine. Once upon a time, I would have been holed up in bed for weeks. I'm feeling better every minute."

Darius wasn't convinced. What must she have looked like last night? Did she almost kill herself to save him? That was unacceptable. "Max. You can't be going around healing people if this is the consequence. It is entirely unacceptable."

"It's my purpose Darius, my duty. Do you suppose healing is easy? Healing hurts – as you are both very aware. One cannot be healed and not give back something in return. Balance. The scales must be balanced." She gestured to herself with a hand prominent with blue veins, "This is the price the world demands for balance to be maintained."

He took a deep breath, forcing back his instinctive disapproval that the world could go to hell with its demands if this was the price. But he understood; Max was a Custodian, a being none of them had any real clue about. If her nature demanded she heal, then that is what she would do – regardless of the consequences to herself. "Being a Goddess ain't all it cracked up to be, huh?" He nudged her chin with his thumb, smiling and hoping to lighten the mood. He never used words like *ain't*.

She laughed, causing Zombie to jump around in excitement. "No. It isn't. But still; Goddess! Way cool!"

He laughed in tandem with Ryker – she really was adorable. He desperately wanted to beg forgiveness for his reluctance to join her Order and to rectify that situation immediately but he was a little afraid. He glanced at Ryker for guidance and received a small nod. Okay, he could do this. He had fought in the Crusades, and had jumped in front of a spear of fire and had his face singed off! Pushing himself off the bed, he lowered to one knee; "I hereby swear fealty to you Max, Custodian of nature. I pledge infinite service, protection, loyalty and honour to you, my liege and my Order. This is my solemn wish and I do so freely without reservation." He recited the traditional words solemnly.

"I accept your service, Darius, with great pride and thanks." Max's voice was soft but he could hear the happiness in it. She tapped him on the shoulder, silently asking him to rise. "But don't you want to wait until you have approval from the IDC? Make it formal?" She asked.

No – he didn't want to wait for a formal ceremony. He wanted to be treated like all the others in the Order – like family. Max smiled, apparently seeing – or hearing – his feelings and thoughts. She reached out to place her hands on him but he shied back at the last moment. Seeing the cringe of hurt on her face, he was quick to reassure her, "You're not well. This can wait. I don't want you to over exert yourself."

She rolled her eyes – another common expression for her. "Please. This is easy. I could do it in my sleep. Now come here, Sir Darius."

Ryker gave him a helpful shove so Max could touch him and the second she did, he felt a warmth spread over his left arm from wrist to shoulder. Black lines began inching their way over his skin in a winding mess of organised chaos. He could see feathers and thorns, thistles and leaves, even an eye or two peeking out. A luminescent grey symbol with one horizontal line and three small vertical ones extending from it, appeared in the middle of his forearm; Max's druidic symbol for air. He watched the brand thrash about for a moment as if struggling to settle into a comfortable position, before admiring the lines. He was now Max's official air paladin, her seventh and final element. "Cool."

A booming laugh from Ryker and a giggle from Max drew his attention and he realised he must have said that out loud; he wasn't one to say the word *cool* either!

"It's pretty wicked." Ryker agreed, running his hand over his own coat of arms.

Darius felt the link flare to life and he could feel the others in the Order. Wow, they were an amazing group of humans and the bond in the Order was so natural, he had to believe this was designed somehow. He could also feel Max. He had experienced the awesomeness of her powers twice now and had glimpses of her mind and heart at those times, but now he was bonded with her ... well, damn! The sheer power of her was astounding. He could barely fathom how she was able to contain all that energy. He turned to Ryker, knowing he was looking a little wide-eyed and dumbfounded.

"I know." Was all Ryker said.

"You know what?" Max demanded, scratching Zombie's exposed belly.

"Nothing, babe. All good." Her lover assured her.

Max was completely oblivious. Unbelievable.

"Whatever. Welcome aboard, Dare." Darius tried not to cringe – there would be no escaping that nickname now. His expression must have said it all for Ryker commented;

"Think yourself lucky it's not Inmate!" Ryker growled, causing the puppy to growl back. Ryker thumped on the bed spread and the pup jumped in the air with a yip, before placing his front paws flat and his fuzzy butt up in the air in a play bow. Ryker indulged him, getting down low and moving from one side of the bed to the other as Zombie chased him. What a softy!

"Now, Darius. About Diana ..." Max began.

"I love her!" He blurted out. It was vitally important that they were both aware that he was in love with the Lady Diana and he really didn't think he could give her up. He probably should have discussed it before he pledged his allegiance to Max again though.

"No shit. Everyone knows that, Dare. That's not what I was referring to. I meant; what are you going to do about it?"

He swallowed. *Everyone knew? Who was everyone?* Likely, she was referring to everyone in the house. And here he thought he had been subtle. But to address her question; "What am I allowed to do about it?"

She scowled at him, "Really Darius? Really? You just got back in my good books by saving me from burning alive and now you want to piss me off again? There is no *allow*. Your life; your heart; your choice. You can do whatever you want. The question is; what do you want?"

He didn't need to even think about it. "I want to be hers."

"Great idea! You have our full support. Right, babe?" She smiled at Ryker – who was now patting the puppy into ecstasy. Darius knew he already loved that dog, despite his words to the contrary.

"I've already addressed this with Diana. As long as there are no distractions from your duties and responsibilities as Max's paladins, then I have no objection."

Ryker's words infused him with hope. "I swear, my duty and my loyalty is to my liege." He bowed his head respectfully.

"Ignore him, Darius. He already knows that. You saved me. You have more than proven your loyalty and your honour." His new liege assured him. "But, back to Diana. She likes bubbles."

"I'm sorry, what?" Max was forever going on tangents with her conversations.

"Diana. She likes bubble baths." Max explained, giving him a wink.

Oh! Bubbles? Hmm ...

THIRTY

"Thanks Cali." She bumped her with her shoulder. "I needed that." They had just had a long swim in the calm waters of the ocean, a little further out to sea. Diana was a good swimmer, but she didn't always feel comfortable swimming that far out alone. But throw in a paladin affiliated with the domain of water? And you had yourself the safest swim buddy in the world.

"No worries. Anytime." The blonde assured her, looking fit and lithe in her one-piece swimsuit. Her straight hair was slicked to her neck and back and Diana felt a little jealous. Her own curls were plastered all over her head, face, and neck and were dripping incessantly down her back. If she didn't wash out the salt soon, they would be completely unmanageable. A shower was definitely in order. But she desperately wanted to seek out Darius. She was afraid she was going to launch herself into his arms and never let him go – pride be damned. But she was still unsure of her reception, from Darius anyway. Max had told her that morning to *'balls up and go claim what's rightfully yours, woman!'*. It was good to know she was supported.

Waving to Cali, they separated in the kitchen – Cali going upstairs to her second floor room, while she made her way through the main living space to the opposite side of the house. She loved the privacy and solitude her room afforded her. She also loved the huge, deep set bath tub in her private bathroom. Although the porcelain tub was amazing, it was not self-filling, so she was shocked when she entered the room to see it overflowing with bubbles.

"Hi."

She cursed, her wet feet slipping on the tiles as she pin-wheeled her arms frantically trying to regain her balance. A pair of strong paladin arms caught her to a strong paladin chest and she inhaled automatically, taking in the masculine scent that was uniquely Darius. She looked up and allowed her eyes to feast on the beauty that was Darius's flawless face. Strong angles, hazel eyes, long eyelashes, firm lips ... she was never going to take looking at him for granted ever again. "Hi ..." She finally responded, a little breathlessly.

He smiled and she felt herself get a little damp; it was a decidedly wicked smile. Pushing herself back a little, she asked, "What are you doing here?"

"Max said I'm allowed to keep you."

She felt her eyebrows raise, "Did she just?"

Darius nodded, losing some of his good humour. "She did. So did Ryker. But even if they didn't give their blessing, it wouldn't have changed a thing for me. Do you know why?"

Diana felt her heart clench and her breathing become shallow. "Why?"

"Because I love you. I love you, Diana. I think I have since the first moment I saw you, with your hair flying like a flag behind you, covered in blood and dirt – a fierce warrior, a noble knight, the very epitome of a woman. I love you."

She couldn't move. She couldn't breathe. Darius loved her?

"Yes. I love you." He smiled fondly, "You were talking out loud."

Air returned to her in a rush and she moved without further thought, launching herself at him and wrapping herself around him like an octopus – legs around his waist, arms around his neck. She peppered kisses over every inch of him she could reach, "I love you! I love you! I love you! Thank you! I'm sorry! I am so sorry! All these years wasted and for what? Stupid stubbornness?" She yelled, probably a little incoherently.

Darius pulled back and kissed her soundly on the mouth before lavishing his lips over her face and neck, "Not stubbornness. Strength. You are the strongest woman I know."

She snorted a little at that. Talk about seeing the bright side – eight centuries gone! "Not as strong as Max." She pointed out.

"Ah, but Max isn't a woman is she? Technically, she's a Goddess. That's a whole different kettle of fish. Don't you think?" He grinned and looked so young that Diana felt herself fall in love with him all over again. It had been a long time since she had seen the boy inside the man. He was always so rigid and in control, the mature knight of times long past. She loved this new look on him.

"What now?" She asked, needing clarification and direction.

His grin turned wicked again and he began undressing her without further ado. "Now it's time for a bubble bath."

*****

He peeled the plain black pair of swimmers over her shoulders and down her creamy thighs. Who knew removing a piece of wet spandex would be so erotic? As each inch of glorious skin was exposed, his breathing became more erratic and his body tightened to the point of pain. He had been hard since the moment he had begun filling the bath with the amazingly scented bubbles. No wonder she smelled so good all the time! He tapped her foot, silently asking for her to lift it and step out of the wet material. He looked up at her from his vantage point at her feet and damn near swallowed his tongue. Her stomach was flat and her breasts full, moving with every breath she took. He started at her ankles, running his hands up and over smooth calf muscles and thighs, bypassing her feminine mound, and up to cup her generous flesh. Despite his own raging desires, he kept his movements unhurried – they had all the time in the world. With Max still recovering, they had nothing on the agenda for the day. It meant he could spend the day worshipping the lush body in front of him and he could begin making up for lost time.

"Darius ..." Diana's voice was husky and a just a little breathless. Well, he wanted her *a lot* breathless.

"Yes?"

"Get up here." She demanded. Wasn't she cute? She seemed to think she was in charge.

"Oh, I don't know. I kind of like the view from down here. Besides, it allows for easy access to one of my favourite places." Leaning forward he parted her soft folds and began to devour her with no further preliminaries. She released a thin scream and gripped his head by the ears, pulling him up slightly higher. She knew what she liked and wasn't afraid to ask for it; she was so damn sexy and beautiful. He loved everything about her; her smell, her taste, the way her internal muscles sucked his fingers right in. It took only minutes for her to be bucking and screaming out his name. Instead of backing off, he gripped her butt cheeks hard in his hands and forced her up that precipice of pleasure/pain once again.

After her second orgasm in as many minutes, her knees buckled and he caught her up, placing her perfect butt on the vanity. She smiled saucily and crooked her finger at him, spreading her legs wide in invitation. He didn't need to be asked twice. He stripped in record time – no strip-tease this time, that memory was still somewhat mortifying – and took his place between her thighs. Leaning over, he brushed his lips over hers in a heated, slow kiss, enjoying the play of her tongue against his.

Pulling back, she smiled at him and ran her palm over his new brand. "Sexy." She said.

"I'm glad you think so." He also thought the dark lines against her latte skin were incredibly sexy. "I love you." He whispered then, and thrust inside her in one smooth stroke. He groaned at the exquisite feel of her heat surrounding him and began to move in slow, steady motions. The last couple of times they were together he had been overcome by either lust or alcohol. He wanted this time to be perfect.

"I love you too, but if you don't get your sexy arse into gear, I'm going to kill you." She glared at him, raking her nails over his chest and across his nipples. Seems she didn't appreciate slow and steady. Giving her what she wanted, he began to power into her, their shared cries echoing off the tiled walls. He thought he may have passed out for a moment or two as he came, seeing stars behind his eyelids and going momentarily deaf. Diana appeared just as blissed out, slumped back against the mirror, her dark curls stuck to her face and chest and her gorgeous grey eyes closed. Smiling in satisfaction, he lifted her once again and lowered her into the waiting bubble bath.

"Hmm ..." She murmured, opening her eyes to peer up at him. "Thank you. That was amazing." She said, holding out her hand. He took the offering, slipping in behind her and pulling her between his legs.

"Well, I did owe you after the night you gave me." He admitted, tangling their legs together.

She stilled. "You remember that?"

He ran the soapy bubbles up and over her breasts, loving the slippery feel it created. "I remember everything. Thank you for giving me my deepest fantasies. I'm sorry I forgot, even for a moment. Whiskey and I don't really mix."

She chuckled at that, turning over and sloshing water everywhere. She pecked a quick kiss to his lips but he grabbed her head, prolonging the moment. She pulled back gasping. "I think you're cute when you're drunk, *Dare*."

"No. Hell no. You are not calling me that."

She chuckled evilly and leaned forward to suck up a kiss on his neck "But just think about all the things I could dare you to do ..."

He perked up at that. He never backed down from a challenge. "Like what?"

"Well, I dare you to ..." What she whispered had him surging from the bath in one motion with her in his arms.

Good thing they had all day.

THIRTY-ONE

As it turned out, they had two days, Diana thought as she waited outside for the rest of her Order to join her. Two glorious days, spent largely in her bedroom while she and Darius made love on every surface possible. They had only ventured out for food and water and the good-natured teasing that accompanied such excursions of course. The camp was happy for them both and no-one seemed concerned that another couple had been made in the house. Man, she loved the lot of them. It had also taken the full two days for Max to completely recover and for Ryker to allow her out of bed. That morning however, Ry had received a phone call from the IDC – they were all in town and their presence was requested immediately.

Diana was nervous – they all were. They had been informed that Max was up on charges for forming an unsanctioned Order and assaulting and maiming a Warden and paladins. Naturally, they had reported Ignatius and his Order to the appropriate authorities immediately after returning from Caspian's. Caspian, Leo and Lawson had filed separate charges and Ivy's personal account also held a lot of weight. The Fire Warden and his five paladins had been remanded in custody and would also face charges today. Caspian and his Order had visited the previous evening with thanks and questions. They had all made a complete recovery and Max had revealed to them that she was a Custodian, not a Life Warden as they had presumed. Cas had taken it well, pledging his support and any aid they might need, from bended knee. Max had blushed furiously and all but yanked the poor Water Warden up by the hair to get him to stand; *'Jeez, Cas. Don't do that. It makes me feel like a real dick!'* After that, they had all stayed for dinner and they had finally played the poker game they were supposed to the night of the attack. Max had won – she was a total shark – big surprise. By the Goddess, she hoped today went well. She didn't know what would happen if the council decided to punish Max. Hell, she didn't even know if the council *could* punish Max. Max wasn't likely to let that happen and they sure would not allow anyone to touch their liege. The day was going to be fraught with danger.

"Don't look like that. Everything is going to be fine." A masculine voice resonated from behind her as warm arms wrapped her up tight. Diana basked. She loved being in Darius's arms.

"I'm worried." She confessed. She felt the sigh move through his broad chest.

"I am too." He spun her around. "But it will all work out."

"How do you know?"

"Because it has to. And I think it's supposed to. All this ..." he gestured broadly to the pristine environment around them, "it's meant, I think. I've known it for a long time but it scared the beejesus out of me. I couldn't stop one word from reverberating in my head and it terrified me that I was going to be a part of it."

She didn't need to ask what word he was referring to; revolution. She felt the same way. In fact, Verity had told her as much hundreds of years ago when she had first pledged her allegiance to him. "Verity knew this was going to happen, you know. He told me I wasn't destined to be by his side forever, but that I would be needed elsewhere. He also told me that you were supposed to be mine – that fate was a fickle wench and she couldn't be dodged, no matter how stubborn one's heart." She revealed.

"Really?" His eyebrows winged up. "I'd heard rumours he was precognitive. They were true?"

She nodded, feeling grief well up with thoughts of her previous liege. He was an amazing man and had achieved amazing things in his lifetime. His presence was sorely missed in their society. "They were true. And I trusted him implicitly. I knew if I waited long enough, you would get your arse into gear and –"

"Throw you up against a wall and have his wicked, knightly way with you?"

Diana spun, scowling at Axel for his interruption. "You had better be careful. Darius won't give you his room if you're not nice."

"I apologise. I have nothing to say. Nope, nothing to say over here." He mimed zipping his lips and Bey and Lark laughed at his antics, coming up behind him. Darius was moving into her suite of rooms – she needed her walk-in closet like she needed air – and Axel would be moving into Darius's old attic bedroom. He said his mental health couldn't hold out against the sounds constantly coming from Max and Ryker's room. Diana was only glad that her room was on the opposite side of the house so nobody could hear her begging ... or Darius begging. She loved when he did that.

"So, are we all ready to face the firing squad?" Diana groaned at Max's flippant comment. Ryker, Cali and Max had just closed up the house and made their way over.

"Not funny, Max. The IDC is no joking matter." Her man scolded.

Max just smiled. "Group hug?"

They just rolled their eyes at her, except for Axel who picked her up and squeezed her breathless. Ryker smacked him up the side of the head, "Hands off my woman."

"Boy, you guys sure are possessive. Darius threatened me with castration for patting the lovely Diana's rump this morning."

Darius bared his teeth at the shameless flirt, "It wasn't a threat."

Axel just laughed, not afraid of the older paladin in the slightest. Zombie chose that moment to come gambolling around the house, running around in circles before parking his furry rear on the ground in front of Max and smiling up at her. He was absolutely freaking adorable!

"You can't come, buddy." Max apologised, bending down to give him a scratch.

The puppy was a wonderful addition to the family and though he spread his puppy love equally to every member of the household, Diana knew Max was his master. He had plumped up over the last few days, losing his too-skinny appearance and his coat was now soft and glossy – albeit still a strange mix of colours and patterns. She knew Max had shared some of her vitality with the dog in order for him to heal completely and quickly. Ryker hadn't even chastised her for it. He was just as smitten with the little creature as the rest of them. Zombie gave a kind of growling yip, as if to disagree with Max. Max replied as though she could understand him – and maybe she could.

"I mean it, Zombie. We'll be back in no time. You just hang around here and play with Bert or something, okay?"

Diana couldn't believe the little slater bug was still hanging around. But he could frequently be found out in the garden or in the kitchen. Looks like they officially had two pets now. She wouldn't be surprised if the place turned into a menagerie before long. Max really did have a thing for strays – thank the Goddess for that, she thought.

Glancing toward said woman, she saw the smile on her face and mirrored it. Darius was right; everything was going to be fine.

THIRTY-TWO

Darius gave Diana's hand one last squeeze as he stepped out of the car and watched as Ryker did the same. They had decided not to draw attention to their personal situations at this time. They had enough to deal with, without throwing that into the mix. They were all also wearing long sleeves once again in an attempt to hide their coats of arms. They had every intention of disclosing Max's Custodian status to the International Domain Council but they wanted to get through the hearing first without the added complication of explaining Max's unique – and still unexplainable – origins. He was hoping that the council would be able to provide some answers regarding her lack of memory. As old as he was, half the members of the council were even older. Surely, one of them would have knowledge of Custodians. In addition, Max didn't want the council to be biased by her background or her possible powers; she wanted a fair trial.

They made their way inside, flanking Max from all directions and ignoring the whispers and dark looks thrown their way. They received nods and smiles from their allies; Caspian and his paladins, Kai, Kane and Kellan, Fawn and even Ray from the local council gave small waves, showing their support. Darius saw Beyden nod to his sister across the room. She was at the front under the raised platform where all seven members of the International Domain Council were already seated ... and guarding a very sick looking Ignatius and five shame-faced paladins. Ivy was flanked by two other Rangers – both male. They were big bastards and just as expressionless as Ivy often appeared to be. Although Darius knew she wasn't as cold as she seemed, having also visited in the last couple of days. They had told her about Max also, they didn't really have much of a choice given her eye witness account of the proceedings at Caspian's. She had received the significant information with surprising warmth and equanimity and had given her word that she would tell no-one. Darius believed her. She was cut from the same cloth as him when it came to her responsibilities.

Max paused and he could feel the nervous energy pouring through the bond; Max was edgy now. He couldn't really blame her. The seven figures seated at the front of the room made an imposing image. He had met all of the council members on several occasions and he genuinely liked most of them. Garrett, was the Life Warden representative and was the power house behind the council. His wife, Autumn, was the Earth Warden delegate and they had been married for over a thousand years, back when formal marriages between wardens was commonplace. He believed they could rely on them to be fair and just. Now Cinder, on the other hand, they could not trust. Her domain was Fire and she also happened to be Magda's mother and Ignatius's grandmother. Talk about bias! Ares, from Air and Ravyn from Beast were likewise conservative in their beliefs and were instigators of some of their stricter rules and regulations, Darius knew. Blu was the Water delegate and a funny old bastard. Darius had no idea how old he truly was but he was one of the few wardens around to actually look like he had aged. And finally, there was Mordecai. He was a Death Warden and very serious all of the time. He was reserved, cold and aloof and Darius could never figure out what he was thinking or what side of the fence he sat on. He didn't think they could consider him an ally, no matter what Cali and Diana seemed to think. They thought the Scotsman was '*hot*'. He scowled at the dark haired, middle-aged looking man with the green eyes and Scottish accent. Darius couldn't see it. He also didn't like the way the man seemed to be staring at Max, his gaze serious and intent. Darius shifted slightly, nudging Max to the side and out of the Warden's line of sight. Mordecai's gaze flicked to him but didn't reveal anything. No, Darius thought, he most definitely did not see the appeal of those shark eyes.

"Everyone be seated." Garrett spoke presently, giving Ryker a small nod of encouragement and acknowledgement. Darius exhaled in relief; he knew he was correct about the Life Warden.

The Order made their way to their assigned seats with Ryker sitting on Max's left and himself on her right. The rest of the team lined up behind them and remained standing at attention.

"Max," Garrett began, "it is a pleasure to finally meet you, although the circumstances could be better." His smile was kind as he looked at her from blue eyes.

"Hello. Lovely to meet you too. Thank you so much for recommending your trainers as temporary guides and guardians. They have been absolutely wonderful and are a credit to your society."

There was some rumbling over that one and smirks on some faces but Garrett just smiled. "I am glad they have made you feel welcomed."

"Not everybody has." Max informed him, getting right to the point and eliciting more grumbling.

"So we are aware." He acknowledged.

"That is correct. So let us address the charges, shall we?" Ravyn suggested, snidely.

Garrett sighed as he looked at his fellow council member but did as he bid; "Max, you are accused of forming an Order without authority and without formal sanction from the local council, nor the International Domain Council. You are furthermore accused of attacking a Warden and an Order, resulting in grievous bodily harm. New charges as of this morning, include attempted murder."

"What?" Ryker snarled. They had not been informed of those charges.

"After listening to the statement of the Warden involved, we had no other choice but to add on the additional charges." Blu revealed.

Darius thought it was mighty unfair that Ignatius had been able to spread his lies before the meeting but Max had not been given the opportunity to share her side in privacy. She seemed fairly unconcerned though, smiling and flashing her lone dimple at the male members of the council;

"What if I promised not to strangle any more arsehole creeps – even when they clearly deserve it? Would that help?" She smiled innocently and fluttered her lashes up at the council. Blu actually snorted, even as he smiled and Garrett shook his head, sighing almost in resignation,

"You, my dear, are far too charming for your own good."

Before anyone could reply, Cinder exploded out of her chair and rounded on her fellow council members. "You cannot be serious! Charming? She is an outrage! She has insulted the local council, threatened the local paladins with physical harm, used powers that are untrained, untested and unstable! She has surrounded herself with outcast paladins – even bonded with them – and openly supported deviant homosexuals! She has physically assaulted a Warden, almost killing him and his sworn paladins. And on top of all that ... I have it on good authority that she is having an intimate relationship with one of her paladins without permission!"

The murmurs in the room had grown steadily in volume as the long list of Max's perceived sins were catalogued. Looking around at the disbelieving and shocked faces, even Darius had to admit that it sounded like she had been very busy lately. Lark gave her a friendly nudge with his elbow;

"You are such a rebel! My cool status increases exponentially just by standing next to you!" Darius shook his head. Lark was such a dork.

Garrett cleared his throat as he intoned, "Max, Warden of the Order of Aurora ..." That resulted in even more murmurs – the formal acknowledgement of her Order from the council was very unexpected and surprised Darius hugely. He had taken it upon himself to register their Order with the council the previous evening, wanting Max's Order recognised. He was also hoping to make up for all the time he had been acting like an arsehole lately and hoped that naming the Order after Ryker's suggestion of her name all those weeks ago, would earn him some points.

Max turned shocked turquoise eyes his way and he felt her gratitude down to his very bones; she liked the name. He picked up her hand, kissing the back of it, "My Lady of Aurora." He could feel the rest of his fellow knights gather around her in a show of solidarity and once again felt that lovely warmth spread even more. The message to the room was clear; they were a family and would stand by Max no matter what the verdict was. Max sent out a pulse of energy through their shared bond and Darius immediately felt six separate, smaller bolts bounce back along the link. He added his own to the mix of elements. It just felt so absolutely right and he knew that Max couldn't help the bubble of joy that burst from her lips. Ryker responded in kind with a rare low chuckle of his own and Max gave him a playful wink.

Refocusing on the council chamber Darius noticed the nervous and somewhat uncomfortable movements from those in the audience and the slight frowns on the councilmen's faces. They all felt her joy too – how could they not? She was practically nature itself being a Custodian, and the wardens and paladins were all connected to nature in their own ways. But they didn't seem to understand that joy, except for maybe Garrett, who was smiling indulgently at their antics.

"Max, and the Aurora Order," Garrett began again, "do you have anything to say in your defence?"

Max shook her head, sending her deep red hair flying. Darius noted the way Mordecai's eyes seemed to follow the movement. What was with the Warden of Death? He didn't have time to focus on him though for Max spoke, "Nope. That was all totally me. I'm *waaay* guilty!" He saw Ryker give her a droll stare; *Really, Max?* It seemed to say.

"I have no choice but to find you guilty of all the afore-mentioned charges, then." Garrett stated sombrely.

The resulting reactions were varied but marked and Darius made note of who was shaking their heads in disappointment, shouting their support for Max, applauding the verdict, and the malicious grins on the faces of Ignatius and his supporters. As for Max and the rest of them? They gave no reactions at all. Max wasn't concerned and so neither were they. Why she wasn't concerned, he didn't really understand but he trusted her.

Blu raised a hand to silence the room, "Do you appeal the verdict?" He asked.

Darius was about to yell a *hell, yes* when Max turned to him and gave a small shake of her head. Ryker stepped forward and answered; "We do not."

"Well then, it would appear I have no choice once again." Garrett eyed them all before taking his own wife's hand in his and declaring, "I hereby nominate Max, Warden of the

Aurora Order, to become the eighth member of the International Domain Council."

"Seconded!" Autumn shouted, almost before Garrett had even finished speaking. The silence in the room was deafening. That was until Cinder let out an ungodly shriek, knocking her chair over with a loud bang.

"What? You cannot do that!"

It was Blu who replied, "Actually, he can. Any nomination put forward and seconded ..." he tilted his head in Autumn's direction and wiggled his eyebrows, "... must be put to a majority vote. You, yourself voted that law in Cinder."

Cinder was clearly seething. "It is not the same thing! You cannot just nominate another council member! The IDC has seven members. One from each Domain. That is how it works!"

"That may have been true in the past however, need dictates change and I for one believe that there is now a need for change." Garrett spoke up.

"Even if that were true. There are seven council members for a reason." Cinder argued, "A representative from each domain maintains the balance. It ensures there cannot be a hung vote. With eight council members there will never be a majority vote."

Blu spoke up again, "That is true, but perhaps that is a good thing. A hung vote would lead to more discussions and a more reasoned and perhaps more *just* outcome." He looked directly at Max. "I vote yes."

"This is ridiculous!" Cinder squawked. She was beginning to turn an interesting shade of purple.

"Cinder, please!" Garrett stood to bend over and right her chair, "Take a seat ... and let us vote."

THIRTY-THREE

Diana couldn't believe her ears, or her eyes for that matter. One by one the seven members of the International Domain Council voted to determine if Max – their politically incorrect, train-wreck of a liege, mouth of a drunken sailor Max – would become one of the most integral political figures in their entire society. Sure, she knew Max was a Custodian and therefore pretty much the most important person in the whole damn world, but the council didn't know that yet!

Autumn, representative of Earth, "Yes."

Garrett, representative of Life, "Yes."

"Yes." From Blu, representative of Water.

"No." That was Ravyn, representative of Beast.

"No." Ares, representative of Air.

"Fuck no! Absolutely not! I object! I ..."

"Cinder, a simple yes or no is all we need. Your response in the negative is heard and accepted." Garrett assured her.

All eyes now turned to Mordecai, the Death representative. Given how uptight he was Diana knew he would vote in the negative as well. That meant that Max would be out-voted four to three.

"Yes." Mordecai's insanely unexpected response boomed into the too-still room as he continued, "And so the majority has spoken. Max, do you accept the position of council member of the International Domain Council?"

Holy shit! That was indeed the majority vote which meant Max was officially voted in as the eighth member of the fucking IDC! One day she was going to have to learn to stop being surprised by the things that Max achieved. Diana felt the fine tremor that ran through Max at Mordecai's question. She knew for all her bravado and her earlier positive words that this was still overwhelming for her. She had gone from a human with no-one and nothing, to one of the most powerful women in the world in under three months. Even though her Custodian instincts were strong, as was her sense of responsibility, she was still not comfortable being in the spotlight. She had been trying to remain invisible all her life and now she had her own Order of paladins, a family, friends, and a position of power in their society. Diana could feel her starting to freak out and second guess herself through their shared link, so instead of allowing her to open that sarcastic mouth of hers and ruin this opportunity, she stepped forward and stated simply;

"She accepts."

"Hey! I can speak for myself!" She heard Max say indignantly.

Darius, always having her back and likely recognising a Max-rant coming on slapped his huge hand over Max's mouth saying, "She absolutely accepts."

"Yep."

"Totally!"

"Major acceptance."

"Big yuppers!"

"Wouldn't dream of saying no!" Ryker, Cali, Axel, Lark and Beyden all added. Diana smiled. Gods, she loved these guys!

"As entertaining as you all are; we still need Max to respond." Autumn said, eyeing them all as an indulgent mother would.

"This is blasphemy! Grandmother! You cannot let them do this!" Ignatius leaped up and shouted before abruptly falling on his arse. He still looked like shit from going toe-to-toe with Max.

"Quiet!" Mordecai snarled, "You have no voice here. Do you think we have forgotten your own crimes? You are a disgrace to wardens everywhere. I suggest you remain mute until it is time to receive your own punishment." Diana managed to stop the little shiver his accented words caused. The Scottish Warden of Death was one fine specimen of a man. And that was saying something, considering the pieces of meat she lived with ... and slept with.

Ignatius opened and closed his mouth looking to his grandmother for aid. It appeared her sense of self-preservation was stronger than her maternal bonds for she remained quiet never meeting his gaze.

Mordecai returned his stern gaze back to Max, "Your decision."

Hearing an 'oompf', Diana peered toward the sound and had to quickly smother a laugh as Max elbowed Darius in the ribs peeling his hand off her mouth in the process. Seems Darius had forgotten he still held Max's mouth closed.

"Shit! Sorry my Lady." He blushed a pretty shade of red and oh boy, was she going to remind him of that later. And so was Max if she read her filthy look correctly. Max stepped up beside her and Diana could feel the rightness of this moment to her very bones;

"I accept."

Her liege's voice was strong and true but she was still surprised by the applause that broke out. She knew Caspian, his paladins, and the triplets would stand by them but hadn't anticipated the number of others that clearly desired the changes that would now surely be brought to fruition. She was less surprised by the angry outbursts from the majority of wardens and paladins and could feel the malevolence aimed at Max crawling like ants over her skin. She knew the others could feel it too and felt confident they were carving names and faces into their minds for future reference.

A very loud and very forced cough drew everyone's attention to Magda who stood and faced the council members. "Although I am in no position to appeal any decision the council has made, I feel it is my duty to address one major issue you all appear to have overlooked."

"Of course, Magda. Please speak. Your opinion is always welcomed and respected." Garrett assured her.

Magda preened under the flattery, "Balance. It is the basis of our society, of our gifts, and of the world itself. Yet, the council is now unbalanced. One domain now has two representatives. How can we trust that the council will remain unbiased in the future? Particularly, to those of us who are not bound to Life."

There was a general murmur of agreement throughout the room. Diana noticed that Mordecai was looking directly at Max again as if he could see right into her soul. Through the Order, she could feel Max's odd sense of recognition that the continued stare brought. Had Max met him before? His gaze was knowing, almost as if he knew Max was a Custodian. But how? And why hadn't he already dropped that little nugget? Confirmation came with his next words;

"I do not believe balance will be a problem, will it Max?" His gaze landed pointedly on each of them, "A little warm in here for long sleeves, isn't it?"

Diana saw Max take a deep breath and also Ryker's hand. She was terrified again and Diana couldn't blame her. There hadn't been a Custodian in their society in recorded history. Who knew how the council – and everybody else – was going to react?

"You got this girl." She muttered out the side of her mouth.

"Yeah, girl power!" Cali followed.

Max smiled but still hesitated, biting her lip. Apparently their Captain was unable to take the uncertainty flowing through the bond, for he swooped down and captured Max's lips. Diana felt herself flush a little and look to Darius at the erotic display. Ryker sipped and sampled and plundered until Diana saw all the tension leave Max's body. In fact, Max just stood there, both arms at her sides, face tilted up, surrounded by Ryker's massive palms on either side of her cheeks. Diana figured the only thing that was keeping her standing was probably Ryker's tongue. Some very indiscreet throat clearing finally seemed to penetrate Ryker and Max's lust induced comas. It was Axel and Beyden sounding like they had furballs and Lark slapping them on their backs asking if they needed some water.

Max smiled sheepishly at all of them, refocused on the council and responded as if no time had lapsed. "No. Balance will not be a problem ... because I am not a Warden ... I am a Custodian."

Boom, bitches!

Max shared the thought along the common Order pathway and they all burst into rather insane laughter. She paid no heed to the quiet devastation in the room, nor did she see the knowing smirk on several faces, or the gleam of calculation in several pairs of eyes.

Diana felt Darius brush his hand along the back of hers and sent him a look filled with love, with hope for their future. Not just their own future, but the future of their race and of the world as a whole. A reckoning, she had told him weeks ago. And now here they were, Max an official member of their governing body. She couldn't help but wonder what a fucked-up, marvellous mess Fate must be to bestow such a liege as Max on them. And also to give her a man of honour, integrity, strength and wickedness in the sack ...

But she would thank that crazy bitch every day for it.

MEET MONTANA!

Montana is a self-confessed book junkie. Although she loves reading all genres from romance to crime fiction to sci-fi, her not-so-guilty pleasure is paranormal romance. Alpha men – just a little bit damaged, and Alpha women – strong yet vulnerable, are a favourite combination of hers. Throw in some steamy sex scenes, a touch of humour, and a little violence and she is in heaven!

Her overactive (and overindulged) imagination could only take so much before the many voices wanted out. Thus, Montana's journey into the wonderful world of writing.

She is a scientist by day, having grown up in country New South Wales, Australia. Writing about ancient knights, demons and shapeshifters is such a delicious contradiction to her day job in the laboratory, that she doesn't see the voices stopping anytime soon!

FOLLOW MONTANA!

Email: montanaash.author@yahoo.com

Website: http://www.montanaash.com/

Facebook: https://www.facebook.com/montana.ash.author/

Twitter: @ReadMontanaAsh

45378438R00171

Printed in Poland
by Amazon Fulfillment
Poland Sp. z o.o., Wrocław